"What are you doing?"

"Taking you to the clinic to make sure you don't have a broken foot."

His hand covered hers on the steering wheel and she hit the brakes, bringing the truck to a stop.

"No." Her mouth opened, but before she could speak, he shook his head. "You have no say in this, Katie." He paused. "I can't afford the clinic."

"Are you drowning in medical bills after..." Katie's voice faltered "...what happened?"

"That's not really any of your business, Katie."

He'd hoped to squelch her rescuing tendencies with the blunt statement but failed.

"I'll ice it. Tomorrow I'll evaluate. If it's really broken, I'll go to the clinic."

"How will you get there?"

"Katie, believe it or not, I can do lots of things with broken bones. It's kind of what I do." Or rather what he had done. His rodeo career was over.

After a long staredown, her lips tightened, then she eased her foot off the brake and headed in the direction of the ranch.

Dear Reader,

I enjoy reading stories with rich family dynamics, and that's what the Sweet Home, Montana series is all about. In this first book of the series, Katie Callahan returns home to the family ranch after discovering that the goals she'd worked toward for so long were not the right goals for her. She plans to use her time alone on the ranch to rest and reflect and find a new direction. But the thing is that she'll be sharing the ranch with the new temporary manager—a man Katie had once been madly in love with.

Brady O'Neil has made some poor life choices, and now that he's too injured to continue his rodeo career, he's dealing with the aftermath of those choices. The last thing he needs is to have sweet, warmhearted Katie Callahan living a stone's throw away. Katie is a rescuer, and the last thing he needs is to be rescued—or to mess up Katie's life by succumbing to his feelings for her.

I hope you'll come along with me and read about Katie's and Brady's journeys of self-discovery as they work their way toward a happy ending.

Happy reading!

Jeannie Watt

HEARTWARMING

A Ranch Between Them

Jeannie Watt

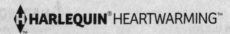

H HARLEQUIN® HEARTWARMING™

Recycling programs
for this product may
not exist in your area.

ISBN-13: 978-1-335-51086-0

A Ranch Between Them

Printed in U.S.A.

Jeannie Watt lives on a small cattle ranch and hay farm in southwest Montana with her husband, her ridiculously energetic parents and the usual ranch menagerie. She spends her mornings writing, except during calving season, and during the remainder of the day enjoys sewing, doing glass mosaics and fixing fences. If you'd like more information about Jeannie and her books, please visit her website at jeanniewatt.com, where you can also sign up for her newsletter.

Books by Jeannie Watt

Harlequin Heartwarming

Her Montana Cowboy

Harlequin Western Romance

Montana Bull Riders

The Bull Rider Meets His Match
The Bull Rider's Homecoming
A Bull Rider to Depend On
The Bull Rider's Plan

Harlequin Superromance

The Brodys of Lightning Creek

To Tempt a Cowgirl
To Kiss a Cowgirl
To Court a Cowgirl
Molly's Mr. Wrong
Wrangling the Rancher

Visit the Author Profile page
at Harlequin.com for more titles.

I'd like to dedicate this book to Wanda Gooby. Thank you, Wanda, for all you do for the people in your life.

CHAPTER ONE

BRADY O'NEIL GRITTED his teeth, mustered his strength and tried to pull his foot free from the boot trapped beneath the four-wheeler. No luck. His lower leg was going numb beneath the weight of the heavy machine that pinned his foot to the ground, and if something didn't change soon, he'd be spending the night in a cold, damp ditch at the edge of the river pasture. Hello, hypothermia.

Cursing under his breath, Brady rested his forehead on the wet ground, and debated his options.

It didn't take long to conclude he had no options other than to try to get his foot free. He was hidden by grass and no one had any reason to look for him. He could be there for a long, long time. A meadowlark trilled nearby, its melodic notes reminding Brady of better times. Times when he wasn't about to die in a field due to his own inattentiveness.

He sucked in a breath, squeezed his eyes

shut with grim concentration and once again tried to wiggle his foot free of his boot, his leg muscles burning with the effort. His foot moved ever so slightly and then…nothing. Brady relaxed his muscles, allowed himself a couple of deep breaths as he did his best to fight a growing sense of panic. This wasn't happening. Not on top of everything else. He let out a choked laugh, startling the meadowlark into silence.

Until six months ago, he'd have been the first to admit that he lived a charmed life. He'd had some serious issues with his parents, but he'd had the Callahans to fill the void left by a mother more interested keeping her husband—Brady's stepfather—happy than in paying attention to her son. Brady had accepted his reality early on, and built his own life. Amused himself by taking risks, just as his real father had done when he'd been alive. Enjoyed himself immensely, in fact. Narrow escapes had been his stock and trade for almost thirty years, and his ability to live recklessly and somehow dodge trouble had served him well during his years as a champion saddle bronc rider…and then it had all caught up with him. Today's mishap was the proverbial frosting on the cake.

Brady reached for his phone, which he'd dug out of his pocket after the four-wheeler had hit the rock that started its slow-motion sideways slide into the ditch before it rolled onto his foot, firmly trapping him. Maybe if he stared at the phone long enough, he could will it into showing some bars. The phone's reception icon remained stubbornly blank. He dialed 911, anyway.

The low rumble in the distance brought his head up.

Holy...

The deep throb of a diesel engine vibrated through the ground as the vehicle turned onto the gravel road that passed twenty yards from where Brady lay pinned by the ATV. Ed Cordell, maybe?

Ed had managed the Callahan Ranch until Rosalie Callahan moved to town a little over a month ago. Believing his job was in jeopardy, Ed had found employment elsewhere, leaving Rosalie high and dry, which was why she'd sought out Brady and offered him a three-month contract to manage the ranch until her grandson, Nick, moved back to Montana. Everything had worked out well— until today, anyway.

Brady had wanted solitude, but the downside of living like a hermit had been driven home today. Ranching alone could be dangerous. If he didn't flag down this vehicle, he was going to be in a world of hurt. Make that a bigger world of hurt.

Brady grimaced as he twisted his body and grabbed the ball cap that had fallen off his head when the four-wheeler had lurched over, bringing him with it, even though he'd tried to jump free. His stiff leg had made the move impossible. Brady, who'd made a career of dismounting bucking horses, hadn't been able to get himself free of the four-wheeler in time to save himself.

He got hold of the hat and stretched his arm skyward, hoping the cap showed above the grass as he waved it wildly, yelling for good measure.

The truck didn't slow.

He kept waving; then, as it appeared that his potential rescuer was going to drive by him, oblivious to his predicament, he tossed the cap in the air. It came back down close to his head and he tossed it again. This time a gust of wind caught it, lofting it high in the air before dropping it back to earth well out of reach.

But the truck had slowed. He started yelling and shaking the grass next to him. It was unlikely the driver could hear him over the sound of the engine, even if the window was down—and why would it be down on a cold late-October day—but maybe the moving grass would attract attention. He flailed his arm, making as much of a ruckus as possible, then let out another yell as the truck rolled to a stop. The door opened, and he heard the sound of feet hitting gravel.

He swallowed dryly as his body went limp with relief, his voice sounding all croaky as he called, "Over here."

The grass rustled and the earth made small hollow thudding sounds as whoever had stopped made their way toward him.

Rescue. *Thank you, thank you, whoever you are.*

He looked over his shoulder as the grass parted behind him and then swallowed a groan. Of all the people in the universe that might have found him like this, the Fates had sent Katie Callahan. Nick's little sister. Who had always driven him crazy in a way he'd have never confessed to his friend for fear of getting a fist in the face. Not that he wasn't glad to see her. He was beyond glad. He was ecstatic.

"I thought you weren't coming home any-time soon," he muttered. Rosalie had told him how well her granddaughter was doing in San Francisco and how it was doubtful Katie would make it home for Thanksgiving, which was a month away.

"Change of plans. Been here long?" She walked around him and knelt close to the ATV, sizing up the situation. She shook her head, her long dark hair shifting over her shoulder. Even now, trapped beneath a ton of machinery, he noticed her hair, the way the late-autumn sunlight glinted off the dark strands. Bad sign.

"About half an hour." The pain in his lower leg was getting worse, and of course it was his good leg trapped beneath the heavy hunk of machinery, rather than the one that had been annihilated last May by a rogue bronc named Pinky. "Maybe you should go for help?" he asked from between his teeth. The McGuire Ranch was only three miles away. Surely Travis or his dad, Will, would be there, much as he hated to ask them for help. After all, Will had implied that if Brady didn't go to college he'd end up in a ditch somewhere, and here he was.

"First I'm going to try to get you out from under this thing."

"Yeah? How you going to do that?" Katie was small, but judging from the way her expression shifted, she wasn't going to let her size slow her down.

She got to her feet and dusted off her palms. "Wait here." She started back through the grass.

"Not funny," Brady called. Once again his forehead met dirt and he swallowed, and then started working his foot again. An eternity later, Katie returned with a short thick-handled shovel, the kind one used to put out a campfire.

"You aren't going to pry with that."

"Yeah? I've been working out." She turned the shovel over and worked the cupped metal end under the ATV next to his boot, getting a fairly decent purchase on the rock the caved-in running board rested on.

"Katie… I'm hurting. Maybe you should just go for help."

She pressed her lips together, then bent her knees and pressed down, using the rock as a fulcrum. To his amazement, the machine moved, and Brady managed to move his foot a fraction of an inch before it came back down.

"Again," Katie said.

This time he didn't argue or try to tell her what was and was not possible. He braced his palms in the dirt, waited until the pressure eased, then pulled as hard as he could. This time when the machine came back down, his foot was far enough out of the boot that he was able to wiggle it, then pull it the rest of the way free.

"Never underestimate the power of a lever," Katie said as she got to her feet.

Or a smallish, determined woman. Brady was amazed that she'd gotten him out from under the thing.

Katie braced her hands on her thighs and let out a breath. "Are you okay?"

"Yeah. Better now."

She gave a low laugh, the husky throaty laugh that was at such odds with her delicate appearance. The laugh that had always made him think that she knew something he didn't, which had both intrigued and alarmed him. She'd never been put off by the distance he'd tried to keep between them and a couple of times he'd teetered dangerously toward closing that distance. And then he'd remember why he couldn't do that, and it wasn't entirely because of her brother's fists. Brady had the same wild streak his father had had, and he would not make Katie as miserable as Colton O'Neil had made his mother. Maybe if he'd had a more conventional father, then his mom would have been a more conventional mother...and maybe he'd have found other excuses to stay away from Katie. But regardless, he wasn't going to hurt Katie.

"How's your foot?" Katie stared at his sock-clad extremity. "Shouldn't we take a look?"

"I'd rather get to the ranch first." A shudder went through him, partly due to reaction, partly due to hugging the cold ground for so long.

"I guess so." She got to her feet and held out a hand. Brady ignored it, putting his weight on his right palm and awkwardly pivoting his body to get his feet under him. It was the way he had to do things now. No more jumping to his feet. Or jumping period. He was at the point in his life where he had to let the four-wheeler roll onto him.

Katie ran her hands down the sides of her jeans, looking a touch self-conscious at having her offer of help rebuffed. He couldn't help that, but he could explain.

"I have to move in certain ways now."

Her eyebrows lifted. "Yeah?" she asked softly.

He shrugged, not wanting to get into it. "Can you give me a ride to the ranch?"

"No offense, Brady, but that's kind of a dumb question. What's my other option? Leaving you here to walk with only one boot?"

"Point taken." He took a cautious step forward and pain shot through the foot he'd pulled free. Great. He gritted his teeth, took another limping step; this time his limp was due to his bad leg, which was now slightly shorter than his newly injured leg. Katie made a move as if to put a hand under his elbow, but his expression must have made her think twice, because she took an instant step back. He fixed his gaze on the truck, which was way too far away, and continued through the grass, one painful step at a time. Behind him, he heard scraping noises as Katie pulled her shovel free—or attempted to. Finally, she ran through the tall grass to catch up with him.

"Shovel's stuck good."

"I know the feeling," he said grimly. He could smell the fresh scent of her shampoo or body wash or something. Here in the middle of a grassy meadow, with a dozen other scents fighting for dominance, he smelled her.

"You know, you don't have to be super tough all the time."

He stopped in his tracks, thankful to have a reason to stop moving. "What does that mean?"

She made a face, then surprised him by plopping his rescued ball cap onto his head, pulling the brim too low. He tilted it up again, scowling at her.

"It means you can relax the attitude." She pushed past him without adding more to the explanation, her denim-clad hips swaying as she walked through the tall grass. Brady dropped his gaze, concentrated on making it to the truck. Katie was waiting for him when he got there, one hand on the edge of the truck bed, her long dark hair now captured in the elastic he'd noticed on her wrist when she'd been prying him free. Without a word, she got into the driver's seat and waited for him to make his way around the truck and awkwardly climb inside.

Once his seat belt was fastened, she started the truck, then swung it into a U.

"What are you doing?" The ranch was in the opposite direction.

"Taking you to the clinic to make sure you don't have a broken foot."

His hand shot out to cover hers on the steering wheel and she instantly hit the brakes, bringing the truck to a stop.

"No." The word came out on a deadly note as he met her gaze. Her mouth opened, but before she could speak, he shook his head. "You have no say in this, Katie. If you don't want to take me to the ranch, then just let me out here."

"And you'll walk." Her delicate dark eyebrows arched. "Or die trying."

"I can't afford the clinic."

"Are you drowning in medical bills after—" Katie's voiced faltered before she finished her question "—what happened?"

"What happened" was why he was in the predicament he was currently in—working as a temporary ranch manager while sorting through his life, waiting for his body to heal to the point that he'd be able to get a more permanent job. The only thing he had left from his rodeo glory years was the lump sum of cash that his agent/accountant was sitting on, earmarked as a down payment on a parcel of land that would be his new beginning. He was just waiting for the legalities to be settled. The last thing he needed was to incur debt while he waited. The owner of the parcel, Abe Larson Jr., had agreed to carry the loan, and he was known to be a stickler for prompt payment. Abe Jr. would foreclose in a heartbeat, so Brady was going to make those payments come hell or high water. He didn't need a stack of medical bills gumming up his finances.

"That's not really any of your business, Katie."

He'd hoped to squelch her rescuing tendencies with the blunt statement, but failed.

She gave him a concerned look. "I can—"

He gave her a warning look. No. She would not help him out in that regard.

"I'll ice it. Tomorrow I'll evaluate. I know what a broken foot feels like." As well as a broken shoulder, broken ribs and a severely fractured leg. Shattered, in fact. "If it's really broken, I'll go to the clinic."

"How will you get there?"

"Katie, believe it or not, I can do lots of things with broken bones. It's kind of what

I do." Or rather, what he had done. His career was over, but in his glory days he'd ridden many a rank bronc while healing from injuries.

After a nice long stare-down, her lips tightened ominously, but she didn't say a word as she eased her foot off the brake, drove the truck out into the field for another bumpy U-turn, then headed in the direction of the ranch.

Stubborn, stubborn, stubborn.

Repeating the mantra made Katie feel less like smacking her passenger, who sat silently staring out at the gravel road ahead of them. She chanced a sideways glance. He pretended not to notice, but his mouth tightened, telling her that he knew she was looking at him and he was purposely not looking back. Not making any kind of a connection at all.

Fine, Brady. Have it your way.

It shouldn't bother her. They'd never been all that close, even though she wanted to be, but he had helped her out a time or two. Laughed with her a time or two…left her wanting more a time or two. She hadn't gotten that more. He'd mostly held her at arm's length and she'd never figured out why he could be so friendly with Nick and her older sister, Cassie, but shut her out. It had stung— when she'd allowed it to. It had also irritated her, so she'd made it a point to never let his standoffishness affect how she treated him. If anything, it made her talk to him more.

"Thank you for the rescue."

Katie jumped at the unexpected sound of his voice. "Not a problem."

"I guess I'm lucky that you were on your way to the ranch."

"Looks like it."

"*Why* are you on your way to the ranch?"

She shot him a curious look. "Grandma didn't say anything?"

He shook his head, but she read the intensity in his expression before pulling her gaze back to the road. He wasn't going to like her answer. She gave a mental shrug and answered, anyway. "I'm on my way to the ranch because I'm staying there." With no plans to leave in the near future. Or the distant future for that matter.

She felt him go still beside her as she slowed for a corner, the last one before the wooden bridge over the Ambrose River, which separated the Callahan Ranch from the pastureland they leased, the pasture Brady had probably been checking when he'd had his accident.

"*I'm* staying there," he said, as if there was a mix-up.

"Yes." Katie's peripheral vision was good, honed from her daily walk to work through the city and a near-miss mugging, and she could see that he was frowning fiercely as he studied her profile. "We'll be fine. The ranch is big."

"Why… What happened to your job? Rosalie told me you were doing well."

"Big layoff. I was one of the casualties," she said in a light voice, even though she wasn't feeling particularly light about it. She'd discovered that her dream job wasn't as perfect as she would have liked, but she'd rolled with it, planning to put in five years— the magic number that would give her the experience necessary to move up the food chain at another firm. She'd never dreamed that the job would quit her before she quit it. In the land of sky-high rents, she'd yet to accrue much of a cushion. Frankly, she hadn't thought she'd need a cushion, but she did, and what she'd managed to save wasn't enough to support her while she looked for another job in San Francisco, so back to the ranch she'd run. And the closer she'd gotten to home, the more right it felt to have cut and run.

That was something she hadn't expected.

Running home was supposed to feel like failure, but instead, as she put miles between herself and the Bay Area, she'd experienced a sense of relief, as if she were escaping something she hadn't realized was trapping her. *What-ifs* and *should-haves* and important next steps faded into the background, and as she approached the Montana border she'd come to the startling realization that her old life didn't have to be her forever life.

But you worked so hard for that life. Made so many sacrifices...

Maybe that was part of the problem.

She'd conditioned herself to believe that she *had* to make sacrifices in order to succeed, and if she wasn't making sacrifices, then she was doing something wrong.

She'd wanted to be a gardener when she was younger. Wanted to have her hands deep into the soil whenever possible. Wanted to feel that sense of peace that filled her whenever she was tending plants. But watching her older siblings charge into first college and then careers in engineering and education convinced her that responsible adults built responsible careers, and following a passion instead of an official profession with a 401K and health insurance seemed irresponsible. And when Nick had left engineering to develop his contracting firm, she hadn't really considered the fact that he'd left something he didn't like so well to do something he liked better.

Now she was wondering. Was it possible that he'd been more in tune with his needs than she'd been with hers?

She hadn't even indulged in hobbies during her career-building years. There'd always been a fire to put out, either in her professional or private life. Life was all about fires, and she knew that, but there were times when she felt like she was encroaching on inferno territory. Even yoga classes hadn't helped—but that might have been because she rarely had time to attend. The instructor must have loved her—more than once she'd paid for six weeks of classes, only to show up once or twice.

She was tired of being on edge full-time. Tired of drama—a sentiment Brady could probably identify with, given the drama he'd recently been involved with. And the consequences of said drama. It had killed her to watch him limp across the pasture to the truck, and to slow her pace to match his when she could so clearly remember scrambling to keep up with his long-legged stride the few times she'd accompanied him and Nick as they worked around the ranch. And she had questions—or rather, one big question.

Had he really been sneaking around with the girlfriend of the bull rider who'd punched him out just prior to his last ride? It didn't seem like something Brady would do, but she hadn't been around the guy in a long time.

After the fight, Brady had insisted on making his ride, because there was an additional purse for the cowboy who could ride the unrideable widow-maker he'd drawn. She didn't know how much being punched had affected him, but the horse had reared over backward four seconds into the ride and crushed Brady beneath him. So, fight or no fight, Brady's career was over.

"So, you're heading to the ranch to…" Brady's voice trailed, inviting her to fill in the blanks.

"Stay. There are two houses. One for you and one for me." She glanced over at him. "Are you living in the main house?"

"Hardly."

"The foreman's house is nice." It was about half the size of the main house, but still had two bedrooms and a bath and a half. A big kitchen that Katie had painted and wallpapered when she was a teen, while Ed, the cranky ranch manager, had been on vacation. He'd asked for the kitchen to be painted, but he hadn't expected cherry wallpaper and bright red cabinets.

"It suits me."

Brady fell into silence, and after a couple of quiet miles, Katie poked the bear. "Do you have a problem sharing the ranch with me?"

"No."

"Right." He'd made it pretty clear that he *did* have a problem sharing and she figured it stemmed from all the stuff he'd been through over the past several months. Stuff she wanted to know more about, but didn't dare ask.

"It's not personal." Brady straightened in his seat, grimacing at the small shift in body position. Katie wished he would have allowed her to take him to the clinic to be checked out. If the foot was broken, something would need to be done, whether he had good insurance or not. "I thought I'd have the place to myself."

The tires clattered as she drove onto the single lane bridge. The lifeline to the ranch. It was just big enough for a cattle truck or hay wagon, but it was always a nail-biter driving over it in a big rig.

"Good thing you don't, or you would have probably died of hypothermia lying under that four-wheeler all night. Who would have come looking for you?"

"Touché." The word came out flatly. "I owe you."

"No. You don't." She meant it. She didn't want anyone, least of all Brady, feeling beholden to her.

Katie drove under the tall archway that marked the entrance to the ranch and her heart swelled. It felt so good to be home. Away from the stuff that had seemed so normal at the time she hadn't noticed it was chipping away at her soul. Maybe that was why, upon receiving her pink slip, the third emotion she'd felt after shock and fear was a brief and quickly squelched twinge of relief.

After parking the truck next to the main

house, she half expected Brady to bolt—or to come as close to bolting as he could with his injuries, both old and new—but instead he turned toward her and regarded her for a long moment from under the brim of his ball cap, giving her a moment to study him back.

He'd been good-looking in high school, but now he bordered on spectacular with his dark hair and green eyes. The planes of his face had become more pronounced with age, as had the laugh lines around his eyes. She doubted that Brady had laughed a lot lately, but the lines made her realize how much time had passed since they'd seen one another. They'd both aged, changed. They weren't the people they'd once been.

"I'm hurting, Katie."

The candid admission startled her. Brady O'Neil admitting weakness. Brady, who'd refused to go to the clinic. Brady, who'd never let on that his parents were not the loving parents they appeared to be. Nick had clued her in on that small fact.

"Hurting inside or out?" She half expected him to pull into himself after she asked the question, refuse to answer or deflect the question. He didn't.

"Out." His jaw shifted sideways, and he

sucked in a breath before saying, "Both. Which is why I need my space. Maybe, before I go, I can explain everything. But for now..." He made a frustrated gesture. "Like I said, I need my space."

"Do you think I'm going to try to mother you, or smother you or something to that effect? Because that isn't the case. I'm here to sort my life out, too."

There was color in his cheeks. This wasn't easy for him, but now that he knew she was going to be sharing his domain, he was establishing boundaries. Like she would encroach where she wasn't wanted. Although perhaps he had cause to think that. She hadn't exactly taken the hint when he'd tried to shut her out when they were teens.

"What makes you think I'm going to insinuate myself into your life?" she added.

He ignored the remark. "You're a helper, Katie, and I don't want help. I want to find out what I'm capable of alone."

"Well, we now know your capabilities in the wrecked four-wheeler department." Katie instantly held up her hand. "Low blow. Sorry. But what makes you think I'm going to pay any attention to you at all?"

"Katie," he said softly, "you rescue things. Puppies, kittens, leppie calves."

Okay. So, she'd rescued a few orphan calves. Some abandoned puppies. A few kittens. Big deal. She propped a hand on her hip. "And that's your big fear? That I'm going to try to rescue you?" She lifted her eyebrows in a speaking expression. "Like I did today?"

Brady didn't bite.

Katie let out a frustrated huff of breath. "Fine. We'll make a no-rescue pact. I won't rescue you, *again*, and you won't rescue me." She lifted her chin. "Not that I would need to be rescued."

He cocked an eyebrow and the color rose in her cheeks as she got his point. "I can now change a tire by myself, and if I get stranded after midnight, I have a cell phone." And a lot more street smarts than she'd had back in the day.

"How about instead of a pact, you treat me like Ed Cordell? An employee of the ranch."

Ed, the former ranch manager, had kept to himself, did his job and did it well. He'd been all business, and Katie had never been able to warm up to the man. But he'd kept the ranch running smoothly, she'd give him that.

"If you're asking me to treat you like Ed, you're serious about this leave-you-alone thing."

"It's not personal, Katie," he repeated. "It's what I need right now."

Katie lifted her chin. "If you need to be left alone, I'll respect your wishes. Believe it or not, I no longer need to tag along where I'm not wanted. I've changed over the past decade."

"I noticed."

She frowned at the unexpected remark, but before she could come up with a comeback or a question, Brady held out a hand. Katie stared at it for a second, feeling as if she was teetering on the brink of something dangerous, which was crazy because how dangerous could it be shaking hands with a guy who didn't want her—or anyone for that matter—around? She resolutely put her hand in his, her nerves jumping as his warm, work-roughened palm made contact with hers and his fingers closed.

"Deal?"

Katie nodded briskly before pulling her fingers free. "Deal." She felt as if she'd just gotten a slow-motion electrical shock. That was the only way she could describe the tingle that gripped her body when they made contact, ultimately making her stomach tumble.

The vestiges of a crush from the distant past. That was all it was.

She reached for her door handle, her heart beating harder than before, and still feeling the warmth of his fingers on hers. She pushed her hands into her back pockets and met Brady's gaze. "This is where we go our separate ways, living our parallel lives on the Callahan Ranch?"

He gave his head a slow shake, those mossy green eyes full of an emotion she couldn't quite read as he said, "I doubt we'll be able to do that, but when we do meet—"

"You're Ed to me."

CHAPTER TWO

As soon as Brady made his way into his house and the door was safely closed behind him, he stopped and scrubbed his hand over his face. Well, he'd handled that poorly. And now he knew why he'd had a message to call Rosalie waiting for him when he came in for lunch. She'd been out when he'd tried to contact her, and then he'd had to leave to check the fence before turning out the cattle on new pasture.

After that he hadn't been able to call because he'd been stuck under a four-wheeler.

Brady squeezed his forehead with his palm before dropping his hand loosely back to his side. Katie Callahan, who was supposed to be enjoying her dream job in San Francisco, had shown up out of nowhere to rescue him. And he'd been borderline rude as he'd tried to set boundaries. He probably hadn't needed to instantly jump right into it as he had, but he wasn't thinking as well as he used to as he coped with life changes.

While Katie might say that she wanted to be left alone, too, her brand of alone wasn't the same as his. And he'd never seen Katie *not* pitch in and help. It was as if it was hard-wired into her brain to lend a helping hand and rescue the less fortunate. She was the person who stood up for the kid who got picked on. The person who hand-raised the orphan duck. Who yelled at people who treated animals poorly with no regard to how they might react to her scolding. And here he was, a walking-talking rescue project. He was curious to see if she *could* treat him like Ed.

He moved to the kitchen table and sat down in a sturdy handmade oak chair. His foot was throbbing, as was the thigh with the metal rod holding his femur in place. He stiffly leaned down and felt his foot and ankle through the thick cotton sock, which was soaking wet and caked with dirt, wincing as he touched the swollen area. Katie might be taking him to the clinic, after all.

Biting his lip, he took hold of the wet sock and gently peeled it down over a purple ankle and swollen foot. It got hung up and clung to his damp skin, but eventually he pulled it free and dropped it on the floor, turning his foot to get a look at it from a different angle.

Broken?

Gingerly he probed. He thought not. He'd had enough broken bones as a result of his chosen profession to be fairly certain of his diagnosis. Or maybe he was just fooling himself to keep money in the bank. All that mattered was that he was able to walk, kind of, and that meant, with the help of the four-wheeler, he'd be able to do his work. It'd be better if he were closer to ambulatory, but one thing bronc riding had taught him was to suck it up and look for a work-around in order to continue with the job. He'd ridden with broken ribs, a dislocated elbow, a stress fracture in his tibia. And he'd won money every time. People had told him not to ride, but he'd never listened, because he knew his abilities. He'd figured out how to do things then, and he'd figure out how to do them now. He'd also figure out how to live peacefully with Katie here on the ranch and somehow ignore the attraction that was just as strong now as it had been back in the day when she'd seemed way too young, and way too sweet, to hook up with a loose cannon like him.

According to Rosalie, it would be a matter of months—no more than three—before Nick finalized the sale of his contracting business and moved from California to Montana to take over management of the ranch. Surely Brady could maintain a level of polite professionalism with Katie until then. All he had to do was stay out of her way.

But one question kept niggling at him. Did Nick know that his little sister was back on the ranch? If so, why no heads-up? They'd talked only a day ago when Brady had called him for some tips on maintaining the wood splitter.

Brady limped to the counter where he'd left his phone, wondering if 911 calls went through retroactively once the signal was restored. Apparently not, because his screen showed no activity since he'd returned to the ranch. He went into his contacts, punched a name. Nick answered in three rings, a harried note in his voice.

"Brady, what's up? Everything okay on the ranch?"

"Your sister is here. Katie," he added, since Nick had two sisters.

"On the ranch?"

His friend's surprised tone answered Brady's

first question, which was, did everyone know but him?

"Yes. She'll be staying awhile."

"Thereby interfering with your fortress-of-solitude scheme."

Brady had never once mentioned his need for privacy to anyone except Katie, but Nick knew him well. He should. He'd talked him down a time or two when things had gotten rough with his parents.

"Pretty much."

"Why is she there? Did Grandma know she was coming?"

"My guess is no. And you should probably discuss the whys with her, since I only got the bare-bones story."

"Yeah. I'll do that."

Brady heard a distinct "Daddy!" in the background before Nick answered in a muffled voice, "I'll be there in a second, Bailey. Just hang tight." He came back on the line. "I've got me a situation here, but I'll call Katie and see what's up."

"Sorry to butt into your family business." And it was crazy to think of Nick, former wild man, as a single father. He'd lost his wife just eighteen months ago, and in Brady's opinion, returning to Montana, where he'd be closer to Rosalie and now Katie, was a good move.

"Hey...you're family, too."

Brady didn't think so. The Callahans had provided him a refuge when he needed it most—twice now—but being part of the family? He wasn't sure about that. But he loved them like a family, and maybe that counted.

"I'll talk to Katie," Nick said. "Tell her to let you be."

"Don't. We'll be fine. I just wanted to give you a heads-up."

"Thanks." Another "Daddy!" came through the line, this one more plaintive than the one before, so Brady said, "I'll let you go. Be in touch."

He hung up before Nick answered, and once again ran a hand over his face as he stared across the kitchen. What was up with Katie, who was apparently in the middle of some big life change that only Rosalie knew about? He wondered how serious an event would have to be to send tenacious Katie back to Montana.

Brady let out a breath.

That was the kind of thinking that was going to get him into trouble if he wasn't careful. Better to focus on matters at hand—such as the four-wheeler, which he had to get out of the ditch. Soon.

How was he supposed to do that without Katie tagging along? Because she would, despite promises made. Brady went to the window and stared out, seeking inspiration, which he got in the form of a gnarly truck parked behind the barn.

The Beast. Nick's old truck had a winch on the front.

Problem solved.

KATIE HAD BARELY gotten her suitcase into the house when her phone rang with her grandmother's special ringtone. She scooped up the phone and held it to her ear as she closed the door behind her. The late-October air was frigid, and she gave a little shiver as she said hello.

"Hey, Grandma…Yes, I got here all right. Sorry I didn't call sooner. Time got away from me." She wasn't going to tell her it was because she was helping the ranch manager out from under his all-terrain vehicle. Her grandmother had enough on her plate helping her friend and business partner, Gloria, refurbish their house and turn the bottom level into a gift and garden store, without having to worry about the goings-on on the ranch. One reason she'd moved to town after her husband's death was to start a new life that didn't revolve around ranching.

"Have you talked to Brady?" Rosalie sounded concerned.

"Yes, I have." She kept her tone casual, as if talking to the guy who'd just made her pulse race with a simple handshake had been nothing more than a casual exchange of words. "We're in a good place."

"He didn't respond to my message and I didn't want him to feel ambushed."

"He was busy in the river pasture," Katie said before adding, "It *is* our ranch, Grandma. I assume we can come and go as we please without asking permission. It isn't like we're renting the place to him."

"Let's just say he was expecting a certain set of circumstances, and it isn't what he's getting."

"We talked," Katie repeated. "He's hurting and healing and wants his privacy. I totally get it. I won't be running hot meals to his door." As she'd done to her down-the-hall neighbor last year after she'd fallen and broken an elbow.

"Good." Her grandmother sounded relieved. "I promised him some solitude, but you also need a place to land."

And it was clear that Rosalie had been torn between their two needs—her granddaughter, who'd just lost her job, and her grandson's best friend, who'd taken refuge on the ranch during his teen years and then gone on to make something of himself, only to have his world crash down around his ears. Katie totally got it.

"No need to feel guilty, Grandma. Brady will get his solitude. We'll perfect the fine art of compromise."

"I wish Cassie would learn to do that," Rosalie murmured.

"Why? What's up with Cass?" Her sister could be a real hard case, which was why she was so good at her job as an assistant school district administrator in a small town in Wisconsin.

"She's having issues with a group of parents. I'm sure she'll tell you about it when you talk to her next. In the meantime, I have trim that needs painting."

"I'm so excited to see your house." She was familiar with the house, since it was one of the Three Grand Ladies of Gavin, Victorian homes that had once housed the local gentry before falling into disrepair.

"And I can't wait to give you a tour. Hopefully I'll be done painting by then. The problem with a big house is that it has lots of walls."

"And trim." Katie smiled. "Go paint, Grandma. And don't spend one more minute worrying about me and Brady. He'll have his space. Promise."

After her grandmother said goodbye, Katie set down her phone and rolled her suitcase down the hall to the room she'd occupied as a child after her widowed father had brought his three kids home to grow up on the ranch like he'd done. Katie had been the only one who hadn't instantly embraced the cowboy lifestyle, as all good Callahans did. She loved riding horses, but she wasn't into riding fence and roping calves and participating in rodeo like Nick and Cassie. She preferred tending to her menagerie of small animals, gardening, reading.

She'd toyed with the idea of becoming a veterinarian, like her father, but dissection had done her in during high school biology. A good vet didn't have to turn away at the sight of blood and guts. Then, because she loved plants, she'd considered botany, but the hard sciences were so not her thing, despite her natural green thumb, so ultimately she readjusted her goals and majored in psychology and business administration with an emphasis in human resources—a great career for a person who got along well with others. It was also a career that involved living in a city, which she'd loved until the new started wearing off.

Being surrounded by crowds of people had been energizing at first, but later began to take its toll. She had stubbornly refused to acknowledge the truth to herself, but as time passed, she'd grown tired of being nudged and bustled along. Tired of having to watch everyone around her...just in case. And she grew tired of her then-boyfriend, a techie with money to burn, trying to convince her to become something she was not, as in sleek and sophisticated. Her "candid nature and refreshing air," which he said had drawn him to her, began to wear on him, too.

After breaking up with her techie, and shortly before her layoff, a guy had grabbed her purse at the BART station and taken off at a run, dragging Katie, who'd had the strap wrapped around her hand, behind him.

When bystanders had converged upon him, he'd abandoned the purse and taken off, leaving Katie bruised and shaken. After getting her layoff notice, it hadn't taken long to decide to head home—and to feel good about the decision. It was as if her eyes had been opened. She still loved the city in a lot of ways, but she'd had enough. Small-town Montana looked pretty good to a girl with a pink slip in her hand and bruises on her shoulder from the attempted mugging.

Her roomies had been happy to buy her furniture at bargain prices, and she'd boxed up her other belongings and shipped them home. Actually, she'd beaten them home. Her dishes, books and the bulk of her clothing would arrive in Gavin early next week. Thankfully, her grandmother had only taken about half of her furniture when she'd moved to her new smaller house in town, so Katie had chairs to sit on and a bed to sleep in.

Katie opened the door to her sunny room at the back of the house, which had glass-paned double doors that opened onto a back deck and surrounding garden. All the ground-floor bedrooms had access to the deck, thanks to Nick, who'd remodeled the aging ranch house before moving to California to start a contracting business. A business he was now in the process of selling.

Katie dumped her suitcase on the bed and started unzipping it when scratching on the deck door brought her head around. She smiled as the big orange tabby cat blinked at her. Tigger, her last rescue before leaving for college. She opened the door and Tigger slipped through, jumping easily up onto the bed, despite his crooked back leg. She sat down beside him and stroked his orange fur as he rubbed his head on her sleeve and purred. "Yep. I'm home, big guy. We can read in the garden like we used to once it warms up again."

That was probably a lie. If she was going to figure out a way to earn a living on the ranch, there wouldn't be a lot of reading time. But she'd try to squeeze in a little— for Tigger's sake.

She quickly unpacked the necessities and then set her suitcase back on the floor. Her stomach growled and she checked the time on her phone. Yes. Definitely time to eat.

"Let's go see what's in the cupboards," she said to the cat. He jumped off the bed and trotted to the door, looking over his shoulder before heading out into the hall. As she suspected, he was waiting for her in the kitchen, staring expectantly up at the treat container. She shook out a couple of fish-shaped treats, and Tigger pounced.

"Eat hearty, my friend." She opened a cupboard door and found the interior jammed with canned food and dry goods. She opened another. Same thing. Her grandmother had always kept a lot of food on hand—the better to deal with a veterinarian son who worked crazy hours, and three hungry teens, with Brady often making it four—but Katie had assumed that once the hungry hoard was gone, her grandmother would adjust her food storage habits.

Apparently not.

She was just closing the cupboard when a movement outside the kitchen window caught her eye. Brady. The guy she was supposed to treat like brusque, cranky Ed. She could do it, because he was acting like brusque, cranky Ed.

He's in pain.

Okay. So he has an excuse. Now. There was no excuse for the way he'd treated her before. The friendlier she'd gotten back in the day, the more distant he became— except for those two rescues. She went to the window and leaned on the dark blue quartz countertop, another of Nick's upgrades, and craned her neck to see where Brady was going. He wasn't moving fast, for obvious reasons, but he definitely had a purpose. When he let himself in through the gate of the machine yard, she had a good idea of his destination. Nick's old truck had a winch on the front, and since Brady had to get the four-wheeler out of the ditch, it made perfect sense to fire up the Beast. But since Nick had pulled the engine from the Beast a little over a year ago and broke it down for parts, she didn't think Brady would find the vehicle all that useful.

She turned and leaned back against the counter, folding her arms over her chest as she watched Tigger down his last treat. Would she have helped Ed out under these circumstances? No. Ed would have soon figured out that the Beast was going nowhere, and Brady would do the same. However, there was still the problem of the ranch four-wheeler lying on its side in a ditch that could easily fill with water if there were to be a rainstorm. She hadn't checked the forecast lately, but rain was always a possibility.

Good enough. If Ed had been endanger-

ing the ranch four-wheeler, she would have
intervened. She pushed off the counter and
headed for the door.

CHAPTER THREE

The engine was gone.

Brady slapped his hand on the fender of the Beast and tipped his chin toward the sky as he debated plan B. Tractor. Chain. Utility trailer. The winch would have been faster, but he was fine with whatever got the job done.

But could he drive a standard transmission with his swollen foot? He'd planned to start the Beast and see what he could do with an automatic transmission, but that was now out of the question.

The sound of the gate opening startled him. He was more than aware that he wasn't alone on the ranch, but he hadn't expected Katie to show up so soon after promising not to.

"If you were Ed, I would have told you that the Beast isn't an option. The engine went south a while ago, and Nick pulled it when he was home last Christmas."

"It does appear to be missing." And she appeared to have been watching him, if she came out to deliver the sad news he'd already figured out on his own. He'd enjoyed three days of solitude on the Callahan Ranch, and now he was going to spend every waking minute feeling as if he was under surveillance.

Get real.

Katie had her own issues. He felt as if she was watching him, because he felt an incredible need to watch her. His fascination with Nick's little sister was still as strong as ever.

She cocked a hip, settling her hand on it. "How are you going to get the four-wheeler out of the ditch?"

The exact question he was pondering, but the answer was simple enough, because the viable options were few. "I'll tow it out with the tractor. Go back with the truck. Load it onto a trailer."

"That's a lot of trips to and fro. Tractor. Truck and trailer."

"It isn't like I don't have time."

"But you don't have a lot of daylight," she pointed out in a very reasonable way. "What if it rains tonight?"

Something he'd already thought of. It

wasn't like he couldn't work after dark, but if it was anyone but Katie hinting that he should accept help, would he refuse? As self-conscious as he was about the limitations of his healing body, the honest answer was no. He'd accept help.

She held up her hands as if in surrender. "No worries. I was just wondering if you wanted help. Not *needed* help, mind you. Wanted."

"I want help." The stubborn part of him wanted to turn down her offer. The logical part knew that was a stupid thing to do.

Katie's mouth fell open, but she quickly closed it.

He'd stunned her. It felt like a small victory. "The job needs done," he said matter-of-factly. "It'll be quicker with two people. I'll pull the ATV out with the truck and ride it back to the ranch. You can bring the truck back." He cleared his throat and looked past her at the bluish mountains behind the ranch. "Plus, I don't know if I can work a clutch with my foot. You might have to drive both ways."

She gave him a cautious sideways look, as if suspecting a trap. "You're being very…"

He lifted his eyebrows, silently encouraging her to continue and perhaps insult him. He could take it. When she didn't finish his sentence, he said, "Reasonable? Is that the word you're looking for?"

"No. Honestly, it wasn't."

He had a feeling it was.

She slipped her hands into her back pockets. "If you want help, I'll go find a pair of Nick's gloves."

"You won't need gloves."

"I'll get them, anyway." She spoke in a no-nonsense tone he wasn't familiar with. It made him frown a little. Katie had changed.

"Suit yourself," he said to her back as she walked away. It wasn't like he was going to waste his breath arguing with her. They'd pull the ATV out of the ditch. He'd ride it back. They'd go their separate ways. She wouldn't need gloves to do that. Not if everything went according to plan, anyway.

He'd found a tow chain by the time she got back, and was carrying it back to the truck, his injured foot slowing his progress even more than usual. He was still fairly certain it wasn't broken. There was no crunching of bone on bone. Just a whole lot of swelling and bruising.

"Just so you know," Katie said as she

picked up the end of the chain and helped him carry it the rest of the way, "I'm doing this more for the ATV than you." She dumped her end of the chain into the truck.

Good. That was the way he wanted things.

No, being alone on the ranch was the way he wanted things, but he wasn't getting his way, so he needed to adapt. Katie had every right to come home, and he had no business making her feel like she wasn't welcome on her own ranch.

"Who's driving?" she asked, not seeming to mind that he'd never answered her.

"I think you'd better drive."

He limped around the back of the truck while Katie crossed in front. Once they were both inside and she closed the door, he once again smelled the floral scent he'd noticed in the field. It tugged at his senses.

Not good.

She put the truck in gear and swung it around in a wide arc. She was good with a clutch, as kids who grew up on ranches tended to be. He'd only had one girlfriend who'd been able to drive his truck, due to it having a standard transmission.

"About those things I said earlier."

"You meant every word?" she asked mildly.

He somehow kept from growling. "You make apologizing difficult."

She shot him a surprised look, her blue eyes widening. "You're apologizing for me crashing your party? I did show up unannounced."

And saved his butt in the process.

"I'm apologizing for handling things wrong." His fingers tightened on his thigh as he fought to find the right words to explain further, but before he could come up with something, Katie reached out and lightly touched his coat sleeve.

"None of us handles every situation correctly. And you have reason to react as you did." Her expression turned wry as she said, "I probably would have continued trying to rescue you, you know."

Like you are now? He kept the comment to himself, but felt his features relax an iota. "Can't help yourself, can you?"

She gave a small shrug. "I usually don't even try."

AFTER HIS SURPRISING APOLOGY, Brady reverted to form, sitting silently as Katie drove to the river pasture. She thought he winced as the truck bounced over the bridge, but kept her gaze focused dead ahead. She tried to imagine Mason, her techie ex-boyfriend, sucking it up and heading back to rescue the four-wheeler after being injured. Couldn't do it. He might have foregone the clinic, as Brady had done, but he wouldn't have pushed himself to do anything other than make himself as comfortable as possible and watch foreign movies on Netflix.

He'd been fun, in his own way, and she'd learned a lot from him. Like while opposites might attract, they don't last. She glanced at Brady out of the corner of her eye. That was exactly what Brady was. Her opposite. She was outgoing, and he was introverted. She'd taken measures to have a safe, predictable career. He'd bypassed college and embarked on a career where he took risks every time he went to work. She'd come from a warm, supportive family, while his upbringing had left a mark.

Did they have anything in common?

Nick?

"The turnoff is just past that post," Brady pointed out.

She knew where the turnoff was, but had been so deep in her analysis of her passenger that she'd almost driven by it. "Thanks."

Katie slowed the truck, shifted down to grandma gear and turned onto the narrow muddy track that disappeared into tall yellowed grass a few yards into the pasture. She started traveling in the general direction of the ditch, using the path she and Brady had beat through the grass as a guide.

"You're lucky I saw you," she murmured. The tops of the dried-up grass blades were well past the bumper. "It was the hat, you know."

"Pure desperation." He looked out the side window. Let out a breath. She wondered if he was thinking again about how things might have turned out if she hadn't happened by.

"Pretty genius, if you ask me."

But he wasn't, as the silence that followed her remark attested to, so Katie focused on finding the ditch. Opposites. She was a talker and he wasn't. But he'd said that before he left, he might explain everything. She wondered if that included the truth about what had led up to the incident in the Vegas parking lot that could have killed him. Somehow, she doubted it. Brady had secrets. She was an open book.

"We're close."

Katie pulled the truck to a stop and they

got out. She walked to the front and saw the wheel of the ATV poking up out of the ditch. Rubbing a hand over her hair, she glanced over at Brady. "How'd this happen?"

"I swerved."

"Really?"

He looked uncomfortable. "There was a rabbit all nestled down in the grass."

Brady O'Neil had almost killed himself for a bunny? Katie pressed her lips together and directed her attention back to the ATV. Wow. It wasn't that she didn't think Brady would swerve for a rabbit, but she was very surprised he'd told her when he didn't have to. He could have given any number of excuses, but instead he'd fessed up to rabbit.

The silence between them was broken by the call of a lone goose and then Brady turned and limped to the back of the truck, where he let down the tailgate and pulled out the chain. Back to business.

"I'll, uh, swing the truck around."

Katie got into the truck and turned it around, following Brady's hand signals until he gave her the stop signal. She left it running and went to the back to help with the chain. Brady stood a few feet from the

ATV, and when she approached, he shook his head.

"With the angle it's at, this could get ugly. We could do some serious damage."

He practically oozed frustration, and Katie understood. A year ago, he probably could have righted the thing and manhandled it while she towed. Today, not so much.

"I think we should contact the McGuires."

Brady shot her a grim look, then nodded. "We need to do something." He raised his gaze to give her a long hard look. "Just one favor, okay?"

"Sure."

"Don't tell him about the rabbit."

"What were you supposed to do? Run over it?"

"No." He tipped his hat forward. "But I should have been able to maintain control of the four-wheeler."

But he had issues because of his injury.

"Fine. I'll tell him it was a bear."

"Katie…"

She propped her hand on her hip. "Tell you what, Brady…you can do the talking. That way you can maintain your image."

"Thank you—and it has nothing to do with image."

"Give me a break," she muttered. "You're a man."

"Thank you — and it has nothing to do with that."

"Give me a break," she repeated. "You're a hard"

CHAPTER FOUR

THE DRIVE TO the bridge, the nearest place to get a cell phone signal, was silent. And it was not a comfortable silence. Brady was practically smoldering in the seat next to her, but Katie refused to let his demeanor affect hers. She kept her eyes on the road and focused on her driving.

A rabbit.

Katie gave her head a quick shake to clear it. She was not going to think about all the facets of the man sitting next to her that he tried so hard to hide. It was as if he expected someone to plunge a metaphorical knife into any area of weakness he might show.

Perhaps something he learned from his parents?

According to Nick, Brady's stepfather didn't have a paternal bone in his body, and Brady's mother felt more of an allegiance to her husband than to her child. They'd provided Brady what he needed while growing up, went through the motions of being parents, but they'd ignored him. Nick had a theory that Brady looked and acted too much like his wild father, who'd lived hard and died young, and that neither his mother nor his stepfather wanted to be reminded of that painful episode in her life. Even so, it fried Katie to think of them treating Brady that way. It had to have hurt so much.

You can't rescue him.

Words to live by. She would treat him like Ed as she'd promised.

She pulled the truck to a stop in a wide spot just before the bridge and checked her phone. "A signal. Great." She spoke more to herself than to Brady as she dialed the McGuires. Will, the elder McGuire, answered.

"Hi, Will. It's Katie Callahan."

"Katie?" He sounded mystified, as well he should, since as far as he knew, she was in San Francisco, and also somewhat alarmed. "Is your grandmother all right?"

It took Katie a split second to realize that he'd assumed she was calling from California to give him bad news about Rosalie.

"No. I mean, yes, she's fine. I'm the one in trouble. I just got back to the ranch, and, well, there's an issue with the four-wheeler."

She felt Brady stiffen beside her, but resisted the urge to glance over at him.

"You're at the ranch?"

"I quit the city," she said. "Anyway, is Travis around? The four-wheeler is in a ditch in our river pasture and I need some help pulling it out."

"Travis isn't here, but I'll head over."

"I have a tow chain. All I need is some help righting the thing."

"Where's Brady? I heard he was managing the place after Ed took off."

"He's here," Katie said lightly. "But—"

"Yeah. His injuries." There was a note of disapproval in the older man's voice, which puzzled her, since his son, Travis, had ridden his fair share of broncs and had been injured more than once. He just hadn't made a career of it. Her gaze slid sideways, hoping for a clue from her seatmate, but Brady stared straight ahead, a carefully blank expression on his face.

"I'll be there in a few," Will said. He hung up without a goodbye, and Katie slowly lowered the phone.

"Travis isn't there, but Will will be here shortly. I guess we'd better head back to the site."

"Yeah."

She had to bite her tongue to keep from saying something to gloss over the situation in an attempt to make it all better. Fact was that Brady had to deal with his own demons. But another fact was that she was probably going to ask about said demons eventually, even though it was clearly none of her business.

She and Brady drove back to the four-wheeler and got out of the truck. Brady leaned against the hood while Katie paced the ditch. Ten minutes later a pickup turned into the field.

"Help has arrived," Katie said, wishing she didn't feel the need to ease the tense mood by stating the obvious.

"So it has," Brady said in a tone that made her mouth tighten.

"You can quit bristling up, you know. I got the message a while ago."

His expression softened an iota as his gaze moved first to her flattened mouth, then back to her eyes. "I've never been good about accepting help."

His candid statement surprised her almost as much as his apology had.

"I know." *And apparently you have issues*

with the McGuires. Her older sister also had issues with McGuires, but those were based totally on an ancient rivalry between her and Travis. One of those "anything you can do, I can do better" things. Cassie was ridiculously competitive.

Will got out of his truck and, after giving Brady a brusque nod, joined Katie at the edge of the ditch. "I see your dilemma. How'd this happen?" Will asked.

"Error of judgment," Brady answered from behind them before Katie could say anything.

Will pushed back his hat as he looked at Brady. "Kind of a habit with you."

There was a hard note in the older man's voice that Katie didn't like. "Maybe you should know the circumstances before you start judging," she said more sharply than she intended. Definitely more sharply than she ever would have spoken on the job, where she was the one who smoothed the waters.

Both men gave her a surprised look. She was a little surprised herself. "I mean…" She wasn't sure what she meant or why she'd instantly jumped to Brady's defense—especially after promising not to.

Will's cheeks went red, but he didn't apologize. He picked up the chain and eased himself into the ditch, where he fastened the chain to the axel of the four-wheeler, then handed the end up to Brady.

Moments later, the chain was attached to the tow hooks on the truck's front bumper and Katie was behind the wheel. On Brady's signal, she started to slowly back up while Will worked to bring the machine back onto its wheels, then keep it upright as it came up out of the ditch. When it cleared the top, Katie pulled forward, allowing the chain to go slack.

Despite his injuries, Brady disconnected the chain from the four-wheeler and the truck, looping it over his arm before limping to the back of the pickup to drop it into the bed.

"Thanks," he said to Will.

"Glad to help," the older man said solemnly, although the undertone of irony was hard to miss. He turned to Katie, and it was apparent from his expression that he didn't hold her defense of Brady against her. "And glad you called me, even if it did scare the hell out of me. I couldn't think of any reason you might be calling me other than a bad one."

"Well, it was kind of bad."

Will finally smiled. "Yeah. I guess it was, but not in the way that I was thinking."

"Appreciate the help," Brady said as Will headed to his truck. The older man raised his hand to indicate he'd heard without looking back.

"What's with you two?" Katie asked. As far as she knew Will and Brady had gotten along well. Will had even coached him in high school rodeo bronc riding after Travis had gone off to college.

Brady straddled the four-wheeler and turned the key. The engine started without so much as a cough. He revved it, but Katie didn't take the hint. "I thought you agreed not to defend me."

"Rescue you," Katie corrected. "I promised not to rescue you, unless it was a circumstance in which I would rescue Ed, of course."

"I don't want you getting sideways with the neighbors because of me."

"Fine. I won't defend you."

"Good."

"Okay."

Brady revved the engine again and this time Katie reluctantly let go of the moment.

There was something about him that tugged at her, drew her toward him, but whatever it was needed to be brought firmly under control.

"I'll see you around," she said.

He gave her a pointed look. "Circumstances being what they are, I guess so."

"Yep. That's life for you. Dealing with circumstances." Katie dusted her hands off. "Drive safe."

He gave her another look but Katie merely raised her eyebrows before swinging the truck door open and climbing inside.

THE SUN DISAPPEARED behind the trees as Katie followed Brady to the ranch, where he pulled the four-wheeler into the barn while she parked next to the house. As she pulled the keys out of the ignition, she heard Brady close up the barn, the rumbling of the heavy door on its metal track bringing back memories.

She was home.

Her former roommates were convinced that she would retreat to the ranch, collect herself, then head back out into the dog-eat-dog world. The world she'd embraced with gusto upon graduating college. The world she was pretty darned sick of.

Was it nuts that she felt more at peace being jobless in Montana than she'd felt while gainfully employed in a city she still loved?

She'd been so focused on making something of herself in college and then in the big city, on proving to herself that she was as much of a go-getter as her successful older siblings, that she hadn't slowed down enough to take stock of her feelings. Maybe because she'd been afraid of what she would discover if she'd done that.

It was all about sacrifice. Maybe she'd learned that from Cassie. If you weren't sacrificing, you weren't serious. Cassie had sacrificed her social life to succeed and appeared to have found the tradeoff equitable.

But perhaps…just perhaps…she could be like her grandmother and embark on a new career, one that spoke to her in a personal way. Did she dare do such a thing? Pursue a passion instead of a sure thing?

She was actually in a good place to do just that. She had a roof over her head. Resources. She'd pay rent, of course, because she wasn't a freeloader, but rent at the ranch would be a tiny fraction of rent for a third of a city apartment.

The crunch of boots on gravel brought her gaze to the rearview mirror in time to catch sight of Brady heading to his dark house. Her house wasn't dark. She'd left on a light in the kitchen before heading out on her rescue mission, and the warm glow now spilled out of the window onto the leaf-covered lawn. Tigger sat on the sill, staring through the glass at her, as if wondering what the deal was. Why wasn't she in the house feeding and petting him?

Katie took the hint and reached for the door handle.

There was an old saying about home being where the heart was, and for several years, Katie had thought her home was on the Bay. But she'd never felt this sense of peace coming back to her apartment. Depending on the day, she'd felt happy, relieved, excited, weary, overwrought, outraged, but never serene.

Katie mounted the single step leading to the porch Nick was going to rebuild when he took up residence on the ranch. The old boards echoed beneath her feet, bringing more memories.

Maybe this was a mirage. Maybe she wanted to feel safe and warm and protected, so she was making the ranch into something it wasn't.

That was possible, but when she closed the kitchen door and stood on the mat just inside, soaking up the atmosphere of her childhood home, she felt nothing but a deep sense of belonging—as if this ranch had been waiting for her to come to her senses and move back home.

Tigger jumped down from the windowsill and arched against her calves. She reached down to stroke his back with the tips of her fingers. "What do you think, Tig?"

He thought he was hungry and told her so by trotting to his dish.

"Yeah. Got it," she said on a laugh. He could eat in the barn with the wild barn cats—heaven knew there was enough food out there in the giant tub next to the grain bins—but a little TLC never hurt anyone. Well, except for Brady.

After dumping a small can of gourmet cat food into the ceramic dish she'd made in junior high art class, she walked to the window and peered out across the graveled expanse that separated the two houses. Brady limped by the window, then back again, probably cooking his dinner. How badly was he hurting?

And what was the deal with him and Will McGuire?

None of your business.

Katie pulled the curtain across the window and headed for the fridge. As expected, it was sparkling clean inside—and empty. She'd remedy that tomorrow when she went to town to visit her grandmother. She was excited to see Rosalie's new house, even if the trim was not painted. Excited to be close to her grandmother's calming presence. Rosalie had seen her husband through a short series of strokes before the big one claimed him, and not once did Katie see her break.

Tough woman.

You're tough, too. Maybe not as in-your-face as Cassie, but tough.

Tough enough to take chances?

Katie let out a soft snort. Yes. She was.

ROSALIE CALLAHAN SAT back on her heels and studied the length of wooden floor molding she'd just painted rose pink. The color wasn't working, which meant headaches ahead.

After buying the beautiful yet run-down

Victorian house in partnership with Gloria Gable, her best friend since grade school, everything had been smooth sailing. They'd worked up a business plan for the gift and garden store, the Daisy Petal, which would occupy the entire first floor as well as the backyard, without a single issue. They'd set goals and delineated responsibilities in the straightforward, cooperative manner that was the hallmark of their long friendship. Everything had gone well until they'd spread out the paint chips on the long knotty-pine potting table and started discussing color.

Gloria had immediately gravitated toward the bright saturated hues that looked so beautiful on her. Rosalie had done the same, picking neutrals and pastels that didn't overpower her delicate Irish coloring. A long multiday discussion had followed, involving many pots of tea, and culminated with a beer at the Shamrock Pub. Finally, a series of coin tosses had decided matters. The walls of the shop were now pale yellow, the cabinets a pretty aqua that perfectly matched Gloria's favorite necklace. The rose pink, a color they both loved, was supposed to tie the room together and give it a funky floral appeal.

It wasn't.

Rosalie got to her feet and stretched her back. This time she was going to suggest that she and Gloria skip the tea and go straight to alcohol while they hashed things out. Life was too short.

The back door scraped open and Rosalie glanced over her shoulder, glad that she had a nice pinot grigio chilling in her apartment on the second floor of the three-story house, because she wasn't going to paint another inch of trim this disastrous color. "Gloria?"

"It's me, Grandma."

Rosalie's heart jumped at the sound of her granddaughter's voice. She loved each of her three grandchildren to the depth of her soul, but Katie was the grandchild she understood. The one most like herself.

All Callahans took to ranching like a duck to water—except for Katie. Because they'd spent so much time together while the rest of the family was out chasing cows and mending fence, she and her youngest grandchild had forged a special bond.

"Katie!" Rosalie jumped to her feet and a second later was enveloped in a warm hug—and it seemed as if Katie hung on just a little tighter than usual. Understandable, considering what she'd gone through over the past several weeks. Her granddaughter's life had been totally upended.

Katie leaned back. "It felt weird coming home and not seeing you immediately."

"Was the house okay?"

"Once I got the heat cranked up to above fifty-five degrees, it was cozy and wonderful—just like it always is."

"I hope you found something to eat. I left the fridge empty."

Katie laughed. "It would be almost impossible to *not* find something to eat. The fridge was empty, but the pantry and the freezer were overloaded."

"Are you okay?" It was more of a statement than a question. Katie always had a smile in her eyes, but today the smile lacked its usual wattage.

Katie gave a vague shrug. "I'm getting there. It's been a rough month." She surveyed the kitchen, nodding as her gaze traveled over the pale-yellow walls and aqua cabinetry. "This place has so much potential." She let out a small breath and shook her head. "I used to drive down this street on my way to school and imagine the Grand Ladies as they used to be back in their glory days. I can't believe you own a Lady."

"Half a Lady," Rosalie corrected. But the fact that she had half was still something that made her feel like doing a victory dance. She'd admired the ornate Victorian homes that dominated an entire block on High Street since she was a girl. The people who owned the houses had eventually moved to more modern houses as new areas of town developed, and the old mansions had fallen into disrepair. However, the owners stubbornly refused to sell until last summer when the first Lady went on the market. Gloria had scooped it up before the for-sale sign had been planted in the lawn. It paid to have contacts.

Katie ran a hand over the unpainted trim of the arched doorway where she stood, then raised her gaze to the ceiling, which was embellished with plaster ornamentation.

"If you ask me, half a Lady is far better than no Lady at all."

"Amen to that." Because Vincent Taylor, the man who'd bought the two remaining Grand Ladies after they went on the market two months ago, made no secret about the fact that he wanted Rosalie and Gloria's Lady also.

Fat chance that he was going to get it.

Katie let out a small sigh and turned to Rosalie. "I want to apologize for showing up out of the blue and upsetting things on the ranch. Like you said, Brady expected one thing and got another."

"But you two worked things out?"

Katie sucked in a breath, just as she'd done when she was younger and was about to confess to some petty crime, which often involved adopting yet another stray animal. "Pretty much. You know how things have always been between us."

Actually, she did, probably better than Katie. She'd watched Brady avoid Katie for years and she had a very good notion as to why he'd done that. She loved Brady like another grandson, which was why she'd invited him to stay on the ranch while he healed, but looking at the family he'd come from… well, his parents had done some damage, and Rosalie wasn't certain that damage could be undone. That, coupled with his habit of not always paying attention to consequences before acting, just as his father had done, made her thankful that Brady had chosen to keep his distance from Katie.

"But don't worry," Katie added brightly. "We'll play nicely. I've learned a thing or two about interpersonal relationships in my former job."

"Good. Maybe you can help me and Gloria." She gestured to the length of rose-pink trim near the dining room entrance and Katie wrinkled her nose.

"Are you guys married to that color?"

"I certainly hope not." She went on to explain the color drama and how she was not looking forward to round two. "We both liked the pink so well, it seemed like the perfect way to give the gift shop a fun, funky feel, but I don't like it now that I see it on the wall."

The shop door opened behind them and they turned together as Gloria came in, wearing a purple and green tunic over skinny jeans and carrying three totes of various sizes.

"Katie!" Gloria dropped her totes and crossed the room to envelope Katie in a motherly hug. "Let me look at you. It's been forever!"

Katie's lips twitched at the corners, but she didn't mention that she'd seen Gloria not that long ago when she and Rosalie went to San Francisco on a buying trip.

"It's been a tough month, hasn't it?"

"Does it show?"

"Not in the least. Although…well, your face is a little pale."

"The downside of living on a foggy coast."

"Well, we're glad you're home." Gloria glanced over at the pink trim and made a face. "*That* doesn't work."

Rosalie felt a rush of relief, which evaporated the instant Gloria said, "Maybe a deep blue?"

"White?" Katie ventured from behind them.

Gloria shook her head and Katie caught Rosalie's eye to give her a sympathetic look.

"We want something colorful to go with our garden vibe," Gloria said.

"I agree." Katie folded her arms over her chest as she studied the wall and cabinets. "But you don't want to look like you're competing with Annie Get Your Gun." The eclectic quilt and gift shop on Main Street was a bastion of bright colors and glittery bling. "You want to be charming, but slightly more…elegant, maybe?"

They'd given that matter a lot of thought, going so far as to meet with Diana, the owner of Annie Get Your Gun, to discuss how to fill different niches. The meeting had ended with an agreement to act as sister stores rather than competitors. There would be crossover, of course, but Annie Get Your Gun would focus on quilting supplies, jewelry and Western-themed gifts and clothing. The Daisy Petal would handle flowers and garden supplies, teas, spices, soaps and lotions.

A rattling at the back door brought Gloria's head up. "Lizzie Belle wants attention. I swear, we need to get her a little dog for company."

"You still have Lizzie Belle?" Katie sounded delighted.

"How could I not have Lizzie Belle?" Gloria asked in fake outrage. She'd asked her husband for a pet a few months before his untimely death two years ago, obviously thinking a dog or cat, but he'd gotten her a baby goat. Gloria had been horrified for almost two seconds, she always said, before falling head over heels in love with the dwarf goat. "I'll just get her a treat and be right back."

Katie fought a smile as Gloria bustled into the kitchen, then opened the back door and began crooning to the goat about eating the carrot slowly so as not to upset her stomach.

"I know you're laughing at me," Gloria said as she came back into the room. "And I agree. On first glance I am definitely not a goat person." She came to stand next to Katie and regarded the pink trim with a frown. "Maybe black. It's elegant and goes with everything."

Rosalie's eyes went wide before she realized that her friend was kidding. "Ha. Ha."

Gloria laughed. "We'll come up with something."

"White?" Katie said again.

Gloria shook her head. "What are you going to do now that you're back?"

Katie let out a sigh. "Excellent question. Everything happened so quickly I haven't had time to fully process." She smiled at Rosalie. "Which is why I'm so grateful to have a grandmother to give me shelter from the storm."

Gloria leaned closer. "So far you've been totally sensible, Katie. You've gone to college. Went to work in the big city. Probably saved money. Now you need to do something you love. Do not wait until you're over sixty, like we did."

Over seventy actually, but Gloria had never been that good with numbers. Rosalie lifted her chin. "Katie is going to let the dust settle, I imagine." She hoped, anyway. Katie had always been driven to succeed, like her brother and sister, and she'd been secretly thrilled when Katie had asked if she could stay at the ranch for a few weeks while she processed. Now, if she could just get Cassie to come home and relax for a nanosecond or two.

"Yes," Katie agreed. "I need some thinking time." She got to her feet and slung her purse strap over her shoulder. "I have to buy groceries, but I can come back and help you here if you'd like."

"I'd love to have you," Rosalie said, "but maybe you should take a day and settle in. Read with Tigger." Give her and Gloria a chance to hash through the color scheme again.

Katie gave her a roguish smile. "I don't know if I can sit still for that long anymore. Do you want to know how long it's been since I read a book?"

"Open the book, apply your eyes to the page, do your best to sit still." Rosalie walked with Katie as far as the door. "I'm driving out to the ranch to find some more display pieces tomorrow. We can talk then, and you can help me choose the right pieces now that you've seen the shop." Rosalie adjusted the edge of the bandanna she wore over her unruly curls to keep them under control while she worked. "I can talk to Brady, too."

"We're going to be fine, Grandma. I'm staying out of his way. He does his thing and I do mine."

"Perfect," Rosalie said. "The last thing I need is to referee a feud while trying to agree on the perfect trim color."

"No feud. I promise." She opened the shop door, but hesitated before walking through it. "I honestly do appreciate you giving me a place to land during tough times."

"It's your home, Katie. For as long as you want."

Katie patted the door frame. "Thanks, Grandma." There was a note of sincerity in her voice that made Rosalie wonder if her granddaughter was considering coming home for good.

"She looks like she needs a rest from the dog-eat-dog world," Gloria said as the door closed behind Katie.

"Yes." Rosalie watched through the multipaned window as her granddaughter climbed into that truck she'd kept the entire time she was in San Francisco—an impractical decision that hinted at the fact that maybe, deep down, Katie always knew she'd be coming home. Now if she would only stay.

DO WHAT YOU LOVE.

Katie turned into the parking lot of Hardwick's Grocery and Hardware. Doing the things she loved didn't pay well, which was why she'd ignored the things she loved for so very long. She honestly couldn't remember the last time she'd read a book. Indulging in me-time took away from building-her-career time. Despite extolling the virtues of balancing home life and work to avoid burnout to the people she worked with, she hadn't practiced what she'd preached. "Next month" had always seemed like the very best time to join the running club, take a class that wasn't related to her future master's degree, read her toppling pile of books.

Now that all was said and done, what did she have to show for all that dedication?

Five years of experience that will look really good on a résumé.

Well, there was that, but mostly, she felt tired. Used up.

In need of…something.

Maybe she needed to stop by the animal shelter. See what needed rescuing.

Excellent idea if she had any clue as to where she might be in the coming weeks. But she couldn't rescue an animal when she didn't know her own future. However, once Nick came home, perhaps she could rescue something. Her nieces could help pick out a new pet. Nothing like a rescue to perk up the spirits—in most cases, anyway. Brady had admonished her not to try to rescue *him*, which she took to mean not to try to help him out around the ranch—unless, of course, there were dire circumstances, such as a four-wheeler in a ditch.

She understood. He hated having to ask for even a small amount of help. His parents had proven untrustworthy in the emotional-support department and Brady was a guy who felt best when he was going it alone. But Katie couldn't help but wonder if he'd also clued into the fact that she'd had a crazy crush on him until she'd left for college and was fearful of a relapse if they spent time together.

Embarrassing, but a real possibility. She needed to remember that small fact.

Katie palmed her keys instead of putting them into her pocket as she crossed the parking lot, letting her fingers close tightly around them. Brady was one hot individual, but she was older and wiser, and he still had issues—new issues atop the old. Yes. She needed to focus on getting her own life on track. Then she could worry about everyone else's.

Hardwick's had remodeled since the last time she'd shopped there almost two years ago. There was a coffee counter near the bakery and an expanded hardware area on the opposite side of the store. Gavin was growing, but thankfully, it was too far away from the larger Montana cities to become a bedroom community. Change was good, but as far as Katie was concerned, the little town she'd left after high school was perfect the way it was.

She grabbed a cart and cruised the aisles, buying milk, butter and local eggs. The produce was a bit on the scrawny side compared to what she could get in California, but life was a series of tradeoffs. Lower cost of living versus scrawny produce. At this point in her life, she'd take the lower cost of living. If she stayed in the area, she could grow her own garden next year. The idea appealed.

The big question was, was it possible for her to stay in the area?

She wheeled past the bakery on her way to the checkout area, hoping that the store still made the awesome apple fritters that had seen her through stressful times in high school, when someone said her name from behind her.

"Katie Callahan? Is that you?"

Katie turned and found herself staring into a familiar and not altogether welcome face.

"It *is* you." Mellie Taylor gave Katie the same less-than-sincere smile she'd given all the lesser beings back in the day—the one that didn't come close to her eyes. Katie had never noticed before, but it was really more of a grimace than a smile.

"Mellie," Katie said as though she were greeting an old friend. She might not have been in Mellie's sphere in school, but life had a way of evening things out. Although... judging from Mellie's beautifully tailored navy blazer, lace blouse, high heels and artfully distressed jeans, she was still part of the Gavin elite. "How are you?"

"Super." She gestured with her left hand as she spoke, and Katie took note of the glistening diamond that nearly blinded her as it caught the light.

"Congratulations. Do I know him?"

"Jace Kenworthy?"

Katie shook her head. "I've been gone awhile."

"He moved here from Bozeman. He wanted to live in a place that has potential for development."

"But hasn't been developed yet?" Katie asked. The sarcasm went straight over Mellie's head.

"Exactly." Mellie spread her hands in a graceful gesture. "We're revitalizing a block of High Street. Even though the wedding is still eight months off, we went into partnership with my parents."

"That's the street where my grandmother's new shop is located." Even though she didn't want to see Gavin change too much, revitalization might be a boon to her grandmother's business.

"Yes. Maybe *you* can talk some sense into her."

"Excuse me?"

"We've purchased the entire block, with the exception of Gloria's old house. We've offered top dollar—more than the house is worth. It's silly not to take the offer and buy up. They could get a much nicer place downtown. Why…the old grainery is for sale."

"I don't think my grandmother wants to live in a grainery." Not when she was half owner of a beautiful Victorian in a perfect part of town.

"That building is an excellent investment. It just cries out *condo*."

"Why don't you guys buy the grainery?"

Mellie's mouth flattened ever so slightly. "Because we bought the houses on High Street, with the intention of building a business there."

"What kind of business?"

"I'm not at liberty to say just yet."

"Has the planning commission approved your plan?"

"We have it on good authority that they will once we procure all the property. The last time we spoke to Rosalie and Gloria, they became defensive and, frankly, a little unhinged."

Katie had to work to keep her tongue under control. Unhinged? If anyone was likely to come off as unhinged in an argument, it would be the perfectly dressed woman in front of her. Also, why hadn't her grandmother told her about this offer to buy? Had she told Nick and Cassie? And should she drive back to the shop and ask her what the heck was going on?

"Can *you* talk to them?" Mellie asked in a conspiratorial tone, oblivious to the change in Katie's demeanor. "Make them see the sense of selling and buying elsewhere? Jace's offer is more than generous."

The Katie who worked in human resources would have come up with a tactful response that offended no one and allowed all parties to move forward to address the problem before them. That Katie was officially unemployed, however, so the Katie who'd put up with Mellie and her snotty ways in school was free to say, "Maybe you guys should have made certain everyone on the block was interested in selling before starting."

Mellie's mouth opened and then closed with a snap. Katie allowed herself a faint smile.

"Don't mess with my grandma," she said mildly as she reached for an apple fritter.

"As if—"

"I mean it." Katie was dead serious, and judging from Mellie's incredulous expression, it showed. Fine. The woman needed to understand that whoever messed with her grandmother messed with her—and her siblings. "So, it'd be best if you and Jace figured out a way to work around my grandmother and Gloria."

"Or what?" There was a spark of battle in Mellie's eyes.

Katie gave the blonde a long hard look and had the satisfaction of seeing the woman shift her gaze uncomfortably after a few seconds. The Katie that Mellie knew would *never* have stared her down. Corporate Katie had developed skills, and they weren't all the warm and fuzzy kind.

"I guess you'll find out what happens when you tangle with the Callahans."

CHAPTER FIVE

YOU'RE GOING AT this all wrong.

Brady stopped forking hay as the idea took hold. He'd felt edgy and jumpy all afternoon, wondering if Katie was going to stop by his house after returning from town, just as she had this morning when she'd offered to help feed if he was still having issues with his foot.

He assured her he was not, taking care not to put any weight on it as they faced off at the door. She didn't ask about the state of his injury, didn't push to be allowed to help, but after she'd left, he'd been twice as tense as before he'd answered his door. He couldn't stop thinking about her and this was not how he wanted to spend the next several days, weeks or months.

He lifted another fork of alfalfa and pitched it into the weathered wooden feed bunk, where the bulls threw it in the air as they went for the leaves, which were far tastier than the stalks.

If he continued to avoid Katie, this jumpy feeling was going to continue dogging him, but if he *didn't* avoid her, if he met the situation head-on, then maybe the tension would dissipate, and maybe he'd stop fixating on her.

The truth was, judging from the way he couldn't stop thinking about her, he was afraid of falling for Katie all over again, at a time when he was busy scraping himself up off the rock-bottom level of his life, and that had made him defensive. He needed to rethink tactics.

After tossing the last of the hay into the feeders, he jammed the pitchfork into a bale, then started limping toward the house. Due to his swollen foot, he'd worn his driving moccasins to feed the bulls and the few cows he'd kept in, and now hay pricked his skin through his socks. He couldn't wait until he got back into his boots.

The sound of a truck brought Brady's head up. Katie was home, which meant it was decision time. How should he play this?

He'd play it by ear.

He walked through the large open bay

door and headed for Katie's truck as it rolled to a stop. She opened her door and dropped to the ground, then gave a violent start as she saw him coming around the back end of the vehicle.

"Oh." She pressed a hand to her heart. "Hi."

"I didn't mean to startle you." He was surprised he had.

"Aftermath of the mugging," she said lightly, reaching into the truck to haul out a bag of groceries.

His insides went still.

"What mugging?"

Katie pushed windblown hair back from her forehead when she turned toward him. "It happened just before I got laid off. I still have a little bruising."

A curse rose to his lips, but he swallowed it. "I didn't know."

She gave a casual shrug. "Not much you could do about it." She reached for her purse and closed the door. There were two more bags sitting on the passenger seat, so Brady limped around the truck to get them, still working on the fact that someone had hurt Katie.

"Is the mugging one of the reasons you came home?"

"It added to the decision." She reached for the bags he carried, but he shook his head.

She wrinkled her forehead. "Is everything okay?"

"Uh, yeah. I just…well, I'm making stew later and wanted to know if you'd like to join me for dinner." The invitation came out awkwardly, but at least it was out, hanging in the air between them. He'd asked many women to dinner and couldn't remember another time when he'd sounded like a junior high kid asking a girl to the big dance.

Katie's eyes narrowed as she gave him an openly suspicious look. "You're asking me to dinner?"

"Yeah."

"Because of the mugging?"

"No."

"Did my grandma call you?"

"What? No. Hell, no." His face started to feel warm as he fought for words to explain his change in attitude. "We're here on the ranch and it's kind of stupid of me to assume that we're not going to see one another and, well, I've rethought the Ed thing, and maybe we could just…you know…share the ranch."

"But I can't rescue or defend you. Are those caveats still in place?"

Brady moistened his lips. "No rescue."

"Will you accept help?" He hesitated, and she clarified. "Will you *ask* for help if you need it?"

"Maybe?"

Katie bit her lip, then that smile of hers, which touched him in ways he didn't want to be touched, broke through. He loved seeing her smile—always had—but he couldn't afford to be attracted to her. It was okay to feel protective of a woman he'd grown up with. Not okay to allow feelings to grow that had no business in their current relationship. He was at such an iffy place in his life as he prepared to embark on another risk-taking venture, this one of a financial nature. If he failed, and Abe Jr. repossessed? Well, he'd have nothing.

Was there a place lower than rock bottom?

He didn't want Katie there if he were to find out.

"You going to help me carry those bags in? Or just hang on to them?"

Brady scowled at her, but felt slightly less tense as he followed Katie into the house and then set the bags on the table. How many hours had he spent at that same table, eating with the family, learning to play cribbage, taking part in the occasional poker game Katie's dad would rustle up among the locals? That was how he'd become acquainted with Will, who'd known his dad and, more than that, was willing to talk about him with Brady. He'd been hungry for information since his mom had never allowed the subject to come up. She hadn't even kept photos of his father.

"About dinner," he said, taking hold of his belt buckle with both hands as she opened the fridge to put milk, butter and eggs inside. "Nothing fancy. Canned stew and biscuits that pop out of the tube."

"That sounds great." The big orange cat sauntered into the room and threw himself against Katie's shins. She leaned down to run a hand over the cat's back. "What time?"

"Around six?" He had a few things to do before calling it a day.

"Sure."

"Okay. See you then." The words came out sounding as stilted and uncomfortable as he felt. Why was it that the only woman in the world who made him feel tongue-tied was this one, whom he'd known forever?

He let himself out into the brisk October air. The wind was starting to pick up as it often did in the afternoon. Winter was due to blow in soon, but he hoped it held off until he could get his injured foot into boots. Otherwise, he'd have both snow and hay in his socks.

He made his way across the drive to his small house with the cherry kitchen decor that must have driven dour Ed nuts. Once inside he went straight to the cupboard and pulled out two large cans of stew. He had nothing fancy to offer, and that pretty much summed up his life at that moment—not only did he have nothing fancy, he essentially had nothing, except for the down payment on the parcel of land.

But he did have that, and with it, he would build, one day at a time. A fight in a parking lot followed by an unfortunate ride on a gnarly bronc may have ended his career, but he was down, not out.

And it was important that he remember that.

IT HAD BEEN a day of surprises—first, Mellie Taylor's bombshell, and then Brady extending an unexpected invitation to dinner. Katie had already hashed over the Mellie situation on the way home, so now it was Brady's turn.

Why the sudden change in attitude?

Katie debated as she put away her groceries and then made a simple lunch—apples, cheese, crackers and peanut butter. It was possible that he'd simply come to his senses and realized that sharing a ranch meant teamwork.

Katie shook her head as she put away the peanut butter. That seemed too simple.

Time would tell—or more accurately, dinner tonight would tell.

Several texts came in over the course of the day from Katie's roommates and former coworkers, checking to see if she'd landed all right. She answered all in the affirmative and as she wrote to Amanda, her closest friend and former roomie, saying that it felt good to be back in Montana, she was struck again by how true those words were. She was home and she wasn't leaving unless it became impossible to stay for some reason.

I think I'm staying.

It's early days. You've taken a beating recently. No hasty decisions.

She had taken a beating. Did she want another? Was the payoff of a corporate job enough to make up for everything else? Every time she thought about going back to the grind, her stomach tightened.

She honestly loved the city, but it had exhausted her. And her job... Lots of people worked at jobs they didn't like all that well due to necessity. She'd been one of them. Why? Because of the way she'd defined success.

She was about to tweak that definition.

Katie didn't attempt to protest. All that would do was further the argument. Instead, she texted, I'll keep you posted. Don't water the Christmas cactus too often.

She got a smiley face in return and set her phone on the counter.

After feeding Tigger just before six, she pulled her hair over her shoulder and started to braid as she headed to her bedroom to see about changing into a sweater. It was getting colder as evening approached and Ed had been notorious for scrimping on heat. She didn't know if Brady was the same, but she didn't want to shiver through dinner.

Brady was at the stove, stirring a pot, when Katie rapped on the door before letting herself in. He glanced over his shoulder and for a moment her breath caught. Was there anything sexier than a guy at the stove?

"Hey." He set the spoon on the plate next to the stove, then bent down to look through the oven window.

"Hey," Katie echoed softly before looking around. The red paint on the cabinets was worn in places, as well it should be after a good decade of use, but the cherry wallpaper was as cheerful as ever. "Thanks again for the invite."

"Yeah." He sounded uncomfortable, like he didn't know what to do with her now that she was here.

"Can I set the table or something?"

"I thought we'd dish up at the stove. I'm not fancy."

Katie smiled as she moved closer, hoping she didn't make him jump out of his skin. "I'm not fancy, either. Nothing makes me happier than leftovers or a box of crackers, a brick of cheese and a knife."

"I kind of like cooking." He shrugged without looking at her. "But never had much time for it while I was on the road. And I had to watch my diet pretty carefully to stay competitive. Lots of protein. Not many carbs."

"Now you're free to eat what you want." Brady's shoulders stiffened, and Katie wished she could yank back the words. Nothing like reminding a guy that his beloved career was over and done.

"Yeah. Kind of a tough way to get dietary freedom, but now I can eat what I want."

"I didn't mean—"

He turned, and the rest of the sentence died on her lips. A sort of bitter acceptance played across his face. He didn't want sympathy or help or, well, anything. The fact that he was talking at all was huge.

"I know." He pressed his lips together, then opened a cupboard to reveal mostly empty space. There was a small stack of plates and bowls and a few assorted coffee cups, all mismatched. "Big bowl or small?"

"I'll go small and refill if necessary."

"Done." He set two bowls, a large and a small, on the counter next to the stove.

"I'll put my biscuits on the stew," she said.

"Good idea. Fewer dishes to wash."

"I'll wash."

"No, you won't." He'd handle his own household chores.

Brady pulled the sheet of golden biscuits out of the oven, then picked up the measuring cup sitting next to the stove and dunked it into the stew. "Pretty uptown, but I don't have a ladle."

"It works."

He filled Katie's small bowl and his larger one. Once he finished, Katie used a fork to carefully set a biscuit on top of her stew, then held her fork back over the baking sheet. "One or two?"

"Two."

She set two biscuits on top of the stew in his bowl.

There they were, going through the motions of having a companionable dinner even though neither of them was anywhere near comfortable. Maybe because they were play-acting. Pretending all was well when it was not.

After setting her bowl on the table and taking a seat, Katie set down her spoon instead of digging in. "Do you know anything about the Taylors buying up a block in Gavin to build some new business?"

Brady felt a swell of relief at her choice of topic. "I don't, but I haven't been back all that long."

"Apparently that's the block that Grandma's new shop is on, and the only building they haven't snapped up is hers." Katie tore a piece off the biscuit and popped it into her mouth. When she was done chewing, she said, "For some reason, Grandma didn't tell me."

"Well, she either considers it a nonissue or she didn't want to worry you."

"It didn't sound like a nonissue when Mellie Taylor told me about it."

Brady gave a small snort. "Mellie Taylor likes to upset people. It's what she does."

His instant answer surprised her. "How well do you know Mellie?"

"Well enough. She's of the opinion that she's a prize and that makes it all right for her to pick on others."

"In other words, she's a bully."

He gave a casual shrug and focused on his stew. "As I learned the hard way."

An unwelcome thought formed. "Did you guys date or something?"

Now his gaze came up. "For a while, when I was training in Missoula for my second rodeo season and she was going to college there. You know how it is when small-town folk connect in a city. We had a drink together, and then…"

And then.

"Huh." And double "huh" for the uncomfortable zap of jealousy that struck her out of nowhere. Really? Jealous of something that had happened years ago?

It was just that the idea of he and Mellie being a couple didn't sit right.

"It didn't last long," he said, as if reassuring her he'd regained his senses.

"Have any of your relationships?"

The shutters dropped. Just like that. She should have known better. First of all, it was a very personal question, and second, relationships were a touchy subject for Brady. Maybe she should have kept her mouth shut.

"Yes. Nick and I are still close friends."

Katie was tired of the awkwardness between them. She'd known him for decades; she was practically a sister, even though he'd never treated her like one. "That wasn't what I meant, but I get that the subject is off-limits." She scooped up a big spoonful of stew, popped it in her mouth, then instantly regretted it as hot broth burned her tongue. Somehow she got it down and managed a weak smile.

"Hot."

"Yes. Some of us let the food cool before eating."

"Sparring with you distracted me."

"Is that what we're doing? Sparring?"

She tilted her head, her spoon poised over the bowl. "Isn't that what we always do? It's one of the hallmarks of our relationship." She emphasized the last word, then told herself to stop baiting him—even subtly. Getting a reaction out of Brady, a guy who took great pains not to react, was satisfying, but she needed to back off.

"Whatever," he muttered as he started to eat.

"I'm sorry."

His eyes came up.

"You invited me to dinner. Put forth an effort to make peace and I'm not playing nicely."

"You're pretty much being yourself."

Katie's eyebrows shot up. "Not nice?"

He shook his head and focused again on his meal, making Katie wonder just what he did mean. To her surprise, a few seconds later he put his spoon down and met her gaze dead-on. "You say things to get a rise out of me."

Her mouth started to fall open before she caught it. "I..."

Now he raised his eyebrows, daring her to deny a solid fact. She couldn't do it.

"And it's not sparring," he continued, "because I don't usually hit back."

"Touché." She pushed a couple pieces of potato around with her spoon. "Pretty classic approach, really. One person pursues, the other engages in avoidance tactics." Her gaze flashed up. "Not that I was pursuing you."

Liar. She'd totally been pursuing him back in the day, and he'd given her zero satisfaction. She felt her color rising and started talking, hoping to distract him from her pink cheeks. "Classic Psychology 101 stuff."

He gave her an uh-huh look.

Katie took another bite—this time it didn't sizzle—then wiped her mouth. "The trouble with holding things in," she continued in her professional voice and hoped that her cheeks cooled soon, "is that they build up, cause additional issues."

"More Psych 101?"

"You're a perfect example. You said you're hurting inside and out… Maybe if you didn't hold things in, you'd heal faster on the inside."

She'd expected the statement to shut him back down, but it seemed to have the opposite effect. Brady's gaze traveled over her face, settled on her mouth, making her cheeks feel hot again. When he slowly met her eyes, she swallowed.

"You think if I talk, it'll make things all better?"

"It might."

"What are you going to do now that you've lost your job?"

The sudden shift in conversation tilted Katie off balance. "I...don't know."

"If you talk, you might feel better."

Fine. Gauntlet dropped—she'd talk. "I'm thinking that instead of doing what I should do, I might follow Gloria's advice and try to do something I love."

"Good advice, if it's possible."

"You don't think it's possible?"

"Let's just say it can be difficult for people who like security and savings accounts and the certainty of knowing where their next meal is coming from."

She almost said, "Like me?" but it was so obvious he was talking about her that she said, "Nothing wrong with those things."

"Which is why so many people work at jobs they don't like. Because when one counts the cost, it's pretty obvious which path is best. I'm a perfect example. I did what I loved, until I couldn't, and here I am. Dependent on the generosity of others…which is not where I want to be."

"Are you trying to talk me out of doing what I love?"

"I'm telling you to think hard."

"This may be the longest we've ever talked," Katie said musingly. She wanted to change the subject, because she didn't want to dwell on the consequences of failure.

"Maybe."

"Yet I feel like I know you pretty well."

"You haven't even scratched the surface."

The statement brought her up short, perhaps because he spoke so definitively. "You might be an easier read than you think."

He gave her a look that made her feel as if she was wading too deeply into dark waters. That he was right—she didn't know him at all, and maybe it would be better if she kept things that way.

Unfortunately, Katie had a problem backing down when she wasn't in a professional setting. She didn't do it unless she had to. She wasn't yet at the have-to stage.

"All right," he said slowly. "Give me a read."

"You pretty much already told me everything. You're hurting. You want solitude." She wasn't about to delve into the deeper things in his life—that he had trust issues due to his parents' sick relationship. That he wanted a home, which was why he'd practically lived with her family during his high school years. "You need help on the ranch due to injuries, old and new, but you're too stubborn to ask for it."

He gave a slow nod, as if agreeing that her superficial read was dead-on. "How about you, Katie, what do *you* need?"

It was crazy that the simple question, coupled with the way he was looking at her, made it seem as if the air had evaporated from her lungs. He looked at her as if he knew that she'd thought about him way too much in the past, that her secret wasn't so secret.

Was he doing this on purpose, to make her back off? Allow him the solitude he cherished so much?

Possible. Very possible.

Allow him that. You've made your point.

Although at that moment she was rather confused on just what point she'd been trying to make. He was right—she'd fallen into her old habit of saying things to see if she could get him to react; only this time, he gave her a dose of her own medicine. Had her backing up.

"I don't know." She idly rubbed the bruise on her shoulder from the mugging before realizing what she was doing and dropped her hand.

"Here's what I think is going to happen. You're going to stay here for a few weeks. Enjoy the fantasy of not going back. Then you'll regroup and go back."

"Why do you think that, Brady?"

"Katie, you couldn't wait to get out of here. Off the ranch. Away from Gavin."

What he said wasn't exactly true. She hadn't wanted to get away from the ranch and Gavin; instead, she'd been anxious to prove herself in a larger arena than Gavin could offer. To be successful in her field, step out from Nick's and Cassie's shadows, and the place to do that was with a major corporation in a big city.

She frowned up at him. "Where did you come up with that idea?"

"Nick and I are friends. Remember?"

She swallowed the bubble of disappointment. He hadn't thought about her, noticed things. Nope. Her brother had simply discussed his little sister with his best friend.

"I've done the corporate thing, proved I could do it and got it out of my system." She leveled a look at him. "Now I'm going to stick around."

"I guess we'll see." He didn't attempt to disguise his disbelief.

"You don't think I will."

"I think you still have things to prove."

Katie carefully scooped up another spoon of stew before saying in a mild voice that didn't fully mask subtle notes of both annoyance and resolve, "Yes, Brady. Maybe I do."

And this time it wasn't that she could be as successful as her driven older siblings.

WAS HE EVER going to stop making tactical errors with this woman? All he'd accomplished during their conversation was to fire Katie up. It was more than obvious from the expression she'd worn during the remainder of their short meal that she now intended to stay come hell or high water.

But hey—he'd shifted the focus from him to her. Maybe that was a win.

And maybe she'd go broke trying to prove him wrong in his assessment of her. He'd hate to have that happen, even if she did have a pretty cushy safety net here.

He touched his forehead to the glass of the small window in the door as he watched her cross the driveway to the main house. The orange cat bounded out of the bushes, much nimbler with a damaged leg than Brady was with his, and raced ahead of her to the door. When she reached for the handle, the cat bumped her leg with his head in a show of affection.

Katie was special. The cat knew it. He knew it.

There was no way she was burying herself on this ranch. Katie was a people person. She'd been a sophomore when he'd been an impatient senior, anxious to leave high school and his family behind. He'd paid next to no attention to what went on in the school social strata, but had still been aware that Katie was on every committee known to man. She organized, she rallied, she cheered. She liked being around people, and they liked being around her.

Unlike him, Katie wasn't meant for an isolated lifestyle, nor was Rosalie. After Carl died, Rosalie had quit the ranch and headed to town. According to Nick, she'd always preferred town life, but had stayed on the ranch for forty-eight years, working shoulder to shoulder with her husband, out of love.

Brady's mom and stepdad shared a similar bond. They were tight—so tight they had essentially squeezed him out, and he was still wondering if it had been purposeful. He wanted to believe that it wasn't, that his mom simply wasn't cut out to be emotionally supportive, and that, coupled with painful memories of his father, had led to her being a distant parent.

Not long after he'd graduated high school, they had moved to Washington state to be closer to his stepfather's parents. He hadn't been in contact in years, and his mom seemed good with the deal, only reaching out to him on the major holidays when he got a duty call. He'd also gotten a call after his wreck in the rodeo arena. One freaking call.

Katie disappeared into the main house and Brady turned back to the ridiculous cherry-infested kitchen. How had Ed not whitewashed the room?

Maybe he never saw the cherries. Maybe he was so locked in his dour world that all he saw was the work ahead of him and his half-empty glass. That wasn't how Brady wanted to go through life—and he needed to take pains to remember that. He had a goal. Almost everything he'd loved had been yanked away from him when the bronc had gone over on him, but while he was in the hospital, under the heavy influence of drugs, a realization had struck him with startling clarity.

He'd been given a second chance. He could let disappointment rule his life, or he could move past it and rebuild. Replace what had been taken from him.

After the pain drugs had dissipated, the epiphany remained, as if it'd been laser etched into his brain. He could have died. He didn't. He needed to take advantage of this gift. He was not a guy who asked for help easily, even when he needed it, so Rosalie's offer to manage the ranch until Nick's return had been another godsend.

Since she needed to fill the position, he could pretend that they were exchanging favors, even though they were both aware that he needed her favor a lot more than she needed his. There were a lot of guys Rosalie could have hired for the job, but he hadn't had many options as to where to work and live. After being discharged from the hospital, he had the small chunk of change his agent was sitting on—the money that hadn't gone to co-pays and medical bills—a truck and a camp trailer. He'd needed a job and Rosalie had come through. That had given him the incentive to approach the Larsons about a land purchase when he'd heard that Abe Jr. was getting ready to divide the property, and he hoped to eventually parlay that purchase into something bigger and better as time went on.

He was not going to blow his second chance by *not* considering the future and the consequences of his actions, which had been his hallmark for almost the entirety of his teens and twenties. And he wasn't going to be so foolish as to try to engage Katie in personal conversations again—but he wasn't going to avoid her, either.

If he needed help, he'd ask. He'd managed to be around her for years without her catching on to the fact that he had a thing for her, and there was no reason he couldn't continue to do the same.

AFTER RETURNING HOME and brewing a pot of herbal tea, Katie settled at her grandmother's kitchen table with her trusty yellow legal pad and started brainstorming ways that she could run a business from the ranch. She wanted it to be something she enjoyed, but wouldn't ruin by turning it into a business. She didn't want to end up hating a former passion because business had taken all the joy out of it.

The first few items were pure fantasy, but sometimes fantasies could be translated into reality—or so she'd read. Soap making. Oils and vinegars. Rare chickens. Herbal lotions and soaps.

Herbs.

Healthy, leafy herbs, unlike the scrawny ones in Hardwick's.

The idea took hold and she started expanding, pausing to do research on her phone, then expanding some more. Her head came up when the lights went out in Brady's house, which was visible through the kitchen window, then she focused back on her pad and continued working.

Her grandmother's chiming clock struck midnight before Katie put aside her pad and phone.

She had to do more research, of course, study markets and costs, but as far as she could tell, her idea was solid. And more than that, it felt right.

"So right that it can't be wrong," she said

to Tigger, who was sound asleep on the chair next to her.

Okay, maybe it could be wrong, but the idea of going in a totally unexpected direction, doing what she loved and combining it with her business degree—well, why hadn't she thought of this before?

Because she'd been too focused on a traditional career path, and maybe a little afraid to step off that path into the unknown.

She was no longer feeling that same fear. She was lucky to have a place to land, so why not take advantage of it? If she was making a mistake, well, she was in the perfect position to fail, pick herself up and head back down the traditional path. A path she truly didn't want to head down again, but it was there if she needed it.

She drew a curlicue beside the list of names she'd jotted in the margin of the pad, next to her list of things to research. *Katie's Herbs. Callahan Country Greens. Katie Grows Greens. Herbalicious.*

She hadn't come up with the right name yet, but she would.

After flipping the legal pad back to the first page, she leaned back in her chair and yawned. Tigger raised his head and she reached out to stroke his orange fur.

Tigger's Tasty Herbs?

Naming greenery after a carnivore seemed wrong.

Katie got to her feet and stretched, a smile on her face. She had the beginning of a road map—the first step toward her new future.

Thank you, Brady.

Because if he hadn't been so certain she wasn't going to stay, then she might have put off making this first important move.

Fast easy, and he certainly isn't talking. He hasn't gone to the doctor.

Rosalie made a mental note to talk with the doctor.

CHAPTER SIX

"WHAT HAPPENED TO BRADY?" Rosalie leaned toward the window to get a better look at her ranch manager, who limped as he moved around the tractor while fueling it up. She glanced back at her granddaughter. "You didn't hurt him, did you?"

"No more than he deserved," Katie dead-panned, and then the smile broke through. Finally. She'd been distracted since Rosalie arrived to look for display items for the store half an hour ago. "He had an accident with the four-wheeler."

"An accident?" Rosalie had reared a son and three grandchildren. She knew what it meant when one of them spoke just a little *too* casually about some matter.

Katie made a dismissive gesture. "In the river pasture. Uneven ground."

"Is that a new injury?"

"I don't know what his old injuries are, so

I can't say, and he certainly isn't talking. He hasn't gone to the doctor."

Rosalie gave a snort. "As if that's an indicator."

Katie emptied her cup and carefully set it back on the gold-rimmed saucer. Drinking tea together was a comforting ritual that had sprung from teddy bear tea parties Rosalie organized shortly after her three motherless grandchildren arrived at the ranch twenty-one years ago. Katie had been six, Cassie eight, Nick ten. When his dad or grandfather had joined the parties, Nick had, too, but usually it was Rosalie and the girls, and then, eventually, just Rosalie and Katie. Many tears had been dried and crises averted over tea.

"On the bright side, the four-wheeler is fine."

"I don't like those things."

"They are kind of necessary."

"Your grandfather used a horse for years."

"Until four-wheelers came along."

Rosalie rolled her eyes, but Katie was right. Toward the end of his ranching career, as his body started to rebel against hard use, Carl had used the four-wheeler more and more. Nick, on the other hand, was old school. He used a horse, and as soon as he sold his business, he'd be back on the ranch with his adorable daughters, working cows, farming fields, mending fence.

A talented carpenter and artisan, he'd made big money working as a contractor in central California, and Rosalie had been happy to travel to visit her grandson and great-grandchildren. But now that she'd lost her husband and Nick had lost his wife, she wanted Nick and the kids back in Gavin. Close by.

And honestly? She didn't want Katie to leave, either.

Maybe she was selfish, but so be it. She'd toss out the offer she'd been turning over in her brain during the past several days and see what Katie thought.

"I don't know if Brady can ride a horse like he used to." Katie removed the cozy from the teapot and divided the last of the Earl Grey between their cups. "By the way, what's the deal with him and the McGuires?"

Rosalie added sugar to her tea, took a sip. "Ancient history," she said softly. "Brady should be the one to fill you in."

"Yeah, right." Katie tilted her head, giving Rosalie a rather direct look. "Can you tell me a little? Enough to keep me from getting into trouble? You know, by putting my foot in my mouth?"

"Will was a talented bronc rider in his day. He mentored Brady's father, Colton, and did the same for Brady. The only problem was that Will tried to exert a little too much control over Brady, fearing he'd follow the same path as his father, and took it personally when Brady rebelled." Rosalie gripped her teacup a little tighter. "I don't know much more." And she didn't want to talk about Will McGuire. There was something about the man that made it impossible to relax around him. She hadn't noticed it until a few months ago when they ran into one another at Hardwick's—and literally bumped grocery carts. He'd gruffly apologized and moved on, but there was something about the encounter that had stuck with her. Something she couldn't put her finger on.

"Ah." Katie turned her teacup in her hand, her expression thoughtful. "That explains why Will was pretty sharp with him when he helped with the four-wheeler."

"Will helped with the four-wheeler? How serious was this little mishap?"

Katie gave a small shrug. "It was no big deal. We simply needed muscle to get the thing righted, and Will was close. But I promise, if there's anything you should know, you will."

"I'll hold you to that, young lady."

Katie's dimple appeared—the one that had charmed the socks off everyone since the time she was a toddler—but it wasn't going to work today.

"I'm serious, Katie."

"Grandma, you moved to town to run a shop, start a life *off* the ranch. You have a competent manager. Let him handle things." Katie's smile faded. "Which brings me to Mellie Taylor."

Rosalie set down her cup at the mention of her nemesis's granddaughter. "What about her?"

"Her family and fiancé are trying to buy your house?"

Rosalie lifted her cup again and took a bracing sip of tea before beginning her explanation. The neighbors were the only downside of owning one of Gavin's Grand Ladies, but at least she now knew what had been bugging Katie.

"The Taylors bought the houses on either

side of ours this summer. They want our house so that they can turn the block into some kind of a corporate retreat or bed-and-breakfast complex... I'm not certain of the details, but they could have bought our house when it came on the market. They didn't. We did." She sipped again, then set the cup down. "Granted, our house come on the market months earlier than the others and Gloria might have snapped it up before the sale became common knowledge..." Which only told Rosalie it was meant to be.

"But they're not getting the house. Right?"

"Nope." Neither she nor Gloria had the slightest interest in selling. Where else would they find a perfect house in an area zoned for both business and residency so close to downtown?

"Is there anything going on? I mean, are the Taylors getting pushy?"

The last thing Rosalie wanted was for her family to worry about her, when she was perfectly capable of fighting her own battles. She met Katie's gaze dead-on. "Gloria and I can handle matters, Katie. But if I find that I need more muscle, I will ask. I promise."

"Why do I feel like things would have to

be pretty desperate before you asked for said 'muscle'?"

"I guess it's because I'm old enough to know what I'm doing." She made a small gesture with her teacup and deliberately changed the subject. "We didn't have time to talk at the shop yesterday. What are your plans now that you're home? Will you start looking for a job immediately? Or are you going to take time to assess possibilities?"

The second option, please.

She was usually better at sounding neutral, but she did not want to see Katie head back into the fray just yet.

"I want to rebuild the greenhouse, grow herbs and maybe get some chickens."

Rosalie set her cup down a little too abruptly, making the saucer clatter. "I... That wasn't what I was expecting." Katie had always loved plants and pottering around in the greenhouse before it'd become storage central for the ranch. When the grandchildren had become teens, Rosalie had simply been too busy to use the greenhouse.

"Neither was I." Katie set down her own cup more gently. "I assumed I'd come home, take a breather, then dive into the job hunt."

"What happened?"

Katie gave a half laugh. "I feel good being here."

Rosalie's eyebrows rose. "You haven't been feeling 'good'?" She'd sensed that in their conversations over the past year, but Katie had been adamant about everything being fine in her life. Just fine.

"I know what you're thinking," Katie said with a wry half smile. "If you'd asked me how I felt a few weeks ago, I would have said, 'Just fine,' and believed it. But now..." Katie turned her cup in her hands before continuing with a faint frown. "I counseled people on burnout, but never listened to my own advice."

"Because you were *fine*."

Katie bit her lip, but the rueful smile broke through. "I wasn't. Looking back, I totally see why I burned out. I finished a double college major, then went to work within a week of graduating and, until I got my pink slip, I haven't slowed down. I haven't read books, or knit a sweater, or done any of the stuff I used to like to do."

Rosalie stared at her, her heart sinking. "I thought Cassie was my problem child in that regard." Katie had been driven like her siblings, but Rosalie had no idea that she'd been *this* driven.

"No," Katie said on a sigh. "I'm pretty much the same. I grew up feeling like a slacker because Nick and Cassie were so good at everything, so I never let myself stop working. But on the bright side, because of that, I have no encumberments. No car payment or house payment. No student loans. I didn't save much in SF, but I saved some."

Katie fell silent, and when she showed no sign of going on, Rosalie said, "You haven't knit a sweater?"

"Or a mitten or a scarf. Nothing."

"What did you do with your free time?"

"I took classes toward a master's degree."

"Katie Lynn Callahan."

"Am I going to get into trouble for not knitting?"

Rosalie just shook her head. "I think you should get some chickens."

"I've always secretly envied people who majored in things they loved, even if their chances of getting jobs in their field of study were close to nil."

"We all do."

"There's money to be made in herbs, but starting a new business is always a risk."

"Preaching to the choir," Rosalie murmured, thinking of all the work she and Gloria had already put into the Daisy Petal hoping that in a few years the business would turn a profit. But would it? "There are no guarantees."

"Are you glad you're making the leap?" Katie leaned forward as she spoke.

"I have some nerves, but yes. I'm glad I'm starting the business. It's…energizing."

Katie leaned back again, a rueful expression on her face. "I wish I would have been brave enough to take that chance earlier. Look at Nick. He majored in engineering and ended up being a contractor."

"He's happy as a contractor."

"I know. He did things his way. Your shop is kind of the same, isn't it? A chance to do your own thing."

"I loved working the ranch with your grandfather."

"I know." There was something in the way Katie spoke that told Rosalie that despite her efforts to hide the truth, at the very least her youngest granddaughter had clued into the fact that she wasn't really cut out for rural life. She'd made the best of it and knew how blessed she was living with a man like Carl for nearly fifty years.

Rosalie reached out to cover Katie's hand with her own. "I came here with the idea of trying to talk you into staying for a few months to help me around the shop. I really don't need help around the shop…but I wanted you to stay for a while." Because she'd suspected that Katie wasn't as happy as she'd insisted she was.

The corner of Katie's mouth quivered ever so slightly, and Rosalie felt her own do the same. "I'm going to stay awhile, Grandma. Find a new dream to chase." Her voice came close to cracking, and then she regained control and worked up a half smile while turning her hand over to squeeze Rosalie's fingers.

"Perfect, because I want you here. Maybe when Nick comes and Brady leaves, you can move into Ed's house, so that you can have some privacy and a little peace and quiet to run your business. And yes—" she guessed what her granddaughter was going to say next "—you can pay rent then if it makes you happy."

An odd expression crossed Katie's face before she squeezed Rosalie's hand again.

"That would be lovely, Grandma. Exactly what I'd hoped for."

THE FOUR-WHEELER HAD come out of the ditch with little more than a scratch on the gas tank. Brady wished he could say the same for himself, but while it might hurt to move, he *could* move. He wasn't stuck in a hospital bed mourning the end of his career. He had his second chance and he wasn't going to waste it whining about bad luck—not when he'd also had his share of good luck.

After fixing a broken strand of wire on the boundary fence, Brady rode the four-wheeler to the top of a hill and looked out over the Hayden Valley on the back side of the Callahan Ranch, where his new home would be once the purchase was finalized. Even though his driveway would be miles from that of the Callahan Ranch, they would still be neighbors.

Most of Hayden Valley belonged to the Larson Stock Company, the owner of which had died while Brady was in the hospital. There were issues with the will, but once the legalities were settled—and it appeared that would happen soon—the heirs intended to break the land into parcels to sell. As soon as he heard the rumors about the land sale, Brady had approached the family and was able to make a deal to buy the parcel with the decrepit homestead house and barn. The price was fair, considering the current state of the Montana real estate market, due to the difficulties accessing the place, and more importantly, Abe Larson Jr., had agreed to carry the loan for a higher than usual interest rate. Injured rodeo riders weren't prime candidates for loans and mortgages, but Brady had grown up with a slew of Larson kids and his former rodeo coach, Stan, was a distant cousin who worked in the Larson land office and had helped broker the deal. Now all Brady had to do was to get healthy enough to get a full-time job so that he could make payments. This property was the springboard to his future, and he was going to hang on to it come hell or high water.

Brady popped the four-wheeler back into gear and headed down the mountain. When he got within sight of the main house, he noted that Rosalie's pickup was no longer parked next to Katie's.

She'd stopped by the manager's house earlier to make certain he was okay with Katie staying on the ranch and he, of course, had assured her he was fine with it. Like he would say anything else to the woman who'd helped him out when he so desperately needed it. And now that he and Katie had spent time together, he decided he *was* fine with it. He could deal with the situation just as he had back when he'd fancied himself falling for her. Besides, he had a strong feeling that Katie intended to stay for at least as long as he'd be there, and he really had no option but to deal with it.

So deal he would.

KATIE PULLED OPEN the door of the old chicken house and made a face as she stepped back. The small building was chock-full of wire—and not the friendly kind. Loose rolls of barbed wire filled most of the interior. She planned to move ahead with her greenhouse plan, but she was also considering other ventures—like hobby chickens. There'd always been chickens and fresh eggs on the ranch while she was growing up, and if she was going to stay, she wanted to indulge in things she hadn't been able to indulge in while in the city.

Chickens qualified.

But if she was going to get chickens, she had some work ahead of her. The roof wasn't exactly watertight, judging from the condition of the floorboards, so she'd have to research how to repair it. Or ask Nick.

"You're a smart girl. You'll figure it out." The muttered words were barely out of her mouth when the sound of a door opening caught her attention. She turned to see Brady emerging from the grain shed and hoped he hadn't heard her talking to herself. He ambled closer, coming to a stop a good ten feet away from her.

"Looking for wire?"

"More like wishing there wasn't so much here." He frowned, and she explained, "I'm thinking chickens in the spring."

"I can help you clean this out if you want."

She blinked at him. "First dinner and now this?"

"I'm here to help with the ranch. That's what Rosalie hired me to do."

"Still a bit of a shift from our first meeting." She didn't know why she was pushing for an answer for his change in attitude, why she couldn't just accept it, but she made no effort to tamp down her curiosity.

"I was feeling raw when you arrived."

"I wonder why, pinned to the ground by a ton of machinery."

"Less than a half ton."

"I stand corrected."

He gripped his buckle, which, interestingly, was one he'd won in high school rather than one of the many he must have won during his professional rodeo career, and rocked on his heels. "I didn't feel ready for company, even when I wasn't pinned under the machine."

"Now you do."

"No." The word came out easily. "But I'm picking my battles."

Her eyebrows lifted. "Okay."

She thought he might have been on the edge of a smile, and the thought of him smiling at her—*really* smiling at her—sent a tingle through her. *Hello, old friend.* She'd felt that tingle so often back in the day when Brady was near. "I'm not going to treat you like Ed. That was a dumb plan."

"Agreed."

Which left the question of how she was going to treat him. "You two do share some common characteristics, however."

"Such as?"

"You can both be surly and distant." There was no sting to her words, and Katie bit the inside of her cheek as she waited for his response. They were once again in comfortable territory, with her gently baiting him while he attempted to keep his cool.

"I have my reasons."

"I know."

His expression started to blank out and Katie made a stab at saving the situation. She hated it when he withdrew. "You aren't your parents."

Big mistake bringing up his parents. His half-closed-off expression became totally closed off. Well, Katie wasn't having it.

"Brady...loosen up. Your big secret isn't such a secret. There was a reason you lived with us more than you lived at home."

He glanced past her toward the open fields, where she imagined he wanted to escape to, and his throat moved. Oh, yeah. The parental wounds cut deeply even after years of being on his own.

"I suppose Nick talked to you?" he said as he looked back at her.

She shook her head. "I heard the two of you talking more than once, and it was pretty obvious that your parents let you run wild because, well—" Katie swallowed, then went with the hard truth as she saw it "—they didn't want to concern themselves."

"I'm too much like my dad. My real dad. I don't think my mom could handle it."

And he might have been hard to handle because of it. Probably easier to let him run.

Katie stayed silent, knowing Brady wouldn't appreciate platitudes after letting loose with some actual information about himself. Finally he blew out a breath, then pressed his lips together as he studied his boots. When he raised his gaze again, his expression was matter-of-fact.

"I had some rough times. But those times are gone."

"Replaced by new rough times." And she had a feeling the physical injuries were easier to deal with.

"Yeah."

He started to move back, and Katie reached out to put her hand on his arm, stopping him. She wasn't done. For a moment they both stared at her hand as it lay on his sleeve, then once again he raised that clear green gaze of his.

"Don't feel sorry for me, Katie. I'm good."

"Are you?" Without conscious thought, she lifted her hand from his sleeve and pressed it to his cheek, her nerves tingling at the sensation of warm, beard-roughened skin beneath her palm. Brady went still, so still that she wondered if he was even breathing. She seemed to be having trouble in that department herself.

Somehow, she found her voice, and it sounded remarkably normal as she said, "Don't you feel sorry for me, either. I'm also good."

Or rather, she'd been good until she touched him and had been unexpectedly warmed from the inside out. Now she felt wildly off-kilter.

Time to retreat, before one of them had a heart attack. She let her hand drop and took half a step back, giving Brady the breathing room he needed. An expression she couldn't read chased across his features before he also stepped back, putting a decent amount of space between them as he slid his thumbs into his front pockets.

"I've got work to do," he said abruptly. "Let me know if you need any help with this wire."

"Will do," Katie said to his back as he walked toward the barn, limping a little less than before. The effect of adrenaline, no doubt.

She blew out a long breath, then clasped

both hands at the back of her neck and focused on the ground near her shoes. What had just happened? A lot more than a touch and an admonishment on her part for him not to shut her out.

But oddly, despite hauling them both further out of their comfort zones than anticipated, she felt better about staying on the ranch. Brady didn't need to be rescued, but Katie had a feeling he might just benefit from some actual human contact while he was healing.

And so might she.

BRADY KEPT HIS gaze so low as he walked away from Katie that he almost ran into the wheelbarrow on his way to the barn. He saw it at the last minute and awkwardly stepped sideways onto his stronger leg. Thankfully. All he needed was to go down in a heap.

Once in the barn, he closed the door behind him and resisted the urge to turn and beat his head against it.

When Katie had touched his cheek with her soft palm and stared up at him with those beautiful blue eyes, it had almost undone him. He thought he was through wanting her, thought he'd moved beyond that stage of his life. He was wrong.

But at least he hadn't kissed her.

What kind of trouble would that bring? He wasn't about to find out. He let out a slow breath. He knew now that he wouldn't hurt her like his dad had hurt his mother as he'd once feared. He still loved a good adrenaline rush, but he could control his impulses. But there was still the small matter of being at rock bottom. He had no profession. Nothing to offer. And he was about to risk what little he did have on a land venture that could evaporate just like that if he missed payments. But as he saw it, that land venture was his only means of building a future in a reasonable amount of time.

Ah, Katie.

He rubbed his neck, then let his hand drop to his side.

You hung out around her before without her clueing in, and you can do it again. Just...act like a big brother or something.

Except he didn't feel like a big brother.

She doesn't know that.

And he was going to make certain she never suspected.

Brady had a strong inclination to spend

the rest of the day working in the barn, aka
hiding out, but if he was going to live around
Katie he needed to man-up. To just go about
his business, treat Katie like a little sis and
somehow muscle through until Nick came
back and he could move to his own land. So
while Katie continued to inspect the premises, making plans for her future on the
ranch, Brady repaired a sagging gate and
then checked the cattle he would move to the
river pasture after they'd grazed the pasture
they were in. Nick was a fanatic about not
overgrazing, and Brady wanted the ground
in good shape when he turned over the reins.

He finally made it back to his house as
dusk was falling, sank down onto the closest
kitchen chair and pulled the moccasin off his
injured foot. It was swollen, but he'd made
it through the day without diving into the
pain meds and tomorrow should be better.
He propped it on the chair closest to him to
let it rest. A little ice and all would be good.

He hadn't bothered with the lights, and
when he glanced out the window, he spotted Katie moving around in her kitchen. It
was hard to pull his gaze away, but he did.

Being attracted to her was no crime. Com-
plicating her life was.

He reached behind him to snap on the light and then gave his foot a few more minutes of being elevated before poking at it. Oh, yeah. Tender. He sucked his breath in through his teeth as he stood, waiting for the pain to subside before he put weight on the foot and headed to the fridge for an ice pack. Dinner would be canned soup and then he'd baby his foot and continue writing up his business plan for his ranch and perusing the local employment sites. He wouldn't abandon Rosalie, who still needed a ranch manager, but he wanted to know what he was looking at employment-wise when Nick moved back home.

As he opened the soup can, he glanced out the window again at the main house, before resolutely pulling his focus back to the simple task at hand. He was not going to think about the fact that Katie was probably just as lonely as he was, and it only made sense for them to eat meals together. But the thing that had just happened between them made that a dangerous proposition.

CHAPTER SEVEN

"HERBS, AS IN...HERBS?" Cassie asked in an astonished voice.

"Yes. Smallish green plants." Katie moved the phone to her other ear as she poured hot water into her teacup. She was a rotten left-handed pourer.

"You're kidding."

"I'm not." Katie knew the exact expression Cassie wore at that moment, having seen it often enough when she'd put forth ideas Cassie hadn't agreed with, be it a prom dress, or a guy Katie had thought was crush-worthy. The trouble was that Cassie was usually right, and maybe that was why she'd kept her feelings for Brady to herself back in the day.

"I assume you've done your research," Cassie said in her stern older-sister voice.

"There's a market. A good market actually." Katie had spent days glued to her computer, first narrowing down business possibilities, and then laser focusing on the ins and outs of growing herbs for profit.

"Herbs." Cassie sounded slightly less gob-smacked the third time she uttered the word.

"I want to stay close to home. Grandma isn't getting any younger. She might need help with her shop, and Nick and the girls are moving back to the ranch."

"All excellent reasons to stay, but have you explored all the possible avenues for employment in the area?"

"I'm tired of the rat race, Cass. I wish I'd never toed up to the starting line, to tell you the truth."

"If you hadn't, you would have always wondered."

"True." So it was probably a good thing she'd pursued her corporate career, but words could not express how happy she was at the thought of leaving it all behind. "But now I know."

"My only concern is that you don't have enough emotional distance yet."

"Emotional distance from what?"

"Failure."

Katie grimaced. "I didn't fail. The company cut back."

"All the same, I'd hate to see you bury

yourself on the ranch due to a temporary career setback."

Katie cleared her throat. "Did you hear that part about me wishing I'd never embarked on that career?" She hesitated, then launched a mild offensive. "Have you ever had second thoughts about your career?"

"Of course," Cassie said a little too quickly. "Everyone does."

The answer surprised her. Cassie's career drive made Katie's look puny in comparison. She was on track to become superintendent of her school district and nothing was going to stand in her way. Katie only hoped it was what her sister really wanted—that Cassie wasn't practicing the same kind of tunnel vision Katie had.

"Second thoughts are normal," her sister continued. "Especially after encountering a rough patch."

"Well, I've had fourth and fifth thoughts, Cass, and now I have a final thought. I'm done with it."

There was an extra beat of silence before Cassie said in a resigned voice, "Tell me about your plan."

Which was why she'd called. She wanted to bounce her ideas off someone who'd be honest with her, even though she knew that Cassie would be initially horrified at the idea of her trading down career-wise.

"I'll start from the beginning." Katie flipped the pages of the yellow legal pad to the beginning and began summarizing her notes, starting with possible markets, working through startup costs and ending with growth potential.

"Health care? Retirement?"

"Grandma will put me on the ranch insurance policy, and I'll give myself three years for the other. If I'm not making enough by then to invest in retirement, I'll rethink the whole thing."

"And lose three years of your professional life."

"I've already lost five years of my real life."

"I'm thinking résumé."

"I'm thinking sanity."

Cassie did not have an answer to that. But she did say something that made Katie feel like the call had been worthwhile. "Then you should start looking into small-business loans and grants."

"Can you think of anything I haven't addressed?"

"Not off the top of my head. You might run this by Nick, too."

"I will. I've also discussed it with Grandma and she's supportive. She might even sell dried herbs in her store."

"Oh, yeah. You'll make a bundle there. Just a sec." Cassie made a small noise, then came back on the line. "I've got a call coming in from the district office. I need to take it."

"Sure thing." Even though it was Friday night. "Thanks for listening. I'll keep you posted."

"You better."

A second later Cassie ended the call and Katie set aside her legal pad and leaned back in the antique office chair. Her coworkers used to tease her about doing more work with a pad and paper than on a computer. It wasn't true, but there *was* something therapeutic about working with a pencil and paper that connected her to her work in a better way than tapping away at a keyboard did. Besides, she could doodle on the margins of a legal pad, and she did love a good doodle.

Tigger jumped onto Katie's lap and butted his head against her chin. She stroked his silky orange coat. "Don't worry, bud. I'm not going anywhere in the near future." The cat seemed to be banking loves and snuggles for the long spell during which he wouldn't see her—a long spell that wasn't coming, but so far she hadn't been able to convince him of that.

Katie pulled the cat up against her chest to give him a proper cuddle, idly stroking his head. She'd missed having a pet more than she'd known. It was crazy how many things she hadn't allowed herself to think about while building her career. Tunnel vision, denial and misplaced focus were to blame.

The pink slip had been a good thing. Otherwise, she might have spent another decade without cat cuddles. Even if she did go back to the city, she'd tackle life differently. She'd carve out time for herself, even if it meant not rocketing up the corporate ladder, and she'd live in a place where she could have a pet, even if it meant a commute.

But you're not going back to the city.

She sincerely hoped not. She liked being home too much. Liked being around Brady too much. She'd given him space over the past several days, because he wanted and needed space, but that didn't stop her from thinking about him, or feeling that little jolt whenever she caught sight of him.

Katie gently set Tigger on the floor, then stood and stretched the kinks out of her shoulders before heading into the kitchen to brew a pot of evening tea. Brady's house was dark, and she wondered if he was already in bed. He did get up early to tend to the cattle.

Even though days had passed, she was still reliving the moment when she'd touched his face and he'd gone so still. Almost as if he was fighting something...and she didn't think it was shock at being touched when he hadn't expected it.

KATIE HAD MADE herself scarce over the past several days and Brady couldn't help but wonder if the near-miss kiss was the reason. Whether it was or wasn't, he had the run of the place while Katie stayed holed up in her house. She'd yet to approach him on the matter of the wire-filled chicken coop, and he decided not to do anything until she did. Why move the wire out when he may well have to move it back in if she abandoned her chicken idea?

Of course, he could talk to her, ask her if she wanted him to move the wire. It wasn't like he wore a blinking hat that read I'm Attracted to You, even though it kind of felt like he did. In the end, he decided that if Katie wanted help, she knew where to find him. She'd never been shy about approaching him, and if she suddenly became shy, well, then it was because she'd figured a few things out and was keeping her distance for a reason.

By the end of the week he found himself in a situation he dreaded—almost out of coffee. And milk. Bread, butter and canned food were also in low supply. He had to go shopping. Although he honestly liked to cook, he hated to shop. Maybe it was all the time he'd spent on the road, but grocery stores seemed like foreign places in a lot of ways. It wasn't that he couldn't navigate them—he knew the ins and outs of perusing aisles and looking for the best buy; it was the feeling of being watched by the people who'd known him when. He didn't like attention and he didn't like sympathy, and what was more pitiful than a guy, who'd once swaggered, limping around a grocery store?

Before he left for town, he did what he would have done for anyone living in the main house. He knocked on the door, and when Katie answered, he ignored the twisting sensation in his chest and said, "I'm going to town. Do you need anything?"

"Actually, I'm going myself tomorrow, so I'm good." She smiled politely. "Thanks for checking."

"No problem." He turned and headed down the walk as fast as his injured foot would allow, which was a little faster than a couple days ago. And he made it to his truck without tripping over a wheelbarrow, so all in all, it was a successful encounter with the woman who would not leave his thoughts.

He needed a distraction. His first thought was to go to the Shamrock Pub after he finished shopping. His second was to stop by the Larson Stock Company office and see how they felt about him taking a close-up look at his property before the snow started flying.

He went with the land office, which was located in an older building near the center of town. The chair behind the desk was empty when he pushed the door open, but he stepped inside, anyway.

"Who goes there?" called a voice from the next room.

"One of your protégées," Brady called

back. Even though Will McGuire had been the man who'd coached Brady to his two High School Rodeo National Finals wins, he'd done it on an unofficial basis, showing up at the practice pen as a volunteer. Stan Larson had been his official coach. Working for the family land company had given Stan the freedom to coach and travel with the rough stock team to the various rodeos, freedom Will hadn't had. But of the two men, there was no question as to who had done Brady the most good. And in return, Brady had broken his promise to the man.

"Brady." Stan came out of the back room carrying a cup of coffee. "Glad you stopped by. Feeling okay?"

He didn't say a word about Brady's injuries, didn't ask how Brady was feeling. They'd covered that territory and neither of them wanted to cover it again.

"Doing all right," Brady replied. "How's it going with the will and the legalities?"

"They're making headway. Things should be settled sooner rather than later. Why a bunch of nieces, nephews and cousins think they have a right to Abe Sr.'s fortune... Never mind. I think we've touched on this before. Like I said. Everything should be settled soon, and then we can sign papers and I can hand you the keys to the house."

Or Brady could climb in through one of the unlocked windows. The house was in rotten shape.

"Have you sold the parcels next to mine yet?" He hoped for good neighbors. Twenty acres was not a lot of land.

Stan fiddled with his pen. "We're working on some stuff, but I can't give any specifics."

"I understand. I just thought I'd stop by and see how things were progressing and ask if anyone cared if I took a drive across Larson land to take a look at my parcel."

"I can't see anyone having a problem with that. The gate combination is 20-1-9."

"Like the year."

Stan smiled. "Some of us are becoming forgetful. That makes it easy."

His former coach did look older, wearier, as if the issues involved in breaking up and selling off the assets of the land company while dealing with a contested will were wearing him down. "Things going okay?"

"Yeah." Stan's featured relaxed. "This whole thing worked out pretty close to perfect for me. By the time the will is settled and the land sells, I'll be ready to retire, the heirs will divvy up the cash and that will be the end of the Larson Stock Company."

"Are you good with that?" Stan was a Larson, but he was a cousin who'd gone to work for the company, not an heir.

"I am. I feel lucky." He picked up the pen again. "And I'm glad you were able to work a deal with Abe Jr."

Stan had a big hand in that, having convinced the heirs that Brady would work his butt off to make his payments. "I appreciate him carrying the loan."

"You're paying a higher interest rate."

Brady was well aware, but that was how private money worked, and since he wasn't able to qualify for a conventional loan, he was happy that Abe Jr. had agreed to carry the loan. "I'm good with it. Maybe at some point I can refinance and pay him off."

"Well, whatever happens, you should be able to move on to your place shortly after the new year—if the snow isn't too deep."

"I'll buy a plow for the front of my truck." Actually, he had his eye on one at the Callahan Ranch that he might be able to buy from Nick, who plowed with a tractor.

Stan grinned at him. "That would be a worthwhile investment." His expression grew more serious as he said, "Everything going all right?" He nodded at Brady's leg and finally addressed the elephant in the room. "Healing okay?"

Brady gave a small nod. "Like you, I feel lucky. If I keep strengthening, I should be able to get a job on another ranch not long after Nick Callahan returns home."

"Have you thought about school?"

"I can't afford school." He preferred to put his money into the property. Something tangible, something that he could build on, one way or another.

Stan had the grace to shift his weight and look self-conscious. He'd been a big part of the reason that Brady hadn't gone to college.

"Hey," Brady said quietly. "I made my own decision then. Enjoyed a ton of success. It just ended badly and now I'm rebuilding." Starting from ground zero at the age of twenty-eight.

But at least he was starting.

DESPITE THE WEATHER being on the cool side, the front door of her grandmother and Gloria's house was open, and when Katie got out of her truck, Gladys Knight & the Pips invited her to take a midnight train to Georgia. Gloria did love her '70s music.

As Katie crossed the porch and walked into the parlor, she understood why the door was open. Paint fumes hit her nostrils as soon as she passed through the doorway.

"Hello?" she called.

"Katie." Her grandmother appeared in the arched doorway leading to the kitchen wearing a bandanna over her hair and latex gloves. "I didn't expect you for another hour."

"I came to town early to talk to the new manager of Hardwick's about the herbs and— Is that white paint I see on that brush?" she asked.

Rosalie winked at her as Gloria joined her in the doorway, wearing paint-splattered safety glasses. "I'm painting the ceiling," she explained. "Not the trim. Messy business, but it keeps me out of trouble."

Despite her light words, there was an edge to her voice and Katie shot her grandmother a questioning look. Rosalie tightened her mouth. "We were going to ease into this, but would you be willing to goat-sit for a while?"

"Goat-sit?"

"Lizzie Belle got into the yard next door

and ate a bunch of ornamental shrubs. The Taylors called the sheriff and pointed out that the property isn't zoned for livestock."

"But Lizzie Belle is a pet," Katie protested.

"According to the state of Montana, she is livestock," Gloria said.

"Can't you have her classified as a comfort animal?"

"If I have a verifiable disability." Gloria's lips tightened even more. "I won't lie and say I do, when I don't. There are other ways around this."

"That don't involve doing the Taylors bodily harm," Rosalie said firmly.

Gloria rolled her eyes. "A girl can dream."

"Of course I'll goat-sit," Katie said quickly. "She's an outdoor goat, right?"

"I had her indoors briefly when she was a kid, but she caused too much mischief. Definitely an outdoor goat."

"She loves going on walks with us," Rosalie added. "The neighbors…well, most of them…got a kick out of seeing two old ladies and a goat taking a stroll."

"Who are you calling old?" Gloria asked with a mock frown.

"We're old, Gloria. It's better than the alternative."

"All right. Maybe so." Gloria's grip tightened on Katie's arm. "Thank you. We'll get this settled and then Lizzie Belle can come home."

"Until then, I'll take good care of her."

"I'm glad that's done. Sit down," Gloria said, whisking the drop cloth off one of the kitchen chairs. "I'll make tea." She shot a look at Rosalie. "I think it's time for a break and conversation on a benign topic—if we can come up with one."

Katie could only imagine the conversations that had occurred after learning that their house wasn't in an area zoned for Gloria's beloved goat. No wonder both women looked a touch frazzled.

"We've had to work in separate rooms to keep from plotting revenge on the Taylor family," Rosalie said darkly before she made an effort to lighten her expression. "Why don't we go up to my apartment for tea? Escape the fumes and the brisk temperatures for a bit."

"Great idea." Gloria unplugged the electric kettle and the three of them headed to the stairs.

Katie waited until they were seated at her grandmother's elegant oak table before asking, "Why didn't you call me when you learned about Lizzie Belle?" Because this was the kind of stuff she wanted to know about. The next time she ran into Mellie Taylor it was not going to be pretty.

"I was still deciding how to handle the matter," Gloria explained.

"Not that there were many options," Rosalie added. "But we *will* be working on this matter in a peaceful and productive manner." She sipped her tea, then set the cup back down. "Now tell me how your meeting went at Hardwick's."

"Good actually. And I have appointments with two restaurant owners. It sounds like I can sell products if I can produce it. Local foods are a big selling point now that people are becoming more interested in green living."

"How much work will it be to restore the greenhouse? I recall a number of broken windows."

"I'll have to bring Nick in on that, but I'll have my hands full. I'm calculating costs now and also working up a packet for a small-business loan and looking into grant opportunities." If she was successful, she'd have to have more than one greenhouse, but she'd deal with that after testing the waters.

"Speaking of Nick, he called this morning."

"And…"

"His buyer is still arranging financing. We are all holding our breath."

"I'll hold mine, too." Because she couldn't wait for her brother and nieces to move back home.

"Will Brady stay after Nick comes home?" Gloria asked brightly.

"He can stay as long as he wants," Rosalie said more to Katie than to Gloria.

Hmm. Might be some kind of a message there. Or maybe, after the near kiss, Katie was reading messages into everything.

"He won't stay long," Katie predicted, and both older women gave her a look. "After Nick comes back, Brady'll assume you no longer need him, and he'll move on." She cleared her throat. "Do you need help painting the trim?"

Gloria nodded and set down her teacup. "We're still debating on trim, but I'm sure we'll come up with something before we open… I hope." She murmured the last words in an undertone before picking up her tea again.

"Nothing looks right," Rosalie explained. "But we'll forge on. If you could take Lizzie Belle to the ranch today, it would be the most help."

"Will she ride on the back seat, or do I need to get the big travel kennel from the ranch?"

"She's used to the back seat," Gloria assured her.

And, indeed, she was. As Katie drove out of town a half hour later, her passenger stood on the back seat, nuzzling Katie's ear and nosing her hair. Katie laughed as the warm goat breath tickled her neck. "Next time we're going to arrange for you to have some kind of a restraint," she said as she gently pushed a snuffling nose away from her ear.

When they arrived at the ranch, Katie led the goat into the front yard, and before she had the gate fully shut and latched, the little nanny was exploring all the yummy dried plants in Rosalie's garden.

"You are cute," Katie murmured.

The little goat blinked her golden eyes at Katie and let out a little bleat.

"Yes. The Taylors are annoying people.

But what goes around comes around." Talking to a goat. Excellent. But it was getting close to nightfall and the lights were already on in Brady's kitchen, so she was fairly certain she had no witnesses.

She headed to the barn and came back toting the big dog kennel, which she fashioned into a goat shelter by tying the door open and filling it with straw. When her handiwork was done, she assured Lizzie Belle that she'd see her the next morning and headed into the house, the little goat on her heels. It broke her heart to close the door and leave the little animal standing on the porch, but she couldn't have a goat in her grandmother's house.

I NEED HELP with the cows.

Why was it so hard to squeeze those words out? Because it appeared Katie was avoiding him? Or because he was sensitive about asking for help?

Regardless of the reason he didn't want to ask, he *had* to ask. The three limping cows he'd noticed while feeding that morning needed to be examined and he couldn't do it alone. He wasn't quick or agile enough to stop them if they decided to make a break for it, as he discovered when he'd managed to corral the limpers, along with seven other cows, into a large holding pen and had slipped as he hurried to close the gate behind them. End result? His foot was swelling up again. He was literally moving one step forward, one step back in the healing process.

Brady drained his second cup of post-morning-feed coffee, glanced out the window and almost dropped his empty cup.

There was a goat standing on the hood of his truck.

How?

The answer was simple. Katie had brought home the beast that was now scratching the paint on his hood.

Brady went out the door without bothering with a coat. The goat was now standing on the top of the cab, surveying her goat kingdom. She let out a bleat when she saw him and did a little dance, then bounded off the cab onto the hood and onto the ground. A second later she butted her hornless head against his leg and then blinked up at him. When he made a grab for her collar, the goat danced out of reach.

Shaking his head, he crossed the driveway to the main house. From behind him came the distinctive sound of hooves sliding across painted metal.

Through the gate he went, not bothering to close it. He gave a couple sharp raps on the door and a few seconds later Katie opened it. She instantly read his mood.

"What's wrong?"

Her hair was hanging in damp waves around her face and she wore a robe. He hadn't thought about how early it was, and he shouldn't be thinking about how good she looked, damp hair and all.

"There's a goat standing on my truck."

Katie gathered her robe more closely around her and looked over his shoulder. "No. She's behind you."

Sure enough, the goat must have followed him through the open gate because she was standing a few feet away from him, cocking her head curiously at him. He turned back to Katie. "She *was* on my truck. Is there any chance that you could contain her so that she doesn't do it again?"

"I'll try." She brushed past Brady and walked to the end of the sidewalk to close the gate. "Step one."

"The gate was closed when I got here," he growled. Meaning the goat had not exited the premises by that means unless she had a talent for locking the latch behind her.

"I'll see about making her a more secure pen." Katie mounted the porch steps and came to a stop a few feet away from him. "Sorry about your truck."

Brady frowned as the goat came to stand between them, gazing up first at Katie, then at him. "You've already been to the animal shelter?" he asked.

Katie's eyes widened. "No. This is Gloria's pet. There are some issues with keeping her at the house, so Grandma asked me to bring her home."

"Maybe she needs a higher fence."

"You think?" Katie asked.

"Yeah, and I can help you with that. In return, I'd appreciate help with the cows." Could he speak more stiffly? Act more self-conscious? His reactions to her were becoming ridiculous. It wasn't as if they'd actually kissed that day outside the chicken house. They'd simply had a near miss.

"What kind of help?"

"I need to cut three limping cows out of the herd and put them in the squeeze so I can figure out what the deal is."

"You have to run the chute. I'm horrible at it. The curse of being short."

"You do the footwork and I'll man the chute."

She smiled and his heart give a stutter beat before regaining its steady rhythm.

This is bad.

Real bad. He was falling for her again. He could deny it all he wanted, but the cold hard truth was that Katie was working her way back into his heart.

"Thanks for asking instead of trying without me," she said, blissfully unaware of the turmoil going on inside of him, and the fact that she knew it'd been hard for him to ask for help made something twist deep in his gut. Just what he needed—stuttering heart, twisted gut. He was feeling a little light-headed, too.

"Yeah. Well…"

She reached out to pat his upper arm. "Don't hurt yourself. I'll get dressed and then we can make a plan. Want some coffee?"

"No. I already had mine. I've got breakfast waiting, so I'll come back in twenty minutes."

"I should have my face on by then." She smiled at her own joke.

"Right." He was pretty sure that Katie didn't wear a lot of makeup.

"Let me just nab the culprit." She moved past him to grab the little goat's collar. "Safe. Make your escape while you can."

Brady headed down the walk as Katie and her little friend went into the house. A second later he heard the door close behind them and the tension that had tightened his shoulders gave a little.

This was going to be a fun day.

BRADY'S LIMP HAD not improved since the accident. Katie sighed and turned away from the kitchen window as he made his way across the driveway to the truck her charge had danced upon. She led Lizzie Belle through the house and out her bedroom door into the backyard, where the fence was higher, and she could keep an eye on the goat while she got dressed. Lizzie Belle started exploring her new surroundings, idly munching on dried flowers and leaves as she navigated the perimeter.

Katie hoped the goat hadn't done much damage to Brady's paint job, because if she had, Katie would pay for it, and she'd much rather sink her savings into her future business than into rectifying goat damage.

Twenty minutes later, her hair was dry, and she was dressed in old jeans, an older sweater, boots and a hooded jacket. The only gloves she could find were her grandmother's pink-flowered gardening gloves, but they were better than nothing, so Katie slipped them into her jacket pocket as she headed out the door to meet Brady.

She found him at his truck, inspecting the hood.

"Bad?"

He shot her a look. "Nothing went to primer, so all the scratches can be buffed."

Guys and their trucks. Nick was the same way. The older ranch rigs could be knocked to death, but the personal rig—that was special.

"I'll try to keep it from happening again."

"I'd appreciate that." He stepped away from the truck and pulled his gloves out of his back pocket. "And thanks for the help with the cows." He glanced down at his injured foot. "I'm not as fast as I used to be, and I need someone who can head them off when they try to escape."

"I'm your woman," she said matter-of-factly, and then, when he shot her a quick questioning glance, she realized how that sounded. Not good. But instead of making things worse by explaining what she did and did not mean, she rubbed her hands together in a businesslike way. Besides…part of her wanted to be his woman. A big part. "Shall we?"

"Yes."

She matched her pace to Brady's without being too obvious about it and together they walked past the barn to the series of corrals where Brady had ten animals penned. Katie picked up one of the long sorting sticks leaning against the corral and propped it on her shoulder.

"You'll handle the gate?" Which was usually her job. Cassie and Nick were better at working the cows, and she was a pretty good gate operator, but that didn't mean she couldn't cut cows out of a herd. If you lived on a ranch, you pretty much had to be ready to do anything.

"As opposed to…"

"Coming into the pen to help when I have trouble sorting out the ones you want?"

"I think I better stick with the gate and let you have all the fun."

Katie's eyebrows went up. "You're being remarkably sensible today."

"My foot hurts like hell."

"Sensible behavior brought on by pain. Very guy-like."

To her surprise, and maybe to his own, as well, he reached out and tapped the bill of her ball cap down low over her eyes.

"Hey," she said, quickly stepping out of reach. "I spent a long time getting the proper angle on my hat."

"Uh-huh." He actually smiled at her, and her stomach gave a crazy little lurch in response.

Katie sniffed loudly and headed for the gate. Brady was playing with her. And she liked it. The big question was, how long until he realized what he was doing and backed off?

"Be careful in there."

"I am not without skills."

"We shall see." Brady followed her through the gate she'd held for him and then latched it before moving to the smaller gate leading to a catch pen. When he was ready, Katie waded into the herd, moving slowly as she looked for the ear tag numbers Brady had given her as they'd walked to the corrals.

She really didn't need the tag numbers, since the limping cows were easy to spot. She carefully cut cows #4J and #5E out of the herd and maneuvered them down the fence line to the pen where Brady swung the gate shut after them.

"Two at once. I'm impressed."

"It was easy," Katie said as Brady moved the cow on through to a smaller inner pen and closed the gate.

"Careful not to jinx yourself," he warned.

Katie rolled her eyes and headed back into the cows, looking for #8H, who, it turned out, didn't want to be separated from her friends. As the cow became more anxious, adrenaline kicked in and she lost the limp. After she evaded Katie for the third time by nosing into the middle of her friends, she decided she'd had enough and put her head down, shaking it at Katie before pawing the ground.

"Let's trade places," Brady called.

"I know what to do in situations like this."

"Yeah? What's that?"

"Pretend I'm Cassie." Who'd put up with no bovine nonsense. Katie judged the distance to the fence, decided she was in good shape in case she had to sprint to safety, then shook her stick at the cow, who raised her head a few inches and gave Katie the equivalent of a cow frown.

"You. Get going," Katie said in a commanding voice. "Now." She took a step forward, brandishing the stick. The cow eyeballed her, then looked toward the open gate where Brady stood. Cows did love an open gate. Katie waved the stick again and the cow started to move in the right direction, only to veer off at the last minute. Katie made a dive to stop her and slipped in the mud. The next thing she knew, Brady was there, hauling her back to her feet by her elbow.

"I'm okay."

"I'll stay here, while you bring her around again."

"Will do," Katie said grimly, heading back into the fray. This time she got #8H and another cow moving.

"Bring them both."

"Exactly what I was going to do." This time, with Brady blocking the escape route, the two went into the pen and Brady swung the gate closed. It only took a minute to separate the extra cow and put her through the gate, leaving #8H alone in the pen.

"Nice work," Brady said, coming to stand next to Katie.

"Yeah." Katie glanced sideways at him and saw his mouth curve up at the corner. She did love to see him smile. "For a limping cow, she was certainly fast."

"And will pay a price later."

"Like you."

He shrugged and Katie knew that was all the answer she was going to get. It took less than half an hour to run the cows through the chute, where Brady determined that they were dealing with a bacterial infection known simply as foot rot. After vaccinating the animals, they turned them back into the smaller corral and Brady used the tractor to bring a bale of hay to feed them while they recovered.

After parking the tractor, Brady returned to the fence, where Katie was watching the three cows eat.

"No goat yet."

"She's in the backyard. The fence is higher." She turned to lean against the rails, crossing. "Do you need help buffing out those scratches?"

"No."

"I understand." She spoke to the gravel at her feet.

"You understand what?"

"I understand that you prefer to work alone."

"I asked you for help with the cows." He came to lean on the fence beside her, their shoulders almost but not quite touching.

"Yes. You did. And it was hard for you to do that, wasn't it?"

He moistened his lips before giving a nod. "It was."

"Would it have been hard to ask Nick?"

"Nope."

She canted her head to one side, narrowing her eyes as she said, "What's the difference?"

He opened his mouth, seemed to think better of what he was about to say, then to her utter amazement, he cupped her chin in his hand and brought his lips to hers in a brief kiss. For a moment all she could do was stare.

"Why did you do that?" She had to say something, so she blurted out the most obvious question.

"That's the difference between asking you and asking Nick."

Katie stilled. She had *not* seen this coming.

"I feel there's a message in your cryptic response," she muttered. Brady didn't come close to smiling.

"I think it's obvious that I've wanted to do that for a while."

"As in how long?"

"Awhile," he repeated.

"That's not an answer."

He turned so he was facing her. "Longer than I should have. The thing is, we weren't on a level playing field. I was older and about to leave—"

"How long, Brady?"

"Years."

She stared at him, then managed to close her open mouth. Was it possible that while she had been crushing on him, he'd felt the same about her? Her brain was having a hard time wrapping itself around the idea. Talk about missed opportunity.

"We still aren't on a level playing field." There was a note of warning in his voice that Katie found patently annoying.

"We're both single, both unemployed. That sounds pretty level to me."

He gave her an exasperated look. "Allow me to point out a few subtle differences." He gestured at his injured leg. "If Rosalie hadn't given me this job, I don't know where I'd be right now, but wherever it was, I doubt I would be making ends meet financially. I have no skills, Katie."

"Are you doing something about that?"

"Trying to, but it's a risky venture."

She narrowed her eyes at him. She could still feel the warmth of his mouth, and she wanted to feel it again. Not now, but maybe sometime in the future, when his defenses weren't a mile high.

Yeah? When might that be?

Katie ignored the small voice. "Are you cautioning me not to fall for you?" She drew herself up. "Excellent application of ego, Brady."

She had the satisfaction of seeing a flare of surprise in his green eyes.

"I'm stating facts."

Katie let out a sigh and leaned her head against the post behind her. "Consider this fact—I'm not a seventeen-year-old kid with no life experience. I am fully capable of recognizing an uneven playing field and adjusting in an appropriate manner."

"Translation?"

"Don't think too hard. We're friends, Brady. And we kissed."

"That's it."

No. Katie lifted her eyebrows in a questioning way. "Are you looking for anything else?"

"No." The word might have come out a little too fast, but she pretended not to notice.

"We almost kissed a week ago. We did kiss today. Don't you think that relieves some of the unexpressed frustration between us? We wondered about it. We did it."

"I don't think it's that simple."

Nor did she. Not for one single second. "Do you want to kiss me again?"

He didn't so much as flinch at the direct question. "I'd be lying if I said no."

"But you feel like you shouldn't, what with the uneven playing field and all that."

"Pretty much."

"Then how about this? The next time you kiss me, do it because you feel like you *should*. Like it's the right thing…the *best* thing…to do."

"Katie—"

"That way we can work together, be together, maybe even eat dinner together— and not have to worry about what's going on in the other's head. If you have doubts about your ability to handle the situation, don't kiss me."

"It's not me I'm worried about."

"I know," she said gently. "Yet you accuse me of being the rescuer."

She heard the low curse he muttered before he said, "Your family is important to me, Katie. I don't want to mess that up."

She rose up on her toes and lightly brushed her lips over his, and even though he didn't kiss her back, she sensed that he wanted to. "Brady...stop thinking so much."

CHAPTER EIGHT

MECHANICKING GAVE A guy a lot of time to think, and as Brady worked on servicing the smaller of the two ranch tractors, he tried to tell himself that kissing Katie Callahan had been a mistake—because now that he'd kissed her once, he wanted to do it again— but in reality it had given them the necessary push to discuss what had been simmering between them ever since she'd arrived on the ranch.

Katie had spun the incident in a way he hadn't expected, sounding a lot like an HR woman as she assured him they were friends. Who'd kissed. And told him that he was supposed to stop thinking so much, which he took to mean stop anticipating dire consequences before they happened.

The thing was, he had a feeling that he wasn't the only one tempted to think too much.

Quick as the kiss had been, Katie had

kissed him back, and when he'd raised his head, her cheeks had been flushed. So, while she was talking about being friends who happened to kiss, all signs pointed to her meeting him halfway on the attraction front.

He just hoped she'd taken his words to heart about the uneven playing field and meant what she said about being friends. Yes, they were both single, and Brady was only temporarily employed, but he had a tough road ahead of him having made life choices that were not conducive to future employment opportunities, because, hey, wouldn't he be young and limber forever?

From what he'd been able to gather from talking to Will during rodeo practice years ago, his father had done the exact same thing. Colton O'Neil had given no thought to what lay ahead, and he'd left behind a wife who'd never forgiven him.

That was the part that bothered Brady most—being so much like his irresponsible dad. Every time he'd mounted a bronc, it could have been his last, but other than saving money, he hadn't given the next phase of his life a whole lot of thought. Maybe he'd been in denial, or maybe he'd been afraid of jinxing his season, but he'd been all about living for the moment. He'd ignored his future, thinking that the money in the bank would stay there instead of going toward medical bills that his skimpy insurance plan hadn't covered and for living expenses while he went through therapy. He was lucky to have been able to hang on to as much as he had and that was because his agent, Chet Jacobs, had put it into accounts that were not easily accessible if Brady had the urge to buy a new truck or pay a medical bill in a lump

Brady'd been irresponsible, and he was paying the price for his lack of planning. Damned if he was going to let someone else pay that price with him.

Maybe some time in the future, when you're in a better place, you and Katie can—

Brady abruptly cut off the thought. If Katie wanted to be friends, he could be a friend. That was all he could allow himself to be, even though he wanted to be so much more.

When he finished checking the tractor's hydraulic hoses, he wiped his hands on a shop rag and headed to the open bay door to see about lunch, arriving in time to see Katie drive over the cattle guard on her way to town.

Crazy how the ranch already felt a little emptier without her there.

Brady shook his head and crossed the drive.

He was in trouble, but he was going to make sure that Katie didn't share those troubles. They were just friends.

Who might kiss every now and again.

KATIE DROVE HOME from Gavin with a still-warm casserole on the seat beside her and little white paint flecks on her wrists and thumb. She'd stopped by her grandmother's place after an informal information-gathering meeting at the local bank to (a) make certain the Taylors hadn't done anything else to Rosalie and Gloria, and (b) to assure Gloria that her goat had settled in just fine. Katie did not mention Brady's truck, but she did insist on helping to sand doors and trim now that the two women had agreed that they needed to stain the trim, which involved removing a lot of old, thankfully lead-free, paint. Some they could do with a nontoxic paint remover, but a lot had to be removed the old-fashioned way—with elbow grease.

Rosalie had handed her a sanding block and a paper face mask without a single word of protest. There was a lot of trim in the old mansion, so Katie spent the afternoon removing paint and listening to Rosalie and Gloria banter. She also did her best to stay in the moment and not think about kissing Brady, but that was a losing proposition.

She'd told him not to think too much, and there she was, thinking too much. She was doing more than thinking. She was reliving. All she had to do was to close her eyes and the sounds of Rosalie's and Gloria's voices faded as she once again felt the warmth of his body, drew in the amazing scent that was all Brady...

She'd gone on that imaginary journey more than once, and the second time, Rosalie had asked if she was all right.

Katie had laughed, because it was kind of funny, and after that did her best to stay in the here and now—until she started driving home and thoughts of Brady began crowding into her head.

She had just crossed the bridge leading to the ranch when her phone rang. Nick. She pulled over to answer instead of waiting until she got home to call back. "Hey. What's happening?"

"Well, the sale of the business is inching

forward. The buyer thinks he might have nailed down some financing. If so, I may be able to start moving home around Thanksgiving."

"That's only three weeks away," Katie said happily.

"It is," he agreed on a wry note.

"And then I can get my hands on those nieces of mine."

"They feel exactly the same about Aunt Katie." There was a smile in his voice, but his tone became more serious as he said, "I'm glad you'll be there to spend time with them."

"I agree, and by the way, were you aware of issues with the Taylors and Grandma?"

"No."

"They bought the Grand Ladies on either side of her house, and now they want that house, too."

"They can't have it," Nick said matter-of-factly.

"They made a stink about Gloria's pet goat, so now it's living with me. I'm afraid that's only their first salvo."

"Keep me posted." He spoke in that dark voice that he took on whenever he needed to take care of business.

"I will. All I have to do is to pry information out of Grandma, and you know how easy that is."

"Keep on her."

She had every intention of doing just that and was about to say so when Nick asked, "How's Brady?"

Katie hoped her voice sounded normal as she said, "He's been better physically," because her stomach had done a slow flip at the question.

"What's this about the four-wheeler rolling on him?"

Katie briefly outlined the events, including Will helping them. "What's with Will and Brady?"

"Are things still awkward there?"

"If by awkward you mean that Brady would have rather chewed his foot off than to have asked for help, and Will being openly rude to him, yes. Awkward."

"How could you not know this?"

"Uh…no one told me anything."

"Will offered Brady that big scholarship the McGuire family gives."

"The full ride to Montana State?" The one she'd thought she was a shoo-in for a couple years later, being a close neighbor, only to be beat out by a kid who majored in chemical engineering. "I had no idea."

"He made a deal with Brady. He'd coach him in bronc riding if Brady went to college."

Katie blew out a low breath. *Wow.* That explained so much.

"And then Brady reneged," she murmured. Which didn't seem like something Brady would do.

"He was riding a wave of glory, and I know for a fact that Stan Larson worked to convince him that he could go to college anytime, but that bronc riding was for the young."

"Guess Stan made his point."

"As you can imagine, Will took it personally. Brady told him he'd go to college after his rodeo career was over, but Will was having none of it."

"Huh." Katie pushed the hair back from her forehead as she watched the river roll by. "Do you have any idea what Brady's going to do when you come back home?"

"He didn't tell you." It was a statement, not a question.

"Well, you know…he's not the most forthcoming person."

"He's better than he used to be. Rodeo kind of brought out the rock star in him."

"The rock star is no longer in residence," Katie said dryly. But what would rock star Brady be like? She imagined the female rodeo fans had loved him. Did he have groupies?

"Did Brady have groupies while he was a rock-star rodeo rider?" She did an excellent job of sounding casually curious, if she did say so herself.

"Seems he had at least one female fan," Nick said darkly.

Of course he did. "The girl he was supposed to have been messing with." The one whose boyfriend beat the snot out of Brady before his last ride.

Katie tipped her chin up to stare at the ceiling of the truck cab. "Do you think he was?" He didn't seem the type, but she never would have suspected that he'd break a pretty major promise to Will, either.

"I don't know, Katie. It's none of my business."

"Just curious," she murmured as her cheeks started to feel a little warm. But she hadn't tipped her hand. She was sure of it. She was just inquiring about the guy she'd grown up with. "I just kind of wonder if he would have wrecked as bad as he did if he hadn't been clobbered in the parking lot."

"He's not doing well?"

"He's hurting," she said honestly. "But we are getting along pretty well. He even had me to dinner."

And kissed me. She wasn't feeling honest enough to drop that little bomb.

"Dinner, huh?"

"He opened a can of stew and baked some pop-out biscuits."

"Sounds about right. He also makes an excellent take-and-bake pizza."

Katie smiled, then looped back to her original question. "Where's he going when he leaves the ranch?"

"He's buying a property in the Hayden Valley, behind our place."

A swell of relief rose inside of her. He'd be close.

"How can he afford a property?"

"I don't know, Katie. We never got into that." There was a hint of warning in his voice. She ignored it.

"I'm just wondering why he wouldn't go to the clinic when it looked like his foot was broken, when he had enough money to buy land."

"He's a rodeo rider, Katie."

"I guess."

"You, um, seem kind of fixated on Brady." He spoke in a tone Katie was well familiar with. Protective older brother was showing his face.

"It distracts me from worrying about my own future, which brings me to, 'Hey I need some advice. I'm rebuilding the greenhouse.'"

"What? Why?"

Katie launched into her explanation, glad to have redirected the conversation from her being fixated on Brady. Unlike Cassie, Nick took no issue with her abandoning the career she worked so hard for and trying something new.

"Maybe it's selfish of me," he said, "but I like that you'll be on the ranch for longer than it takes to find another job."

"I missed it more than I dreamed. And it'll be nice to be close to my nieces."

"Speaking of which, I have to pick up a couple of little mop tops from kiddie ballet."

"Give them a hug for me."

"Will do, and why don't you send me some

photos of the greenhouse, so I have an idea of just how bad the damage is."

"Gladly."

"You probably shouldn't start work without me being there."

"I'll clear it out. Will that be okay?" she said on a dry note.

"Yeah," Nick said, echoing her tone. "That will be fine. Talk to you later."

As Katie put the truck in gear and headed toward the bridge, the foremost thought in her mind was that Brady would soon leave the ranch and attempt to bury himself in his isolated property on the opposite side of the mountain, but he'd be close. Kind of. And that was a good thing, because it gave her time to figure a few things out—like how she was going to get Brady to see her as a strong woman who wasn't afraid to take a few knocks with him.

ROSALIE TUCKED A couple of stray curls into the sides of her bandanna, then sat down on the lowest step of the staircase and settled her elbows on her thighs, cupping her chin.

She and Gloria had decided on a soft opening in March. When they'd first started refurbishing the house during the summer, around the time the Taylors had purchased the Grand Ladies on either side of them, they'd hoped to open the gift part of the store before Christmas.

Wasn't going to happen.

Rosalie was fine with that. She was enjoying the process. Enjoying working toward something she'd long dreamed about.

As long as Carl had been with her, she'd been happy on the ranch. She'd sewn and crafted and, in the years before his death, started her own Etsy store, but now that Carl was gone, she needed more. She needed to fill the gaping void in her life.

The store didn't fill the void, but it filled her hours with things she loved to do. She'd always wanted to own a brick-and-mortar gift shop and Gloria had long talked about a garden store, so when they purchased the house, it was with the idea of fulfilling two dreams in one building. It was going well, too.

Stripping the paint from the original trim had been labor intensive, involving face masks and a lot of open windows, but now that the job was done and the oak was stained and sealed, Rosalie couldn't imagine having done anything else. So much better than that pink that hadn't worked for anyone. The pale-yellow walls and aqua cabinetry looked more elegant than funky now. Exactly what she'd hoped for.

The sound of heavy footsteps on the porch brought her head up.

If it was Vincent Taylor, there to "talk sense" into her again, she was going to throttle the man. She was a businesswoman now, so she'd have to do it inside, where no one could see her.

Smiling at the thought, she pushed herself to her feet and glanced in the small mosaic mirror hanging next to the heavy oak front door before she pulled it open. She looked like she'd been cleaning an attic. Tough. Vincent would simply have to avert his eyes as he tried again to strong-arm her.

Rosalie pulled open the door, ready to do battle, then her hand went to her chest as she found herself staring into a pair of electric blue eyes.

"Will."

Her former neighbor across the river inclined his silver head. "Rosalie."

The years had done their work, but Rosalie was still of the opinion that Will McGuire was one of the handsomest men she knew. Handsome and stubborn.

"Is there a problem, Will?"

"Does there have to be a problem?"

"No. Of course not." She felt her cheeks start to warm as she stepped back to welcome him into the house. "I phrased that poorly. I'm just surprised to see you."

He nodded in a way that told her that he totally understood. He and Carl had worked together innumerable times, and they'd all met at community events and social occasions over the years, but Rosalie could count the number of times she and Will had been together alone on one hand. Given that they'd been neighbors for nearly fifty years, that was saying something.

Will glanced around the house, then gave another nod. "Looks good."

"We're making progress," she said. She bit her lip and tucked another curl into her bandanna. She was certain that on branding days, Will had seen her looking worse, but that didn't stop her from feeling self-conscious about being dusty and unkept while entertaining a visitor.

"Actually, Rosalie, there is a problem."

Her eyes widened. "Is there something I can do to help?"

"No. Because you're the one with the problem."

"Excuse me?"

Will flattened his mouth briefly, then said, "I heard you were having trouble with Vince Taylor and his outfit."

"Where did you hear that?" Even to her own ears, Rosalie's tone had a defensive edge, but she couldn't help it. She did not like being the subject of gossip, and it was no one's business if she and Gloria were having problems with a neighbor...who just happened to be a world-class jerk.

"Word travels. That daughter of his— Ellie, Nellie—"

"Mellie. Short for Melanie."

"Yes. Her. She's been shooting off her mouth to anyone that will listen." Will hooked his thumbs in his pockets, giving Rosalie the impression that he didn't know what to do with his hands. In fact, he seemed very self-conscious.

Maybe because they'd rarely spoken one-on-one?

That made sense.

"I think they're trying to do your business harm before it even gets off the ground."

Rosalie tipped up her chin. "That may well be," she acknowledged. "I appreciate your concern."

"What are you going to do about it?"

"Gloria and I will continue as we are."

Will tightened his mouth again, and she wondered if some kind of male protective gene had kicked in. He needed to understand that while they'd been neighbors for years and she appreciated his concern, she would handle her own affairs.

"There's not really much he can do, Will, unless he resorts to playing loud music and the like, which will not work for him if he's in the hospitality business. He called us on the goat, but I don't see what else he can do."

"Legally."

"If it's illegal, I will not hesitate to call the sheriff." Rosalie smiled at him. "Would you like tea?"

"No." He swallowed. "Thank you. I'll be leaving shortly… What about the goat?"

Rosalie explained about Lizzie Belle and the zoning laws and watched as Will's blue eyes narrowed with irritation.

"That son of a…" His voice trailed off.

"We'll handle it, Will." Rosalie met his gaze dead-on as she spoke. "If we decide we need help, we'll call—if you came to offer help, that is. I don't mean to be presumptuous."

"Of course I came to offer help." Will let out a breath, looked like he wanted to say more, but instead he inclined his head. "I mean it, too. Call me if you need help."

"I'll do that, Will." She walked with him as far as the door. He gave her a quick look before reaching for the handle, and there was something in his blue eyes that made her breath catch, which in turn made it hard to say, "Thank you. Say hello to Travis for me."

BRADY SIPPED HIS beer and watched through his window as Katie circled the old greenhouse, taking photos from different angles, the goat shadowing her every move. Every now and again, the little nanny would stop and stare longingly at his truck, and then trot off after Katie.

The goat was actually kind of cute—when her feet were on the ground where they belonged. Brady pushed back his chair and eased his injured foot into his boot, glad to be done with the moccasins. Picking hay out of his socks was no fun.

His day was done, so he'd see what Katie was up to and if she needed help. It's what any ranch employee might do. What any friend would do.

He wished he only felt like her friend, but the fact of the matter was that he could not stop thinking about that kiss. Mistake? Maybe. But there was a part of him that would never regret having kissed her.

His phone dinged and he picked it up to see an answer to the email he'd sent Chet Jacobs, his agent/accountant saying there was no problem with wiring the money to Larson Stock Company. Chet just needed a few days' notice.

Sounds good, Brady texted back before setting his phone aside and glancing out the window as he put on his other boot. Katie disappeared around the back of the greenhouse, where the lumber stacked inside of the deteriorating structure hid her from view. The goat peeked around the corner, almost like she knew Brady was watching, then disappeared with a dismissive flick of her tail. Yeah. Definitely cute.

He let himself out of the house and was

met halfway to the greenhouse by the goat, who gave him a friendly head butt before following him to where Katie was taking photos. She glanced up as he came around the building, and it might have been his imagination, but it seemed like her cheeks flushed at the sight of him.

Good flush or bad?

Katie pushed her hair over her shoulder with one hand and it fell like a wave of dark silk. "You're moving better."

"Yeah. I am." The swelling had gone down, and the pain was finally letting up. He hooked his thumbs in his pockets. "Big plans?"

"I hope." She patted the metal upright next to her. "The frame is still intact and seems sturdy enough, despite the weather. I'm taking pictures for Nick so that he can advise me."

"You're not waiting until he gets home?"

"Nope." There was a gleam of determination in her blue eyes. "I want the area enclosed before the snow flies, and even though Nick hopes to start moving back by Thanksgiving, everything hinges on the sale of his business. And you know something will come up at the last minute to put a monkey wrench into things."

"It's always good to think positive."

Katie laughed. "Just being realistic."

"What are you going to do once you get it re-enclosed?"

She tucked her phone into her pocket. "I'm going to become an herb farmer. This will hopefully be the first of many greenhouses."

"Herbs?"

She made a face at him. "You sound like Cassie. *Herbs?*"

Katie's impression of her sister was so dead-on that Brady had to laugh, which in turn made him relax a smidge. It seemed that he was always on his guard around Katie, and it was wearing on him. He wanted to relax. To believe that they could be friends without him accidentally hurting her.

So just do it. Be a friend.

"But don't get me wrong," she continued. "Cassie is usually right. She just tends to err on the side of caution."

"I kind of noticed that about you, too."

"Until recently."

Was she talking about what had happened between them, or her new business venture?

Both? Good time to abandon this avenue of questioning.

"After I move the cows to the river pasture tomorrow, I'll have more free time." Which he'd planned to use to service the farm equipment. He was finished with the small tractor and was ready to move on to the big tractor, the swather, baler, bale wagon, but he could spare a few hours here and there. "I can give you a hand if you need it."

Her expression brightened. "I would like help, to tell you the truth. If nothing else, I'd like to cover the broken windows and start moving junk out of here."

"To…?"

"The boneyard. Most everything in there has been ruined by the weather, so I see no reason to protect it anymore."

"True."

"Do you need help with the cows tomorrow?"

"Nope. I'll just open gates and push them along with the four-wheeler."

"Just keep it on its wheels, okay?"

"Ha ha." Once again, he felt like reaching out and tapping her ball cap down over her eyes just as he had the day before. When was the last time he'd felt playful like that?

Long time ago.

Pretty much when he'd been in his element, rodeoing and hanging with his own kind. When he'd dated women who understood the life and the risks and were good with it. None of them had been like Katie, planning every aspect of their life so that nothing was left to chance. Katie was tough, like all the Callahans were tough, but she was all about security. It must have killed her to get laid off—to have the monkey wrench she'd spoken of get tossed into her own carefully planned life.

Yet, here she was, taking a chance.

Although how much of chance was it, when if she failed, she still had a place to live and food to eat?

"I'd love to know what's going on in that head of yours."

He wrinkled his forehead, being very glad she didn't know what was going on in that head of his. "I was just thinking about cars."

"Ri-ight." Katie pressed her lips together, trying to maintain her mock-stern expression, but the smile broke through and something stirred deep in his gut. Protectiveness. As always. He wanted to protect her from getting hurt and he had to get a handle on that.

But helping her with her greenhouse...that wouldn't hurt anyone. Right?

CHAPTER NINE

BRADY MOVED THE cows to the river pasture and managed to keep the four-wheeler in an upright position the entire time. Katie was going to be so proud.

He parked the machine in the barn, then headed for the greenhouse—or what was left of it. He'd researched herb farming the night before and discovered that Katie had found a nice little niche market that had excellent growth potential. Given her drive and attention to detail, he had no doubt she'd succeed. It didn't hurt having family there for moral and possibly financial support.

His situation was markedly different. Whether he failed, or succeeded, he was on his own. There would be no parental support for him, emotional or financial, and the idea of asking for anything from his parents, even in a dire emergency, was ludicrous. They'd made their position clear through their actions while he was growing up, and Brady was good with that. He was happier on his own.

When he reached the greenhouse, Katie was carrying a long board out the door, the goat close behind her.

"Did Lizzie Belle escape?"

"I hate leaving her alone in the yard." She brushed back her hair from her forehead with her free hand. "I'm thinking of visiting the shelter and getting a dog for company."

"What happens when Lizzie goes back to town?"

Katie smiled. "Then I'll have a dog for company."

"Of course." Katie continued on out the door and Brady went to the back of the greenhouse, where lumber had been stacked to supposedly keep it out of the weather. He grabbed three boards and hefted them. The weight tested his injured thigh, so he set down the stack and picked up the top two boards. Better. Katie came back in, picked up the board he'd left behind and together they headed for the boneyard behind the machine shed where she'd started a stack of silvery weathered boards under the eaves.

"You can sell these things, you know."

"The thought has crossed my mind."

They headed back to the greenhouse, walking side by side. Brady noticed that instead of the silly pink flowered gloves Katie had been wearing when she worked, she had on a pair of oversize leather gloves.

"If you sneeze, those will fly off your hands," he said.

"Funny." She sent him a look, giving him that feeling of deep connection that kept coming out of nowhere when he was with her—a feeling he was doing his best not to think about, because if he thought about it, he was going to have to acknowledge his growing feelings, and then he might have to do something about them. Better to remain in limbo for now. No one got hurt that way. Besides, Katie had expressly told him *not* to think too hard.

Brady smiled a little, and the fact that he could smile told him he was doing okay.

Katie stopped just inside the greenhouse doorway and planted her gloved fists on her hips. The interior of the place was a mess. In addition to the broken glass, there were inches of accumulated soil on the floor and a lot of water damage in the form of rust and rot.

"The benches need to be rebuilt," Brady

pointed out. The wood was rotted, and nails hung out at haphazard angles.

"I got an A in shop."

"Of course you did." He'd also gotten an A in shop. He'd gotten straight A's until his senior year, when he'd spent more time on rodeo than his studies.

They moved lumber until the entire back wall was clear and all that was left in the building were some sheets of roofing metal, some asphalt shingles and an assortment of old flower pots. It took the two of them working together to move the roofing and the shingles, and then Katie suggested a break.

"Coffee or a breather?"

"Breather. The weather is due to change soon."

Brady was about to comment that he'd noticed the same thing when he'd checked the forecast that morning, when Katie surprised him by saying, "Nick said you're moving to the Hayden Valley."

"I'm buying a parcel of land there from the Larsons."

"Is there a house?"

He pointed to the butt end of the camp trailer just visible behind the barn. "That is my house." And had been his house for years.

Katie gave a considering nod. "Cozy."

"Well, you know," he said as he pulled off his gloves. "Those tiny-house things are popular now. Kind of the same."

"Exactly the same." She pulled a chocolate bar out of her jacket pocket, broke it in two and handed him half without asking. Then she broke a piece off her half and popped it into her mouth. "I like having space to spread out. Not that I had any in San Francisco. Four of us were jammed into a two-bedroom apartment and could still barely make ends meet."

"Yeah. At least I won't have to share my space."

"It wasn't *that* bad. The biggest issue was closet space, but fortunately, Amanda, the woman I shared my bedroom with, was something of a wardrobe minimalist, so I had enough room for most of my clothes."

"Did you like living there?" He was genuinely curious, because she did not seem to want to go back.

"I enjoyed the energy. And there are parts of the city I truly miss." She leaned her forearms on the top brace. "But as soon as I started home, I felt like I was escaping something I didn't even know I needed to escape from. It wasn't the city itself," she said quickly. "It was the life I'd made there." She gave a small shrug. "I'd love to go back and visit. Hang out in my favorite places, but—"

"You don't want to live there."

"It's not home. This is home." She broke off another piece of chocolate. "And how is it that I asked you a question about your future plans and we ended up talking about me?" She leveled a look his way and he shifted his gaze.

"Not much to tell. I have earnest money down on a parcel that isn't on the market yet."

"What's the holdup?"

"Abe Larson's shirttail relatives contested the will. After the judge has his say, things should move forward."

"What's your time frame?"

"Before the new year." That was what Stan had told him the last time he'd asked.

"It would feel great to actually own something."

He gave her an odd look. "You mean like you own this?" He gestured to the ranch buildings.

"Grandma owns all of it, and then it'll

go to a partnership with me and Nick and Cassie. So I guess I will own part of the ranch, but it isn't like I can sell it or anything."

"But no matter what, you have a place to live."

"Yes. I do." She came to stand a few feet in front of him, folding her arms over her chest. "What of it?"

"I…"

She lifted her eyebrows as she waited, and Brady had a sudden urge to smile. "Are you challenging me?"

"Uh-huh." Her gaze did not waver. "But if you have to ask, then I'm not doing it right."

"No," he deadpanned, wanting very much to reach for her, pull her closer. "You're doing okay."

Don't think too hard.

"You keep pointing out the differences between our circumstances, like I'm too thick to have caught on the first time you said it."

True. But because Katie had always been secure, he didn't know if she understood what it was like to *not* be secure. To live how he'd lived—how he would likely keep living as he figured out how to make payments on his land—with no real safety net.

Rosalie had provided him a net after his last fall, but that had been a fluke. There would be no one to help next time he stumbled, because he was not going to continue relying on the kindness of the Callahan family.

"Just stating facts."

"Again, and again."

"Twice."

Her lips curved. "You've been counting."

He felt like smiling again. She brought her hands up to let them rest lightly on his chest, but she did not move closer. "Trust yourself, Brady. Trust me."

Stop being defensive. The unspoken message was clear.

He was about to tell her that he'd try when the sound of hooves on metal brought both of their heads around to find Lizzie Belle once again standing proudly on the hood of Brady's truck.

Katie started toward the door, then came to an abrupt stop as Brady touched her arm. Her gaze flashed up to his. "I'm sorry. I meant to keep an eye on her."

"I know you got an A in shop and all, but would you like help building a more secure goat pen? One with something for her to climb?"

"That would be fantastic."

"I take it she's not going back to Gloria anytime soon?"

"It all depends on the Taylors." She started toward the truck again and Brady fell in step. "I feel so bad about Gloria and my grandmother starting their dream business, only to find themselves contending with bad neighbors—on both sides."

"I imagine that does take some of the joy out of the operation."

"They're tough women."

"But like you say, they shouldn't have to deal with this kind of stuff."

"Exactly." When she reached the truck, she held out her hand and crooned soft words as she coaxed Lizzie Belle close enough to grab her collar and then swing the little goat into her arms, only getting one hoof in the face in the process.

She set the goat on the ground while keeping hold of her collar. "I'll put her in the backyard again. I found out how she escaped yesterday and plugged the hole in the fence behind the honeysuckle. I can't keep her in there forever, though, because she's eating the honeysuckle."

"Note to self. Do not get a goat for a pet."

"But she is kind of cute." Katie smiled up at him and all he could think was that *she* was cute, or rather, beautiful.

"Yes. She is." He felt his expression soften. The goat was cute. Katie was beautiful. And this time on the ranch felt special. But temporary situations—holidays, vacations—always felt special because of their fleeting nature. He would do well to remember that.

"After we get her corralled, would you like to visit my property?" he asked, ignoring all the warning bells going off in his head.

A look of surprise lit Katie's face. "Yes."

"I want to take some pictures so that I can make plans for a shed and pole barn, and since weather is coming, I need to do it before the place gets snowed in."

"Maybe we should go now."

"Right now?"

She nodded.

"And leave Houdini unattended?" he asked warily.

"No. We can bring her with us."

KATIE GAVE BRADY bonus points for not only agreeing to take the goat, but to also allowing Lizzie Belle into his truck for the trip, although he took the precaution of putting down a protective tarp on the rear seat.

The trip to Brady's property took close to an hour, although, as he noted before starting, it would have only taken ten minutes as the crow flies. The property was located on the back side of the low-lying Granger Range, which separated the Ambrose Valley from the Hayden Valley, and because they were not crows, they had to drive around the toe of the Granger Range to get to Brady's property.

After unlocking a gate that marked the boundary of Larson land, they drove another mile to the small cluster of buildings beneath skeletal trees, and Katie could tell from a distance that the place wasn't inhabited—had probably not been inhabited for years.

Brady drove under a skinny log archway and parked near a weathered barn. The house, which stood fifty feet away from the barn, had broken windows and a hole in the roof. The outbuildings were in similar shape. But despite the dilapidated buildings, the site was beautiful, nestled in the curve of the small river with a spectacular view of the valley.

"You got the homestead."

"I did. But believe it or not, these old buildings didn't add to the value of the land."

Katie could believe it. It might be possible to save the barn, but the house and outbuildings were beyond hope.

"The last time the place was occupied was in the 1970s. But it has a well and power. I could have bought a larger undeveloped parcel nearby for the same price, but after calculating in the cost of bringing in electricity and well-drilling, I was better off taking this smaller piece and tearing down the buildings."

Katie turned a slow circle, taking in the utter loneliness of the deserted ranch, then met Brady's gaze. He was watching her closely, maybe waiting for her to pass judgment.

"Why here, Brady? Why choose a place that's so isolated?" She thought she knew the answer, but she wanted to hear Brady's take. Actually, she wondered if he would even answer. He surprised her.

"The place kind of chose me. Abe Larson Jr., will carry the loan. I can't qualify for a mortgage, so my choices are very limited."

Katie could see that it cost him to confess his circumstances, so instead of asking more questions, she walked toward the old house, Lizzie Belle trotting after her. The insides were wrecked, but there was a beautiful old iron sink hanging from the wall. "You should try to reclaim that."

"Yeah." He'd followed her across the broken porch boards and reached out to take the goat's collar as she started climbing through the window. "I will. It'll look nice in my camp trailer."

She smiled a little and moved down the porch to look in through the next broken window. "You'll probably have neighbors eventually?"

"I'm sure of it. People are always looking for prime Montana land, and this is a perfect spot for some rich-guy getaway." His mouth crooked up at the corner. "Poor-guy getaway, too."

Katie left the porch and walked toward the barn. "What would you have done if you hadn't found this place?"

"I don't know."

He spoke quietly, as if the thought had weighed on him before.

"Well, I guess the important thing is that you did find it."

"Yeah. I'll get a job on another ranch once I'm in better shape and rebuild as I can."

Brady unlatched the handmade iron hasp and opened the barn door. The building was surprisingly empty, and Lizzie Belle showed no interest in going inside. Instead, she pulled up a dried weed and started munching.

"I imagine the souvenir hunters cleaned it out," he said before closing the door again. He stared out over the valley, then shifted his attention back to her. "As to what I would have done, the honest answer is that I would have ended up in a low-rent place in or around Gavin, saving all the money I could and building a credit rating so that I could eventually buy a place of my own. The way prices are skyrocketing, I don't know if I could have saved fast enough to qualify for anything."

"That's a concern," she agreed.

Brady walked back toward the truck and leaned against the grille, folding his arms over his chest as he stared out over the panoramic view. He frowned, as if debating, then glanced toward Katie.

"I actually have a bigger plan for this place."

"What's that?" She was surprised at how softly she spoke, as if she was afraid that if she appeared too interested, he might clam up.

"I'm going to wait until the area starts to develop—and according to Stan, it will— then I'm going to sell at a profit and sink that money into another place. Something closer to town, with a house. And by that time, I'll have a job history and maybe qualify for a mortgage on a bigger piece of property."

"Good plan."

"I kind of lucked out. If it hadn't been for Stan and the Larsons, I would have suffered the consequences of thinking I'd ride broncs forever and then finding out I couldn't."

"If it hadn't been for Stan, you might not have *considered* riding broncs forever." *You might have gone to college like you promised Will.*

Brady didn't seem to notice that she knew more than she ought to, thanks to her discussion with Nick. "Touché," he said with a lift of his eyebrows.

"Were you winding down career-wise before your accident?"

He gave his head a solemn shake. "Nope. I'd planned to keep riding until I couldn't."

"And that's how it worked out."

He frowned at her. "Rubbing it in?"

Katie gave an innocent shrug. "Stating a fact."

He tipped his hat back, staring off across the valley, his lips pressing flat. "I should have been able to ride that mare. I'd studied her, knew what she'd do."

"You couldn't have known that she would fall on you."

"My center was off."

"Did the fight affect you?"

"You know about that."

"I did a cyberstalk," she confessed.

"It didn't help. I got clocked pretty good. My timing was off, that's for sure. As was my balance." He gave her a sideways look. "I didn't do it, by the way."

"Do what?" Katie knew what, but she felt the need to say something.

"I didn't fool around with that bull rider's fiancée. I don't know what she told him or why, but she wasn't even on my radar."

"Did you do something to her by accident?"

"I think she was trying to make the guy jealous."

"Why you?"

"We talked sometimes, but it was never..." He let out a breath. "It was in Laundromats on the road, or while in line at concession stands waiting for a hamburger. I never gave her any reason to think..."

"Well, that ticks me off."

His head came up and he frowned.

"You could have been killed." Katie shifted her gaze to the gravel near the toe of her shoe. And that would have ruined her.

"Hey."

She looked up.

"It's over and done, okay."

"Maybe you've had time to get over the injustice, but I haven't, having just found out about it."

"Katie," he said patiently. "It's not your job to get over the injustice. And for the record, I'm not over it, either, but I'm not going to waste my brain cells worrying about injustice. I've learned to live with it and not let it consume me."

Her jaw muscles were clenched, and Brady reached out to lightly touch her face as if to smooth away the tension. "You look the way I felt when you told me you'd been mugged."

The gentle stroke of his fingers effectively shifted her attention from injustice—for a few seconds, anyway. "Filled with impotent rage?"

"Uh...yeah." He let his hand drop, but his gaze remained locked on her face. "Do you care if we discuss the future instead of the past?"

He spoke quietly, but there was something in his tone that told Katie that he needed to focus on the future—that he'd spent enough time dealing with the past. "Fine," she said simply, even though she still had questions.

He gestured toward the remains of a rock foundation. "I'm going to make use of that foundation and build a pole barn there..."

By the time he finished explaining his planned improvements and taking photos, the sun was getting low in the sky and Lizzie Belle was bedded down next to the rear tire of the truck, chewing her cud.

"It looks like you have things under control," Katie said as she urged the little goat to her feet.

"I don't want to end up in an apartment or a beat-up trailer on the edge of town for the rest of my life. I have to make up for lost time, and if I watch the dollars, this will work out."

When Brady shut the back door after loading Lizzie Belle, Katie realized just how close they were to one another. Really close. Feel the heat of his body close.

Excellently close.

"I'm not going to think too hard," he murmured before leaning down to kiss her.

Katie brought her hand up to caress his cheek as he lifted his head, then let it fall back to her side. "Me, either," she said with a small lift of her eyebrows.

Brady's lips were still curved into a smile as he settled in behind the wheel for the trip back to the ranch, and Katie realized that he looked a lot more relaxed than she felt.

Because at the moment, she wanted nothing more than to kiss him again.

CHAPTER TEN

BRADY HAD JUST drained the oil on the big tractor when the sound of a vehicle caught his attention. Katie was in the main house pricing out windows for her greenhouse and he was in charge of Lizzie Belle, who was bounding around the stacked hay bales, clambering to the top, then bounding down and running in little goat circles.

Brady wiped his hands on a shop rag as he went to the open bay door and watched as the older Ford truck swung in a half circle and came to a stop near the bay.

Travis McGuire.

Lizzie Belle made a dash for the newcomer, but Brady caught her by the collar and pulled her to a stop as Travis got out of his truck. Brady honestly had no idea how much Travis knew about what had gone down between Brady and Will, but he assumed Will must have talked to his son about it. Vented, if nothing else.

"Hey, Brady." Travis sounded a whole lot friendlier than his dad had, which had Brady relaxing his defensive stance an iota. Maybe the son didn't hold the same grudges as the father. Why should he?

Travis had been four years ahead of Brady in high school and had enjoyed a rather stellar rodeo career, thanks in part to his dad's steady coaching. Then, when Travis headed off to college, Will had taken Brady as a protégé, just as he'd taken on Brady's father years before.

Will and Brady's dad had shared a close relationship, more like a father and son than a coach and student according to Carl Callahan, and as near as Brady could tell, Will had decided that if he couldn't save the father, he was going to save the son.

Brady had disappointed him on that count.

Midway through Brady's final high school rodeo season, while he was on his way to a national title, Stan Larson had pointed out that Brady hadn't signed a contract or sworn a blood oath. Circumstances change, Stan had said. People's goals change. It would be criminal for Brady to give up a professional career. But while Stan had argued in favor of rodeo, it had been Brady who'd made the decision to break his promise to Will. Will had every right to be angry and to stay angry.

"Travis. How goes it?"

"Doing okay. Is, uh, Katie around?"

"In the house. Want me to get her?" He was unprepared for the jolt of something that felt a lot like jealousy shooting through him.

"I can knock on the door."

Lizzie Belle tugged on her collar and Brady gently pulled her back to his side. Travis inclined his head toward the little nanny.

"I heard that you had a goat."

"Katie has a goat," Brady corrected as Lizzie Belle lovingly rubbed her head on his knee.

Travis smiled at Brady's stiff tone. "I came to see if she wanted another."

"You're here to pawn off a goat?"

"My niece got a baby goat last summer in the animal scramble at the July Fourth picnic. She went back to Boise at the end of the summer. The goat stayed with us. Goats get lonely."

"She has you." Brady let go of Lizzie's collar and she moved behind him to peek out around his legs.

"Looks like we're in the same boat."

"I'm sure Katie will take the goat."

"Yeah." Travis spoke as if it were a done deal. "Me, too." He tipped up the brim of his hat. "I heard something through the grapevine that I think I should pass along to Katie, but I don't want to stick my nose in where it doesn't belong."

"What's that?"

"Vincent Taylor was at the lumberyard bragging to one of his cronies while I stopped by on my way home from town this afternoon. I guess he had the property lines surveyed at those houses he just bought and Gloria and Rosalie's back fence is over the line. He's going to tear the fence out. I don't know if Rosalie and Gloria know. It sounded like they didn't."

Brady cursed under his breath. "Yeah. It'd be good for Katie to know. Mind if I come along?"

Travis gave a shrug and the two men headed toward the house, the goat tagging along behind them. If the gossip was true, and he figured it was if Travis felt compelled to mention it, then something needed to be done about the situation.

Katie met the two men at the door and invited them inside, her gaze bouncing from one to the other in a perplexed way before she hugged Travis. "I won't tell Cassie I did that."

"Probably better that you don't."

Cassie and Travis had gone head-to-head on just about everything—4-H, rodeo, academics. And it had not been a matter of friendly competition. Cassie had taken her rivalry with Travis very seriously, to the point that it had become something of a community legend.

Travis shot a look at Brady before saying, "Are you aware of a property line issue at your grandmother's house in town?"

Katie went still. "No."

"I heard something today…" Travis went on to outline exactly what he'd heard at the lumberyard. By the time he was finished, Katie's jaw was once again set in that hard line Brady was beginning to know well.

"I really appreciate you telling me."

"I know how parents and grandparents tend to keep things to themselves to save family from worry."

"Personal experience?"

Travis let out an eloquent breath and Katie laughed. He shifted his weight, obviously wondering how to dive into the goat thing after dropping his bomb, so Brady helped him out. "Travis has a spare goat. He thought Lizzie Belle might like company."

Katie's eyes went wide. "I think she'd love company, but…I don't know how long I could keep another goat. If Lizzie Belle goes back to town, I doubt she could bring a friend."

"Maybe we could work something out? He's driving us crazy, to tell you the truth. He thinks he's one of the dogs, and he can go back to being one of the dogs if your goat goes to town, but right now I think he should be a goat."

"I'll take him. We'll figure things out."

Travis's face broke into a wide smile. "Excellent. I can deliver him. Tomorrow if the weather doesn't get any worse. If it does, I might be plowing, so maybe you should give me your number and I can keep you posted."

Indeed, it had been threatening to snow for days, but so far the weather had moved around them, dumping precipitation in the surrounding areas.

Katie took the phone that Travis dug out of his back pocket and put in her number. He smiled as she handed it back, and once again Brady felt a twinge of jealousy, which he instantly tamped down. He wasn't a jealous sort of guy. Never had been and he wasn't going to start now.

But Travis had better not plan to visit his goat too often.

"Is everything all right?" Gloria asked as Rosalie came down the stairs from her apartment, where she'd taken not one but two difficult phone calls.

"Nick can't make it home for Thanksgiving. I knew this might happen, but it's still disappointing."

"Of course it is." Gloria set down the brush she'd been using to paint the clever wood-and-wire turkeys she'd designed. Thanksgiving was a difficult time for Gloria. Her late husband had proposed to her on Thanksgiving Day almost fifty years ago, but she was doing her best to put on a brave face and embrace her second holiday without him. Thus the whimsical turkeys.

"These are cute," Rosalie said, lifting a

bird and turning it in her hands before setting it back down. "Katie also called."

"Don't tell me *she* can't make it."

Rosalie pulled out a chair and sat, giving her friend a weary smile.

"If you have to sit, it's serious."

"No. It's just that she found out about Vince's latest tactic and is ready to go to battle."

"He has every right to take down the fence," Gloria murmured as if trying to convince herself. She was correct—Vince had had a survey done, and the vintage iron fence that Lizzie Belle breached was several feet onto his property, as was the beautiful old ash tree he was threatening to cut down.

"And to sell it for scrap." Rosalie repeated Vincent's most recent threat as she took the cozy off the teapot. Her teacup from earlier that morning still sat next to the pot, so she poured. "Top off?" she asked Gloria, who shook her head.

"That part really fries me," Gloria muttered. "Why not just allow us to move the fence?" Instead, Vince had insisted that because the fencing had been on the property for so long, it was legally his. "How are we supposed to match new fencing to the old without having it custom-made?"

"If he honestly keeps the fencing—and I'm not certain he's actually going to follow through on that particular threat, then one side of our yard will have a cedar privacy fence," Rosalie said.

Gloria shook her head. "That's too classy for a fence shared with Mr. Taylor. Let's find some used chain link. Really used."

"And shoot ourselves in the foot. Anyway, I told Katie not to get involved."

"Did she agree?" Gloria glanced up before dabbing a bit of paint on a turkey beak.

"She wanted me to promise that I would tell her when Vince started acting up again."

"Did *you* agree?"

"I did," Rosalie said on a sigh. Then she smiled and picked up her cup. "But I didn't say when."

"Maybe Vince is done."

"Maybe Lizzie Belle will sprout wings and fly."

"Good point," Gloria said, once again picking up her brush and dipping it into orange paint. "Next year you'll have the entire family home again."

"I assume that means you'll help me kidnap Cassie next year."

"Indeed it does."

"Actually, that's not fair to Cassie," Rosalie said as she sipped lukewarm tea, which was to be expected since the pot had been there since breakfast. "She's on probation this first year as assistant school district administrator, and she warned me she may not be home for the holidays."

"Next year, Rosie," Gloria said in a nononsense voice. "Even if we do have to kidnap someone. Thanksgiving is a special holiday. Family should be together." She blinked and then lowered her gaze as she reached for another turkey. Rosalie saw her swallow and reached out to cover her friend's hand. She didn't say a word and Gloria eventually looked up and smiled.

"Thank you," she said softly.

"Anytime."

LIZZIE BELLE AND her new friend Wendell the billy goat touched noses, their little tails wagging a mile a minute, then Wendell gave her a playful butt on the forehead and scampered away, climbing the hay bales near the back of the barn with Lizzie Belle hot on his heels.

"Is that not the cutest thing you've ever seen?" Katie asked, turning to give Brady a sunny smile. He'd been trying to free up the rusted manure spreader linkage when Travis delivered the goat twenty minutes ago, and now he was watching goats play instead of working. Watching goats and hanging with Katie, pretending he didn't feel a lot of stuff he did for fear of messing things up for her.

"The cutest," he said dryly.

Katie gave him an elbow and Brady laughed. It was becoming impossible to keep his mind where he needed it to be.

"You're coming to Thanksgiving dinner, right?"

"I—"

"Not to be pushy, but 'no' is not an option."

"Oh, that's not pushy at all. Don't worry about it."

"Since Nick isn't going to make it, you have to." Nick had hit a glitch in the sale of his business, just as Katie predicted, but it appeared to be more of an inconvenience than a major roadblock.

"So I'm like a pinch-hitter?"

She gave him a look of mock-exasperation. "More like you're part of the clan."

Truthfully, he'd always liked being part of the Callahan clan. Without them, he'd have nothing close to a family. Another reason not to blow things with Katie.

"Yes. I'll come to dinner."

"You'll have to drive yourself, because I'm going in early tomorrow to help Grandma and Gloria. They've invited a few other people and the small intimate dinner has become something more involved."

"What's your job?"

Katie tossed her head. "I put frozen pies in the oven."

He laughed again, trying not to be overwhelmed by the crazy warmth he felt whenever Katie was near. She made him feel whole in a lot of ways, but also made him super aware of all the shortcomings in his life, the direct result of the decisions he'd made. Consequences, he believed they were called. He wasn't up for sharing consequences with someone he was falling in love with, although he was fairly certain that if he said the word, Katie would wholeheartedly dive into his life and start fixing it. But there was only one person who could successfully do that—the guy living the life.

Katie smiled up at him, making him want to kiss her. He took a step back.

"You're thinking again."

"I am," he admitted before reaching out to slide his hand around the back of her neck, under her dark, silky hair. She went still as he drew her close enough to plant a kiss on her forehead. Wendell came up behind them and rubbed the curve of his horns up the back of Brady's legs, knocking him closer.

Katie laughed again, a low sound, and Brady brought his hand up to cup her cheek. He lightly kissed her lips to show her that he wasn't thinking *that* hard, and stepped back.

"I have work to do."

Katie gave a silent nod, a smile playing on her lips that seemed to say she knew things he didn't.

Brady sidestepped Lizzie Belle and headed back to the linkage he'd been working on when Travis had arrived with his spare goat.

"I'll tell Grandma that you're a for-certain 'yes,'" she called after him.

"You do that." *And I'll just hide out here, trying to get my head on straight.*

The barn door closed behind Katie and Brady let out a breath as he picked up a wrench, then stared at the door. Maybe one of these days he could follow her.

Before he could do that, he needed to dig himself out of the hole he'd gotten himself into. Prove that he was different than his dad by building a life worth sharing. Then he could make his move.

KATIE SPENT THANKSGIVING morning helping her grandmother and Gloria prepare for the afternoon feast, to which they'd invited three neighbors who didn't have family close—a pair of elderly sisters, Mae and Rhea Stenholm, who lived across the street, and Mr. Higgins, who'd been the librarian at Gavin High School, where Gloria had taught until her retirement. True to her word, Katie didn't mention Vince Taylor once…but she wanted to. When she stepped out of the hot kitchen into the backyard to get some air, she walked along the edge of the wrought iron fence that Vince was going to legally steal, thus trespassing on the two feet of Taylor property that was included in Rosalie and Gloria's backyard, and wondered what he would say if those iron panels disappeared late one night.

The only problem with that plan was that Rosalie and Gloria couldn't use the iron panels—but at least the Taylors wouldn't have them. That alone was worth risking arrest—in a hypothetical way, of course. Katie wouldn't actually commit a crime, but she debated about running the scheme past Gloria in an attempt to distract her and perhaps give her a laugh. The older woman had been quiet all morning, and Rosalie had whispered to Katie early in the day that it was because she missed her husband.

"Nothing we can do but allow her to deal with the grief in her own way. If she needs us, she'll reach out," Rosalie had added.

And Katie decided that meant no blatant attempts to distract her. She'd share the scheme later.

Rosalie had spent days preparing for the feast, roasting both a turkey and a small prime rib in addition to making traditional side dishes and desserts. Katie had helped prepare many holiday meals and knew her tasks—making the fruit salad and dressing, overseeing the pies, chopping anything that needed to be chopped. While Rosalie and Katie manned the kitchen, Gloria decorated the house with flowers and the whimsical turkeys she'd made. She lit candles and put on music, creating a warm and welcoming atmosphere that had the guests relaxed and smiling almost as soon as they'd shed their coats.

Brady arrived first, but when Gloria offered to take his coat he shook his head. "I have an errand to run."

"An errand?" Gloria said as Katie entered the room from the kitchen where she'd been helping with the gravy.

"A quick one," he said. "Katie's tire is going flat."

"What?" Katie asked, startled. "Those are fairly new tires."

"But probably not impervious to nails or slow leaks," Brady said. "If you give me your keys, I'll run your truck to Gus's Service Station and pump it up. By the time dinner's over, we should know if it's okay to drive home."

"Sure. Thank you." Katie opened the roll

top desk and pulled her keys out of her handbag. "I'm glad you noticed."

Brady gave her a nod and a self-conscious smile, then headed back out the door.

"How sweet," Gloria said as she slowly closed the door behind him.

"Brady's a considerate guy."

"I can see that."

There was something in the way Gloria was looking at her that made her feel like blushing guiltily. She didn't, thank goodness, but still…

By the time Brady returned, the other guests had arrived, and Gloria set about serving hors d'oeuvres while Katie offered drinks. She gave Brady a beer and thanked him again for handling the tire.

"I can't find a puncture, so it might be a slow leak, or it might be a fluke."

"I'll take fluke, thank you."

He smiled at her, then he seemed to remember himself and tore his gaze away to focus on Mr. Higgins, who sat in the recliner next to his.

"Brady," Mr. Higgins said warmly, "it's nice to be in a situation where I don't have to ask you and your friends to lower your voices."

"I'm quieter now," Brady said with a touch of amusement. "Are you retired?"

"I am. Less than a year, however, so I'm still adjusting."

"It just keeps getting better, Hal," Gloria said as she set another plate of appetizers on the coffee table.

"If you continue like this," Rae Stenholm said, reaching for shrimp toast, "we won't need dinner."

"That's my plan," Gloria said with a grin. "Then I won't have to worry about dinner for at least two weeks."

Everyone laughed and Katie caught Brady's eye, giving him a half smile. It was good to see him off the ranch, looking as if he was actually enjoying himself instead of ready to jump out of his skin as he often did when she was near. Gloria offered him a shrimp toast, then glanced at Katie and gave her a wink.

After cocktails, the group settled for dinner and Gloria insisted that Brady switch seats with her so that he was next to Katie, instead of three seats away. Katie met Brady's gaze with a nonchalant shrug, but inwardly she felt a prick of unease. Was Gloria playing matchmaker?

Please, no.

Katie loved Gloria to death, but she did not need help in the man department, and as dinner progressed, she hoped that Brady didn't notice how much attention the older woman was paying the two of them. He didn't seem to, thanks to the Stenholm sisters, who kept him busy throughout dinner with questions about his rodeo career. Then the subject of Katie's herb business came up, and she was the one answering questions. Gloria may have arranged for them to sit together, but Brady and Katie barely interacted, a circumstance that Katie hoped would quell any urges on Gloria's part to throw them together again.

After dinner, Brady helped the Stenholm sisters carry the leftovers Rosalie had packaged to their home across the street, promising to check Katie's tire on his way back to the house. He'd just let himself in through the front door when Gloria, elbow-deep in soapy dish water, said to Katie, "So, am I mistaken, or is there a little something developing between you and Brady?"

Katie almost dropped the dish she was rinsing. Gloria's teacher voice carried, even when she was trying to be quiet, and Katie was certain that Brady had to have heard, even if he was in the small parlor where his coat had been stashed.

"Gloria!" Rosalie said on a gasp, holding a length of plastic wrap frozen in the air over a bowl of fruit salad.

It was only then that Gloria seemed to realize that Brady was back in the house. But she didn't seem one bit repentant as she said, "It's a reasonable question. There's only one reason two people don't *ever* look at each other, and that's because they *want* to look at each other."

In an effort to counteract Gloria's interest, Katie had made it a point to talk to everyone except Brady during dinner, so Gloria was right. She'd barely looked at him, a strategy that had backfired in a rather magnificent way.

"We are not going to question my granddaughter and my ranch manager about their private lives," Rosalie said as if Katie wasn't there.

"It's not about questioning. It's about realizing." Gloria made a gesture with the ladle she'd been washing, sending little droplets of soapy water to the floor. "Here we are, having Thanksgiving *without* the men we loved. What would we not give to have them back?" She shot Katie a look. "To not be *wasting* the time we had?"

That was when Katie noticed tears shimmering in Gloria's dark eyes. She stepped forward and gave the woman a hug. "Taking time is not necessarily wasting time," she murmured.

Gloria hugged her back, her fingers pressing into Katie's shoulders, then she stepped away as Brady came into the room. One look at his distant expression and Katie could tell that yes, he'd heard Gloria's question. The thing she couldn't tell was whether or not he cared that people were speculating about the two of them. Her guess was yes, he cared, but no, he wouldn't own up to it, because he was Brady O'Neil, who kept his emotions carefully concealed.

"You're sure you don't need help with the cleanup?" he asked.

"You be on your way, Brady," Rosalie said

with an overly bright smile. "Take care of my cows."

"I will. Thanks for the invitation. The dinner was great." He shifted his attention to Katie. "The tire seems okay, but how about I drive your rig back to the ranch tonight? That way if there's a flat, you won't be stranded."

"I can change a tire."

"But it's still a good idea," Rosalie said calmly, and Katie had to concede that it was.

"I won't be back until tomorrow," she said.

"I won't need my truck." He dug the keys out of his pocket and handed them to her.

"My keys are in the roll top."

"I know." He met her gaze briefly, and Katie would have given a lot of money to know what was going through his head. He didn't give her so much as a hint.

"Let me know if you run into trouble," she murmured.

"Trouble and I get along just fine, but yeah. I will. I'll see you on the ranch."

CHAPTER ELEVEN

WHEN BRADY HAD said he'd see her later upon leaving her grandmother's house, he obviously had meant from a distance. Overhearing Gloria must have spooked him, because the camaraderie they'd developed had evaporated. After two days of next to no contact, Katie was 100 percent certain that Brady was avoiding her, but she was only 50 percent certain of what her best course of action was.

Wait him out?

Katie gave a small snort. Brady could easily outwait her. She was much more impatient than he was, even though he had the rep for being impulsive. That impulsiveness had more to do with diving off bridges and climbing onto widow-making broncs. Brady could be both patient and stubborn in other matters, which meant the ball was in her court.

She didn't know what to do.

Focus on the herbs.

Katie tapped her pencil on her teeth before jotting a note on a yellow legal tablet. It was difficult focusing on a business plan when her mind kept slipping to other topics. Aka Brady.

A movement outside the window caught her eye. Not Brady. Lizzie Belle. Katie dropped the pencil. Really? And where was Wendell? The two were inseparable, so if one goat had escaped, the other couldn't be too far away. She just hoped she wasn't going to find him doing a tap dance on Brady's truck.

She slipped into her boots, even though the ground outside was dry. Here it was, the last day of November, and it felt like it was still October.

"Lizzie Belle," Katie called as she stepped out onto the porch. The little goat did a comical double take.

"I let her out," Brady called from the machine shop.

"Did you?" Katie called back from the porch. He stepped out of the open bay door, a wrench in his hand, and Wendell trotted out after him.

"Yeah. All's well." He waved the wrench and stepped back inside.

Conversation over.

Katie started across the drive to the shop, then decided against it. The moment would come when she would engage him and they'd discuss matters, but now wasn't the time, even though her patience was wearing thin. She took a step toward the house, turned and started again toward the shop. Stopped.

Brady, you're driving me nuts.

Finally, she headed back to the house. She'd bide her time a little longer, even though it was slipping away from her. *But…* if the proper moment didn't present itself soon, she was going to force the issue. Otherwise, Brady really would succeed in waiting her out until he moved to his new property.

She had a couple things to say to him before that.

And she was going to say them soon.

IN THE DAYS that followed Thanksgiving, Brady put his head down and focused on doing as much property maintenance as possible before actual winter set in. It was late this year, which was bad for the snowpack, but good for a guy who was trying to keep busy.

Staying busy didn't keep him from thinking about Katie, or from the fact that his secret wasn't secret—even Gloria had figured out he was in love with Katie—but it kept him from having to make any hard and fast decisions. It seemed that when she was near, he forgot all of his issues and simply went with his gut—and his gut said that he needed to be close to her while he had the chance. Once he was on his new property, he would throw all his energies into making improvements and payments, working whatever jobs he could find to make those things possible. Long hours, but if he was successful, then the payoff would be having a decent life to share.

That was why he was glad the snow had yet to fall.

No snow meant he could work all over the property and avoid the temptation that was Katie. On the day that he intended to tighten gates, however, the weather guys failed him, and he woke to a good three or four inches of white stuff covering the ground. So much for radar weather maps and all that.

"This wasn't in the forecast," Katie called from her yard when he let himself out of the house. "It was supposed to go well north of us." They'd barely spoken, barely seen one another in two days thanks to his self-imposed work schedule, but just a couple words and it was all he could do not to head her direction and exchange a few more. He was drawn to her like the proverbial moth to the flame.

"You're a native. You know better than to believe Montana weather forecasts."

"True. Where are you off to?"

"Checking on the cows in the river pasture. The feed should be fine, but I want to take a look." Which meant walking past Katie on his way to the open shed where the four-wheeler was parked.

"Good plan." Katie leaned down as he approached, her head disappearing below the top of the picket fence. With fresh snow on the ground, that could only mean one thing. Katie was going to demonstrate her throwing ability.

"Don't even think about it," he said gruffly as he walked past. His foot was finally on the mend and for once he was covering some ground—or he was until the small snowball hit him square in the back of the neck. His wild rag took most of the blow, but the wet stuff splattered on both sides of his face.

"Really?" he asked as he brushed the wet

slush off his neck and shook his hand before turning to face her. He let out a breath, telling himself he really wasn't enjoying this. "I'm not fighting back."

"Then you're toast." She started forming another snowball. "Besides that, I'm not *fighting*, Brady. I'm playing. Can you play back?"

He refrained from mentioning that he'd never heard of a "snowball play" as she tossed another snowball at him. He leaned to the right and it sailed past him.

"That was a warning shot."

"I'm not engaging."

She picked up more snow and started forming another ball. "So you say." She tossed the packed snow in the air and caught it again, her blue eyes sparkling. "Come on, Brady. Loosen up."

"I'm not in the mood for play. I have work to do."

"You're afraid of me."

In more ways than she knew. He narrowed his eyes as he studied her, taking in her rosy cheeks, flushed with cold and perhaps something else, the perfect curve of her lips, her sparkling eyes. She smiled as if she knew a secret and if he was nice enough to her she might tell.

Part of him really wanted to know that secret.

"Come closer, Brady." She spoke in a sing-song voice.

"I'm not a fool, Katie."

She just smiled at him, holding his gaze, the snow still in her hand, and that was when he realized something had shifted inside of him. That maybe he was ready to play again.

"All right," he said, stepping closer to the fence. "I'm afraid of you."

"As well you should be." She lifted her chin, her lips still curved in a half smile. He took another step forward and she lifted her chin just that much higher. How was he supposed to resist kissing her?

The air was cold, but her lips were warm when he lowered his head to meet her lips. Her snowy mittens came up to his cheeks, the little ice crystals clinging to the wool melting as they touched his skin.

"Still want to put snow down my neck?" He brought his forehead down to rest against hers.

"No," she said as she took a slow step

back, breaking the contact between them. "That urge has passed."

"Just trying to get my attention?"

"Pretty much." She settled her hands on her hips, giving him a challenging look that he had no trouble interpreting. Why had he been avoiding her?

She knew the answer as well as he did. He was trying to keep the status quo, and when he was near her, he had a hard time doing that.

"I am who I am, Katie."

"Yeah? Sometimes I wonder about that."

"What does that mean?"

"I don't think you trust yourself, therefore you don't trust anyone around you." Brady blinked at her, wondering how she could read him so well, but before he could answer, she rubbed her mittened hands together. "What's on your agenda on this unexpected snow day?"

He gave her a wary look. "After I check the cattle, I'm going to service some of the equipment. And you?"

"I'm going to put the finishing touches on the goat fortress in the barn and then go to town for a loan meeting at the Ambrose Valley Bank."

Brady glanced to the north, where the clouds were hanging low, obliterating the view of the Granger Range. "Are you sure you want to travel today?"

"The loan officer is about to go on vacation, so it's now or wait until after Christmas. Besides, the roads will be plowed."

"After you hit the main road."

"I'm not a snow newbie, Brady."

"But I bet you're out of practice."

She smiled sweetly, but there was steel in her gaze as she said, "I can handle it."

AND THAT'S THREE. *Or was it four? Three because one was a mere brush of the lips. Three real kisses.*

Katie hadn't expected even one Brady kiss when she'd first returned home, but now she had a trifecta plus a deep sense of being in limbo with the man. They couldn't move forward; they couldn't go back. Brady was opening up, but his protective instincts were as strong as ever, and she couldn't decide who he thought needed the most protection— him or her. What she did know was that she was falling for the guy. Again.

Katie parked the wheelbarrow next to the

house and let herself into the screened-in porch, where she abandoned her snow boots.

This will all work out.

She'd been repeating that statement more and more as the days passed. In regard to her business. In regard to her personal life.

She'd barely gotten into the house when the phone rang. Nick. She said hello as she walked to the window to stare out at the mountains. The clouds were threatening, but if she made it to town for her meeting, she could spend the night with her grandmother and Gloria.

"Guess what?"

Her brother was not a guessing-game kind of guy, so something had to be up. "Uh…the loan went through?"

"Yes, it did. And I'm in Idaho. Caldwell, to be exact."

"What? Why?"

"Because the girls are with their grandparents and last night I decided to drive my first load of stuff home and pick up a stock trailer to haul the rest. I spent the night in Winnemucca."

Katie shook her head, smiling into the phone as she said, "Because if it's not moved in a stock trailer, it's not a real move."

"Well, I am a Callahan." His voice took on a serious note as he said, "I was trying to take advantage of the clear weather, but it looks like I'd better get my butt in gear."

"How long will you stay?"

"Grandma Alice and Pops are taking the girls to Disneyland. Kind of a last hurrah until they see them in the summer. I'll rest up a day or two, make sure the tires on the stock trailer are up to par, then head back."

"But you and the girls will be here for Christmas."

"That's the plan. I've been working on Cassie to do the same."

"I'll work on her, too. I'm sure she has some professional reason she can't make the trip, so I think we'd better apply guilt."

"Noted. I'll start with little-girl letters to Aunt Cassie."

"Good plan."

"Kendra draws an excellent potato person—sure to melt Cassie's heart."

"Have her draw one for me, too. My fridge is very bare."

"That will change soon. Trust me."

Katie laughed, and then Nick went on to say, "I'm going to call Brady. Let him know my schedule. Any word on his land deal?"

"I guess it's moving forward."

"How's *he* doing?"

"Let's see. He was almost killed, robbed of his career and had a good chunk of his life stolen. All things considered, he's doing pretty good."

"I was talking about physically," Nick said dryly.

"Oh."

"I see you've gone into protect-o mode."

Katie's cheeks warmed. "Brady is not one of my rescues."

"What is he?"

"He's a friend." She spoke a little too adamantly, a little too quickly. "I'm concerned, but I have enough respect for the guy to allow him to solve his own problems. And *you* should do the same for *me*."

"I don't want you to get hurt, Katie. That's all."

"What makes you think I'll get hurt? You're Brady's friend. Has he hurt you?"

"Point taken," Nick said, but Katie had a feeling that he wasn't totally swayed by her argument and she suspected that she hadn't hidden her Brady crush as well as she thought she had back in the day.

"Pretty soon you'll be home, and you can

referee, but for right now, have some faith in me. I'm no longer dragging home every stray I see."

"But I bet you still want to."

"Of course I do," she said matter-of-factly.

Nick laughed. "I've topped off my gas tank, and I'm about to push on. I'll keep you posted on my whereabouts."

"Travel safe." Katie hung up the phone and set it aside before rubbing the stiff muscles in her neck. She couldn't wait to see her brother, but having him worry about her trying to rescue Brady? Well, that simply wasn't going to fly. She just wasn't sure yet what she could do about it.

BRADY CAME OUT to the truck when Katie was loading a backpack with personal items and a T-shirt to sleep in into her truck. The snow had picked up after Nick called, and if it continued while she met with the loan officer at the Ambrose Valley Bank, she'd spend the night in town. If it let up, she'd travel home. She had a feeling she'd try to make it home no matter what. Especially if Nick made it to the ranch.

"I think you should reschedule." He'd said the same thing when she'd caught him on his way to feed the heifers and told him that Nick was on his way home. The snow had barely been coming down then, but there was more in the forecast.

"Noted." Rescheduling would slow her down. Ambrose Valley Bank was her best bet for a loan, but if it wasn't going to work out, then she needed to seek financing elsewhere.

"Katie, don't be stubborn on this."

She gave him a frowning look. Days of no communication and now he had stuff to say. Stuff she didn't want to hear, because she intended to make this meeting. "I have four-wheel drive. I drove to school alone come hell or high water for two years. It isn't like I'll be out of my element." She was a Montana native and she didn't need to be coddled.

"All the same."

For a moment, she thought he was going to touch her, and truth be told, that was probably the one thing he could do to sway her, but instead he jammed his hands back into his jacket pockets.

"I'll text when I get there," she said, her voice sounding unusually stiff. Due to disappointment because he hadn't touched her? Maybe.

"Thanks."

Was it her imagination, or was there a sarcastic note in his voice? "I'm not being stubborn. I'm weighing the odds. If I make it to the highway, it should be clear sailing."

The stretch of highway between the county road and Gavin was especially well-maintained during winter because it was a school bus route. Brady scowled at her, shaking his head and making it obvious that he thought she *was* being stubborn, then took a step back, silently acquiescing—or so she thought until he broke that silence.

"I don't like this."

"I understand." Snow swirled around them, stirred up by a gust of wind, pelleting Katie's cheeks with sharp ice crystals. But it wasn't falling from the sky. That was coming within the hour and she needed to get moving to beat it. "But I've got to go."

Katie got into the truck and turned on the wipers to clear the windshield of the wind-blown snow before putting it into gear. As she drove toward the cattle guard at the main gate, she glanced in her rearview mirror. Brady was standing exactly where she'd left him, hands pushing into his pockets, watching her leave.

She fixed her eyes back on the road, the better to avoid hitting the upright next to the cattle guard, and tightened her jaw muscles. Her decision would have been the same if she'd been discussing the matter with Nick or her grandmother and that was the end of it. She wasn't being stubborn. She was taking a calculated risk. Something Montanans did all winter long.

THE SNOW WAS coming down hard by the time Brady wrapped up his day's work in the shop and started trudging across the driveway to the house. His phone rang in his pocket and he answered it as he walked.

"Brady. It's Stan."

He stopped walking. "Good news, I hope?"

"This isn't about the land. It's about a job."

Brady trudged on. "What kind of job?"

"Nothing certain, but a ranch job. I know the owners of the Bar HM in Wyoming. I assume you've heard of the place."

"Uh, yeah." Who hadn't? It was fairly famous.

"Harp Martin might be looking for a guy

to manage one of their smaller properties in southwest Montana. I want to put your name in for the job."

"Why?" Brady had a feeling it was because Stan felt a touch of responsibility for Brady's current situation, which was off the mark. There was only one guy responsible for that and it wasn't Stan.

"What do you mean why?"

"It's not like I have a lot of ranch management experience." He knew how to run the Callahan place, because he'd practically grown up there. He'd learned a ton from Carl Callahan. But he wasn't ready to manage a place he didn't know.

"You have common sense."

"I need to learn more before I can become a proper manager." Brady hesitated, then added, "If there's something else, though, something I'm qualified for, I'm interested."

"All right. I'll tell Harp to keep you in mind."

"Thanks for the call, Stan. I appreciate the thought." He ended the call, wondering if he'd just shot himself in the foot again by not allowing Stan to put his name in for the job. He checked his phone before opening the door and stepping into his cheery cherry kitchen.

So far there'd been no text from Katie, who'd left an hour ago, but given the conditions, she was probably still on the road.

And regardless of what she'd said, she was stubborn. He'd offered to go with her earlier that day, but she'd turned him down flat. She'd kiss him, but she wouldn't let him ride shotgun.

After shutting down the shop, he stopped by the barn to check on Lizzie Belle and Wendell, who were snuggled deeply into a bed of straw. Lizzie Belle jumped to her feet and bounded toward him as he closed the door, rubbing her nubby horns on his pant leg, while Wendell snuggled deeper in his goat bed. Brady smiled a little and stroked her head. Lizzie Belle headed back to her bed and flopped down next to Wendell. He was glad she finally had a friend. Nobody liked spending all of their time alone.

You thought that you *did.*

That had been true after his injury, when he'd felt like shutting out the world as he mourned. It was still true to a degree, but now it had more to do with the need to focus on his future and to try to make something of himself. It had to do with penance over breaking a promise he should have kept. It had to do with the natural consequences to one's actions and dealing with them.

As he walked back to the house, he stopped to soak in the silence as heavy snowflakes covered his arms and shoulders and melted on his face. Perfect snowman snow.

They'd built a lot of snowmen on the Callahan Ranch as teens and he imagined that one of Nick's first orders of business upon moving back to the ranch would be to make a snowman with his little girls, who'd never seen snow.

Kids.

What would it be like to be a dad?

He stomped the snow off his boots before walking into the kitchen, where he immediately checked his phone. Nothing.

His stomach tightened ominously even as he told himself that Katie had probably driven slowly and then forgotten to text. If she'd had issues on the road, he would have heard—unless those issues occurred in the same spot where he'd had his issues—on the far side of the bridge over the Ambrose River.

Not likely.

But he reached for the phone, then gave a jerk as it rang in his hand. The tight feeling in his stomach became a hard knot as he saw the number.

"Hi, Rosalie—"

"I haven't heard from Katie yet. I called the bank and she's late for her meeting."

His first gut reaction was fear. His second was anger, at Katie for being stubborn and at himself for not being more insistent that she stay home. "She left well over an hour ago."

"Maybe she's driving slowly because of the snow."

Rosalie's voice had an edge to it. She was as worried as he was, but he kept his voice matter-of-fact and reassuring as he said, "Maybe. Tell you what. I'll head out to take a look and call you."

"Do that. I'll call when she gets here."

"Great. Be in touch."

He hung up without saying goodbye and headed back to the hooks by the door, where he shoved his feet back into his arctic boots and shrugged into his coat. Seconds later he was in his truck and heading out the driveway.

If Katie's truck slid off the road, her tracks would be covered in a matter of minutes the way the snow was coming down, so he drove slowly after crossing the river, peering through the windshield as the wipers did their best to beat back the snow.

He went especially slow on the corners, the most likely spot for Katie to leave the road—unless something had happened on the highway going to town. But there was cell service on the highway, and if there'd been an accident, Rosalie would know by now.

Maybe Katie had already made it to town, and Rosalie wasn't able to contact him because he was in the dead zone. Best possible scenario, and the one he was rooting for as he continued the slow drive down the blanketed road.

He was almost to the turnoff onto the county road and beginning to think that Katie probably had driven slowly, and was quite possibly at Rosalie's house, when his headlights illuminated a dark form emerging out of the swirl of snow. A dark form that was definitely not a deer.

Brady slowed to a stop, then threw the truck into Neutral, pushed the emergency brake and jumped out. The form started moving toward him a little faster.

"Katie!"

"More like your friendly neighborhood yeti," she grumbled as she slogged forward.

If she could joke, she was okay, but that didn't stop Brady from moving more quickly through the snow, and when he reached her, he didn't hesitate to put his arms around her and pull her close. She leaned into him, then pulled back to look up into his face. Snowflakes clung to her eyelashes and melted as they hit her cheeks. Her hat and shoulders were covered with snow.

"What happened?"

"There was this rabbit."

"Funny," Brady muttered, pulling her close again before letting her go.

She wrapped her arms around herself as a visible shiver ran through her. "That tire again. I had a flat. Couldn't get the lugs off, so I started walking."

Brady cursed under his breath. A flat. She hadn't wrecked. She certainly hadn't swerved to miss a rabbit. She was all right.

"The very last trouble I expected on this trip was tire failure."

"Let's get you back to the ranch."

She shook her head. "We should get the truck."

He lifted a hank of damp hair that escaped her hat. It was almost frozen. "You've got to be freezing."

"A little, but I'd feel better if we checked on my truck. Maybe you can get the lugs loose."

Freaking Callahan stubbornness. But even though he wanted to get Katie in out of the weather, he wasn't going to have a showdown over it.

"How far away?"

"No idea. It was dark and white. I couldn't get my true bearings. I figured I would be closer to a cell signal if I walked this way, though, rather than toward the county road."

Brady turned the heater on high after they'd got into the truck and the windows started fogging from the inside, telling him just how wet she was.

"Are you sure about the truck?" Because all he wanted to do was to get her home and into dry clothing.

She nodded instead of saying yes, and he had a feeling it was because she knew her teeth would start chattering if she tried to talk.

"If you get hypothermia, I'm not letting you live it down."

"Somehow I think being in a Ford sauna is going to keep my core temperature from dropping too much."

"Fine, but do me a favor and stay in the truck where it's warm while I deal with the flat."

She wrapped her arms around herself. "I won't fight you on that one."

"Good." Because Brady *would* fight back on that one.

Katie's truck finally appeared out of the wall of white, a hulking shape already covered with a good inch of snow. Brady continued driving for another half mile before coming to a turnaround spot. It was dicey getting his rig pointed in the opposite direction without getting stuck, but he got turned around and pulled to a stop next to Katie's truck.

Using a cheater bar—a pipe he carried in the back of his truck for just such occasions—to act as an extension of the wrench handle, he was able to loosen the lugs and commence changing the tire. And he had to give Katie credit for staying in the truck. It wasn't until he began the awkward process of lifting the tire and matching holes to lugs that she broke her promise and joined him. She knelt beside him and, with her shoulder pressed against his, helped maneuver the heavy wheel into position, then stayed beside him until he had all the nuts back on and tightened. He tossed the hub cover into the bed to deal with later.

"Let me drive this one. It's cold and it needs to be turned around."

She nodded and headed back to the warmth of his truck. A few seconds later, Brady had her rig started and was driving toward the turnaround area. As he expected, she was waiting for him, and as he passed her to break trail, she pulled in behind him. Brady focused on the road. His tracks were already close to invisible, but the traction was good, and as long as Katie's headlights were behind him, he was good.

They drove onto the ranch and swung in a wide circle, parking side by side facing the cattle guard that crossed the driveway—the better to get moving again if the snow got too deep.

"I called my grandmother and explained," Katie said as she came around his truck, arms once again hugged around her body. "So all is well. She said I'm to thank you for rescuing me."

"Get in the house," he said gruffly.

"Yeah." Her teeth clacked on the word.

She started across the drive, but before she made it more than a couple steps, he called her name. She turned back, and words he didn't expect came out of his mouth. "I'm making you dinner. Your place or mine?"

"What are we having?" She spoke casually, as if they were discussing dinner plans on a sunny afternoon, but he saw the shiver that went through her after she spoke.

"Steak and macaroni and cheese."

"Sounds amazing."

"I don't know about amazing, but it will be warm and edible. We have to share a steak."

She took a backward step in the direction of her house, hugging herself tightly as she said, "My place."

"Be over shortly."

"And, Brady?"

Instead of telling her to go inside, now, he said, "What, Katie?"

"Thank you for not saying, 'I told you so.'"

"It wouldn't have accomplished anything."

She nodded, then turned and started trudging through the snow. Brady did the same, heading into his house to pack up what he needed to make Katie dinner.

As soon as she got out of her freezing cold clothing, Katie perched on the edge of her bed, fighting shivers as she called the bank, explained the circumstances and set up a new appointment immediately after the loan officer returned from her vacation.

A flat tire. It wasn't fair.

But she hadn't gone into the ditch or had a snow-related problem, so she had to believe that she would have been fine if not for a nail in the road, or some such thing.

She and Brady were now even in the rescue department, but they were not even in the cooking department. This was the second meal he'd cooked for her—and wasn't cooking one of the more intimate things one person could do for another?

Do you really want your thoughts heading in that direction?

She crossed the hall to the bathroom and cranked on the hot water in the shower.

Yes, she did.

Nick was on his way home—he wasn't answering his phone, so he might well be stopped somewhere, waiting out the storm—and after he got home, she was certain Brady would leave at the first opportunity. He had his house on wheels, and he'd soon have his own property, but the sad truth was, she didn't want to let him go—again.

After standing under a hot shower spray until the shivers stopped shaking her body, Katie dried off and dressed in loose pants and a short pink sweater. Her hair she left damp, combing it back away from her face to dry naturally. Makeup? She thought about it and nixed the idea. Brady had seen her at her worst—she'd been stunned to see snow-induced raccoon smudges under her eyes when she'd looked in the mirror before getting into the shower—both with and without makeup.

Brady was seasoning a largish slab of meat when she walked into the kitchen, looking very much at home. And why not? He'd spent years in this very kitchen. He glanced over at her, an expression of concern drawing his dark eyebrows together.

"How do you like your steak?"

Katie gave a little shrug. "I'm not fussy. How to do you like yours?"

"Medium."

"Perfect. Do you want me to do something?"

"Sit back and relax." He lifted the steak

with a pair of tongs and set it in the pan. "Even if it is out of character for a Callahan."

"I don't see you doing a lot of relaxing."

"I'm not in a position where I can relax." He pushed the steak to the middle of the pan, then checked the mac and cheese. "I'm making up for lost time, missed opportunities and errors in judgment."

"As well as broken promises?"

She saw his shoulders go tight, but his tone was mild as he said, "I regret some of the decisions I've made."

"Who doesn't?" It wasn't like he was the only person in this world who'd broken his word. "I half wish that I'd never set out on my gung-ho career path. I mean, I pretty much left my late teens and twenties by the wayside as I marched toward a goal."

"But look at you now," he said to the frying pan. "You have employable skills that can earn you a decent wage. You have work experience."

"Yes, but the longer I hold off getting a job in my field while I chase a dream, the harder it will be to get a job later."

He shot her a look over his shoulder, then poked at the steak.

"All right," she conceded his unspoken point. "I'm in better shape than you are employment-wise. How long are you going to use that excuse to keep your distance from me?"

If she thought his shoulders were stiff before, they were so tight now that she imagined they were starting to ache. Big deal. This was the moment she'd been waiting for—the time to get some answers to direct questions.

In response, Brady did what he did so well—he went silent. Katie forged on.

"I have another question. Why did you keep your distance back in the day? We spent a lot of time in the same places, but you ignored me."

"Maybe I was shy."

"You weren't shy with Cassie."

"Because I wasn't attracted to Cassie." Katie's stomach flip-flopped at the bald statement, then Brady turned to face her, the long fork in one hand. "Did you want me to ask you out back then?"

"Yes." If she wanted the truth, she needed to tell the truth. "I dreamed about it."

He let out a soft snort as if doing such a

thing would have been impossible. "You can imagine how that would have gone over with Nick? His consequences-be-damned friend dating his sweet little sister?"

"It wasn't Nick's business." And she had a feeling it was more than Nick that had kept Brady from asking her out.

"Okay. How about the fact that I was heading out on the rodeo circuit? You were headed to college. Think about how different those two worlds are…and how there was no way to align them."

"Okay. I'll give you that one. What about now? You can live your life regretting and paying penance, or you can move forward."

"I am moving forward."

"And insistent upon doing it alone."

He stepped away from the stove, looking very much like a man deciding whether or not to make a life-changing leap. "Give me a little time."

"If I give you time, you'll slip away from me. I know your ways. And I know what I want."

The expression that chased across his face made her insides quiver.

"Katie…don't do this."

"Oh, I am doing this. I think we can build

something together, given the chance. But you have to give us that chance."

"What happened to not thinking too hard? To being friends?"

Katie shook her head. "Didn't work. We have to change strategies."

He dropped his chin, regarded the floor for a long moment. "You're right."

He was about to speak again when a sweep of headlights reflected off the kitchen window, startling them both. Katie dropped her hands and went to the door, opening it in time to see her brother's truck and utility trailer come to a halt next to the front gate.

"Nick?" Brady asked from behind her.

"Yes, thank goodness. I haven't been able to reach him on the phone."

Brady's hands hovered for a moment, then lightly settled on her shoulders, and Katie allowed herself to lean back into him as her brother opened the truck door and stepped out into the snow.

Brady bent down close to her ear and said, "We'll talk later."

"Promise?" she asked without looking at him. Because she could well imagine him withdrawing into his internal Brady lair.

She felt his nod as his hands tightened on her shoulders. "I promise. Believe it or not, I've learned the importance of keeping my word."

CHAPTER TWELVE

KATIE OPENED THE door as Nick came up the walk, shivering as a blast of cold wind and snow hit her square in the face. Her brother stomped the snow off his boots as well as he could on the snowy top step before Katie grabbed his coat and pulled him into the house. Brady shut the door behind him.

"Some weather," he said as he pulled off his knit hat and shook the snow onto the rug. His dark hair glistened with water despite the hat.

"You're wearing a windbreaker."

Nick glanced down. "I have a warmer coat in the truck, but yeah. I'm going to have to buy some stuff before I go back. Most of my clothes are California warm."

There was a brief pause as she met his gaze, then Katie launched herself into her big brother's arms. "I was worried when you didn't answer your calls."

"Yeah. Like I haven't been in stuff like this before."

"Where have I heard that?" Brady asked from behind Katie. She turned and gave him a scowl and then stepped back as the two men gave each other a bro hug.

"You're looking good," Nick said to Brady.

"Clean living."

"That's not what the tabloids say."

Katie winced at her brother's remark, but Brady seemed to take no offense. "I'll put on coffee."

"Tea. Green if you have it."

"Want some tofu on the side?" Brady asked as he rearranged the steak in the pan.

"Funny. And I like tofu. Have you ever tried it?"

Brady shook his head.

"You're in for a treat." Nick sat in his usual spot at the kitchen table and started prying off his boots while Katie put on the kettle and then went to dig around in the pantry for green tea.

"Score," she called as she emerged with an unopened box of tea.

"Great."

Katie filled the kettle and put it on the

burner next to the skillet. "Does Grandma know you're here?"

"Yeah. I called her from the driveway." He frowned at Katie. "Did you turn around at the Forest Service gate today? There were a lot of snow-filled tracks."

"I tried to get to town before the weather got bad."

"You had to turn back?"

"Flat tire."

"And the weather got bad," Brady added as he poked at the steak. Katie made the mistake of looking at her brother, who raised his eyebrows in a questioning way. The problem was, Katie didn't understand his question. Did it have to do with her and Brady? Only Brady? Just her? If he wanted to know something, he was going to have to ask out loud.

"Are you hungry?" Katie asked. "We can stretch the meal." She was happy to forego her piece of steak and load up on macaroni and cheese.

Nick shook his head. "I ate in Lima." The small town just over the Idaho-Montana border. "But thank you, anyway."

Brady pulled the steak out of the pan, placed it on a plastic cutting board and sawed it into two pieces. Katie added a scoop of macaroni and cheese to each plate, then carried them to the table. Brady followed with forks and steak knives.

"No veggies?" Nick asked.

Katie gave him a *really?* look.

Nick shrugged. "I'm a dad. All about healthy eating."

"How long are you staying, Mr. Healthy-Eating Dad?"

"Two days. The weather is supposed to clear, so I'll have a window for travel. I figure I can get the trailer loaded before Alice and Pops get back with the girls and then we'll set out on a big adventure."

"How are they handling this?"

"They're confused, but taking it in stride, like kids do."

"How many trips will you make?" Brady asked.

"I've sold just about everything in the house except for the kid stuff and my tools, so I'm hoping to get it all in one." He made a gesture toward the living room. "Even with Grandma moving out, there's more than enough furniture. Add a couple hundred toys and the house will be filled."

"You'll definitely be here for Christmas."

Because Katie wanted a full house if possible.

"Oh, yeah." Nick grinned at her. "Bailey's worried about Santa finding us, but I've told her that won't be a problem. I've been in communication."

"I think Santa will find her," Katie said with a smile.

Nick glanced at Brady. "You'll be here, too. Right?" Brady opened his mouth, but before he spoke, Nick continued "I know you have plans, but I don't think you can carry them out in the snow. Hayden Valley has some rugged weather."

"I'm still waiting for the deal to close. The judge is ruling on the will next week. Stan says things will move rapidly after that."

The kettle went off and Nick went to the stove and snapped off the burner, bringing the shrill whistle to a stop. "I think you should consider staying here until after the melt. Why go anywhere else when we have the room and I could use the help?"

"I'll stay for Christmas."

"Good," Nick said in a that's-settled voice.

Katie didn't think things were as settled as Nick's tone indicated, but she was glad Brady would be there for Christmas. The thought of him alone in a rental somewhere didn't sit well with her, not when they still had some things to settle.

"I assume you'll visit Grandma tomorrow," Katie said.

"First thing." Nick brought the cup of tea and a small saucer and spoon to the table.

"Good." Katie set down her steak knife, ready to get to business. "What do we do about this property line dispute between her and the Taylors?"

Nick gave her a surprised look. "If her fence is on Taylor land, there really is no dispute."

Katie's eyebrows lifted. "It's more the fact that the Taylors are being jerks. They're making Grandma and Gloria uncomfortable because they want the house."

"Do you think a little discomfort is going to make Grandma and Gloria give up their house?"

Katie pressed her lips together before saying, "No."

"And since the Taylors plan to make their houses into bed-and-breakfast inns, do you think they'll resort to bad neighbor tactics like loud music?"

"Probably not. But they are stealing the antique fencing."

"Regardless, I think we need to let Grandma and Gloria handle this as they see fit. If they need help, they'll ask."

"Grandma is awful about asking for help."

"She asked you to keep the goat."

Katie frowned at her brother. "I was thinking we'd present more of a united front."

"And I think we should respect Grandma's and Gloria's ability to deal with the situation as they see fit." Katie's mouth flattened, and he added, "We'll monitor, but one thing I found after losing Kayla was that sometimes you have to deal with adversity on your own. In your own terms. It's good to have people to lean on, but they can't take over your life."

"How are your wife's parents dealing with the move?"

Katie glanced at Brady, surprised at both the question and the obvious change of topic, since Nick was unwittingly bolstering Brady's argument for not getting closer to her.

Nick smiled a little. "They're thinking of moving to Idaho or Montana to be near the girls, and I hope they make the move. Their house is worth a lot of money in today's market and they really have nothing tying them to California."

"The winters here might be a shock."

Nick glanced at the window at the white stuff beating on the windows. "You think?" He stretched out his legs.

"They'll be here by summer," Katie predicted. She'd met Alice and Peter, whom everyone called Pops, while living in California, and liked them very much. Despite their grief at losing their daughter, they'd been like a rock to Nick as he put his life back together.

Nick lifted his cup in silent agreement, then sipped his tea while Katie and Brady finished their meals.

Once done, Brady pushed back his chair and picked up his plate. "I should get going."

Translation—he needed to escape. There was an awkwardness between him and Nick that she'd never seen before, and it bothered her. Together she and Brady rinsed dishes and set them in the dishwasher. He scraped and oiled the frying pan, then after putting it back gave Katie a look she couldn't read. Or rather, a look she was afraid of reading something into that she shouldn't.

"I'll see you later," he said gruffly.

"Yes," she said matter-of-factly, not daring To look at her brother. "You will."

BRADY HAD BARELY gotten his boots off when there was a knock on his door.

"Hey," Nick said as he came into Brady's kitchen and closed the door behind him. He glanced around and then shook his head. "I don't know how Ed lived with these cherries. Katie told me she was going to do something to improve his attitude, so she went with a 'life is a bowl of cherries' theme."

"They kind of grow on a guy," Brady said, motioning to a chair. It was pretty obvious that Nick hadn't made his way through the snow after driving all day to chat about the kitchen decor.

Nick sat, resting one forearm on the battered oak table. "I wanted to talk without Katie being around. Is there a reason you aren't staying on until spring? Because there's no way you're getting into the Hayden Valley after a snow."

"Yeah. I didn't figure you guys had the work."

"We can come up with the work."

Brady shook his head.

"Not charity. Real work. There's stuff

that needs done around here. Katie's greenhouse for one. I plan to refurbish the barn so that I can do carpentry in there. And if the snow continues, we'll have to bring the cattle home, so there's feeding."

"Do you *need* me here?"

"Here's the thing. I *want* you here. If you honestly have other business to attend to, fine. If not, then you should stay. Don't let misplaced pride make a decision for you."

Brady blew out a breath. "I appreciate the offer, and I might take you up on it for a while, but I need to stand on my own two feet." His mouth twisted ruefully. "Literally and figuratively. Once I'm in better shape, I'm applying around."

He couldn't stay here forever, and one of the main reasons was because of this thing developing between him and Katie. He had no idea what to do about it, but he was not ready to look at building a future with a woman when he had no idea if he could succeed in anything other than rodeo.

"I totally get that." Nick rubbed the back of his neck and stretched out his legs. One of his knees popped. "Long, long day in the truck."

"I know that feeling." He'd put in a crazy

number of hours behind the wheel, traveling from rodeo to rodeo. Back when he'd been so focused on winning the next championship that he hadn't given half a thought to life after rodeo. He was paying the price now. He glanced up and caught Nick studying him. Did he have an idea of what was going on between him and Katie? That they were circling one another, trying to figure out the best next move?

"Do you have any bourbon?" Nick said out of the blue.

Brady gave him a surprised look. Apparently Nick's thoughts had been miles from his own. Guilt, pure and simple, but he had nothing to feel guilty about. "I do."

"I haven't had a drink in a long time, excluding milk, of course." He grinned. "Does a body good, you know."

"So does bourbon, taken in the proper quantity at the proper time."

"Once my girls get here, the proper times will be few and far between."

Brady got to his feet. "I'll get the bottle."

THE RANCH WAS blanketed in snow and the sun shone brightly, creating a dazzling contrast of white and cerulean blue as Katie trudged through the snow to her greenhouse with Nick after breakfast.

"Good thing you got the patches up," he said, running a finger along the duct-taped edge of the cardboard panel that had done a good job keeping the snow out.

"I didn't know if the cardboard would work, but figured it was better than nothing."

Nick walked the aisles between the rotting benches.

"We'll have to run power to the building, but I'm looking into this interesting half-buried woodstove that apparently works well in cold climates."

"You're going to come out here and stoke a stove?"

Katie gave her brother a look. "I am going to do whatever it takes."

"This is really what you want to do?"

"It is." She spoke with utter sincerity. "I thought I wanted something else, but I was wrong." She pushed her knit hat a little higher on her forehead. "I may discover that this isn't what I want to do in the long run, or I may fail, but one thing that has changed in my life over the past few weeks is that I'm not so afraid to make a mistake.

I know now that I can survive without getting a gold star."

He pulled a piece of broken wood off the edge of a bench. "That said, you don't want to go rushing headlong into stuff."

Why did she have the feeling that he wasn't talking about only her business?

"The rebound effect," he explained.

"Career rebound?"

"It happens, just like it happens in other areas of life."

"Did it happen to you when you quit engineering and went into contracting?" She'd been in college at the time.

"The job market forced me into that decision since Kayla was pregnant with Kendra, so no. That wasn't a rebound."

Katie leaned back against a cold bench and folded her arms over her chest. "Even if this is a rebound, maybe it's a step I need to take."

"Maybe so." He gave her a considering look. "I think you'll do okay."

"You had your doubts?"

"You're my baby sister, Katie."

"What about Cassie?"

"She kind of scares me," he said with a straight face. "You were always more...I don't know...vulnerable?"

"Gee. Thanks."

"Totally capable, but since you never really got smacked by life, I didn't know how you'd handle it. Cassie grew up battling Travis McGuire and anyone else who wanted to challenge her. You battled yourself."

Katie hugged her arms around herself and cast her gaze down toward her arctic boots. "Huh."

"Huh, what?"

She lifted her eyes. "Good call. I'd never thought of it that way. I was just trying to keep up with you guys."

"You did. Kept up and eventually surpassed me. No one surpasses Cass."

Katie laughed. "I assume she's not coming home for Christmas? She's yet to answer my guilt-mail."

He shook his head. "I don't think she is. I texted last night to tell her I was here, and she said something about emergency school board meetings due to some scandal."

"Sounds about right. I miss her."

Nick nodded, then went to inspect the greenhouse frame. "I think we can set you up. You won't be able to do a lot with only one greenhouse, but you can test the waters."

"Exactly. And in the summer I can grow

plants outside as well as in the greenhouse, and dry herbs for other applications."

"You're getting into this."

Katie shrugged and started toward the door. "I always liked working with my hands. The reason I didn't was because it didn't seem like the best path to world domination."

Nick laughed and followed her out the door. Brady was on the tractor, plowing the area between the houses and outbuildings and they stopped to watch him work.

"He's staying," Nick said in a tone that made Katie give him a frowning look. He kept his eyes on the tractor. "For now, anyway."

Was her older brother telling her to work fast? Because that was exactly the vibe she was getting, which was crazy, because Nick had no way of knowing what was going on between them.

"Good to hear," she said briskly. She clapped her mittens together. "Do you want some help unpacking your little trailer?"

"Yeah. I do. Then I'm heading to town to see Grandma. Want to come?"

"Read my mind." She might have to keep her mouth shut about the Taylors, but there was always the chance that her grandmother might bring the matter up.

BRADY PLOWED THE long driveway leading to the county road, following the tracks Nick had made as he'd four-wheeled out of the place on his way to town. He and Katie would have a much easier trip back into the ranch.

After parking the tractor, Brady took a break before heading to the river pasture to check cow feed and called Stan Larson to nail down the time schedule for signing his paperwork, if the judge signed off on the contested will.

"Just a matter of transferring funds and signing a boatload of forms."

"It'll move fast, then." Brady had never bought anything except his truck and camp trailer, and had no idea how the process went.

"That's the way it's supposed to go."

Supposed to go? Brady frowned at the unexpected answer, then told himself that his former coach was talking about the contested will. How often would that circumstance play into a land purchase?

He spent the rest of the afternoon maintaining the one-ton flatbed, plugged into his headphones and convincing himself that all was well whenever he thought again about the odd way Stan had said "supposed to go." It was nothing. He was so used to getting slapped backward that he was reading trouble into situations where there was no trouble.

Or maybe this all mattered to him so damned much that he was manufacturing possible roadblocks.

He tightened the drain plug on the oil pan, then stiffly rose to his feet and put the wrench back in its place on the wall. His foot was better, his thigh wasn't aching as badly as usual and he had a roof over his head for as long as he wanted.

In other words, stop looking for trouble.

Nick and Katie returned half an hour after he'd quit for the day. He heard doors slamming and went to the window as the siblings unloaded a tree from the back of the pickup.

He was glad Nick was home, but it was almost more for Katie's sake than for his own. The last time he'd lived on the ranch, he and Nick had been fairly inseparable. Things had changed. Not that he didn't feel close to his friend, but Nick was working through some serious issues, as was he, and they'd yet to find that middle ground—although the bourbon had helped. They'd drank and relaxed and touched briefly on things they were dealing with before steering the conversation back to safer subjects.

But as they'd talked and drank, he'd been struck by a profound thought—when he'd come to this ranch he'd thought he wanted to be alone. That was no longer true. He wasn't a true loner and never had been. He was a guy who made friends easily, but only let them so close...except for Nick and Cassie.

And Katie.

He was about to drop the cheerful red curtain when he realized that Katie was heading toward his place rather than into the main house. He met her at the door, and she smiled up at him.

"How are Rosalie and Gloria?"

"Vince Taylor hadn't done anything new. I asked about the fence, but Nick poked me in the back with his thumb, so I dropped the matter." She rubbed her hands together as if cold, but since the temperatures were climbing, he had a feeling it was more because she wasn't sure how to dive into the reason she'd come by.

"Is something up?"

She gave him a bright smile. "As a matter

of fact, yes. Would you like to come to the Shamrock Pub with us?"

"Tonight?"

"Tomorrow. The weather is supposed to cooperate, and Nick wants to have a night out before heading back to California. You know—to see who he runs into after being gone for a decade."

"Yeah. I'll go."

"Great."

"Surprised you, didn't I?"

"You did," she admitted. "Want to do it again?"

He leaned a forearm on the doorjamb, wondering if it was his imagination, or if Katie was leaning toward him. "How?"

"Nick and I are putting up Christmas decorations. Want to help? Hot buttered rum is involved."

"It's almost Christmas."

"Your point?"

"Yeah. What was I thinking?" Brady dropped his forearm from the doorjamb and smiled a little. "Just give me a time."

She gave him a sparkling smile. "How about now?"

As far as Christmas traditions went, Brady didn't have many that didn't involve the Callahans. Although he'd spent Christmas Day with his parents, most of the holiday break was spent at the ranch, prepping for Christmas, or enjoying the aftermath. They'd tubed, pulled sleds behind the four-wheeler, rode horses in the snow. Good times. Lots of them.

After he'd hit the rodeo circuit, he hadn't really celebrated Christmas, preferring to spend the holidays recovering from whatever injuries he'd accumulated during the year and getting ready for the next rodeo season.

But here he was, back with the Callahans and feeling more relaxed than he'd felt in maybe years. Months for certain. The hot buttered rum had something to do with it, but it was more about the feeling of warmth and belonging he had when he was with these people.

"Crooked," Katie said to Nick as he adjusted the star on top of the tree.

"I prefer the term *Seussian*."

"No. You'd really have to bend the tree to achieve that. It's just plain crooked." She looked over her shoulder. "Brady? Judgment call."

"Crooked."

Nick blew out a breath, removed the star and held it with one hand as he took nippers out of his back pocket and trimmed the top of the tree. When he replaced the star it bobbed, but came to a fully upright position.

They'd agreed to put on lights and garlands, but to save the ornaments until Nick's little girls arrived in a week so that they had a hand in decorating the tree.

"After this, cookies."

Brady smiled and sipped his buttered rum, remembering the frosting fights they'd once had, and the way Rosalie had kicked them out of the kitchen each and every year until he graduated, swearing she'd never let them near a bag of powdered sugar again.

"After this, bed," Nick said, yawning. Katie gave him a surprised look and he cocked an eyebrow at her. "Just wait until the girls get here. You'll understand."

"I'm not sure I want to," Brady said. "Will you be able to stay up past eight when we go out tomorrow?"

"I'm aiming for ten o'clock."

"You wild man."

Katie caught his eye and made a face and Brady smiled back, feeling warm and…comfortable. But he was also taking care not to engage too intimately with Katie in front of Nick. Not that it was any of Nick's business, but he didn't want anything to ruin his remaining time at the ranch. But after Nick called it a night and headed off down the hall toward the room he'd slept in as a kid, Katie split the last of the buttered rum between their mugs.

"Cheers," she murmured, lifting her glass.

"Cheers." He held her gaze as he drank. "Things are going to be different with Nick and his kids on the ranch. Livelier."

"I'm ready for lively. Are you?"

"I probably won't be here for a whole lot of liveliness."

"True," she said. "But I imagine we might see you every now and again?"

She returned his gaze as she waited for his answer, her expression one of calm acceptance, but he knew better. Katie was a fighter. For reasons unknown, she wanted him as much as he wanted her. And it would kill him if she stopped wanting him because sharing his life was a losing proposition.

"Yes. You'll see me."

She tilted her head, her gaze holding his as she waited for more. It was time to give her more.

"You probably know this," he said slowly, "but my dad was kind of wild."

"That's kind of common knowledge."

One corner of his mouth lifted at her dry tone. "I guess it is. I heard lots of stories growing up. Will told me stories while he was coaching me—mostly the cautionary kind." The smile faded. "My mom told me stories when she was ticked off at me. Told me how much I was like him. And it wasn't a compliment."

Katie raised her hand, then closed her fingers and brought her hand back to her lap. Somehow she seemed to know that he didn't want comfort. He wanted to push these words out of his mouth.

"My dad made her miserable. He rushed into things without thinking about consequences and she paid the price with him." His mouth flattened grimly. "She continued to pay the price long after he was gone."

"And took it out on you."

He nodded and a flash of heat lit her blue eyes. "I'm not going to make excuses for her. What she did was wrong. And the way she treated me encouraged me to act even more like my dad. But trust me, the urge was strong even without her help."

"Oh, Brady." His name came out on a whisper and it was all he could do not to reach for her.

"I need to prove some things to myself, Katie. I can't move forward until I do that."

"What kind of things? That you're not your dad?"

"It's more than that." More than he could explain, because Katie would brush his reasoning aside and assure him that she could deal. But how could she know that when she didn't know what she'd be dealing with? He didn't know himself.

She studied his face for a long moment, a faint frown pulling her eyebrows together. "It's easy to lose track of what's important when you set out to prove something, Brady. I speak from experience."

"And I'm the kid who has to pee on the electric fence."

"You have to find out for yourself," she murmured.

"Pretty much, yeah. I do."

CHAPTER THIRTEEN

THE FIRST PERSON Katie spotted upon entering the Shamrock Pub that evening with Nick and Brady was Mellie Taylor, sitting at a table with people Katie didn't know, her hand resting possessively on the arm of a ridiculously good-looking guy.

Cool. She'd like to have a word with one of the Taylor clan, and tonight seemed as good a time as any. She must have telegraphed her intentions, however, because Brady took hold of her elbow before she could amble in Mellie's direction. "Let's find a table."

"I'm not going to do anything drastic," Katie murmured as she allowed herself to be steered toward the back of the room. She simply wanted to meet the guy who was helping the Taylors harass her grandmother.

"We're not risking the possibility of you having latent Cassie tendencies," Nick said, flanking her on the other side. There were several empty tables near the rear entrance, and Nick picked the one that didn't allow a view of Mellie's part of the room. But she would be able to see the dance floor.

They'd barely gotten seated when a server showed up at the table, did a double take, then enveloped Brady in a huge hug. "Brady. My goodness. How long has it been?"

"Three years?"

The server stepped back, beaming at him before turning to Katie and Nick. "I'm Leni. I used to tend bar in Miles City."

"Where I practiced in the off season after Missoula got too expensive," Brady explained.

"Ah," Katie said in a voice that didn't sound as friendly as usual. Nick shot her a look and she made a conscious effort to sound more her normal self as she asked what brought Leni to the opposite side of the state.

"My sister needed a nanny. I needed something new in my life and here I am."

"Gavin is a nice town," Katie said.

"I know. I love it here." She gave Brady another long look, then shifted the position of her tray. "What can I get you guys?"

"Let's start with a pitcher?" Brady said.

"Sounds good," Leni murmured. "Be right back."

Katie settled back in her chair after Leni left. Her fun night at the Shamrock hadn't started well, what with Mellie Taylor followed by the unexpected jolt of hey-wait-a-minute-he's-mine that had hit her when Leni had hugged Brady.

"I don't want you getting drunk and fighting Mellie Taylor," Nick said from beside her.

"Fun-ny." For one thing, Katie was not a drinker. For another, it looked like Mellie and company were leaving. Katie's view of Mellie's table was blocked, but she could see the front entrance and Mellie and her handsome friend had just walked out of it.

Maybe she could make something of this night, after all.

"Feel better?" Brady asked in a low voice from beside her.

"I do."

Nick was watching the rear door and didn't seem to notice the exchange, and he also missed the part where Brady smiled at her and Katie's heart did the double beat.

"I wouldn't have made a scene, you know," she said in a low voice.

"But Mellie would have if the urge had hit her."

"Good point."

Brady smiled at her, showing creases in his cheeks that had driven her crazy as a teen. Still drove her crazy. "I know you could have handled yourself."

"You flatter me." But he was also correct. She wasn't going to let Mellie get away with the crap she got away with in high school.

Brady's smile widened, almost as if he knew what was going on in her head, and Katie found herself thinking that it'd been a while since she'd kissed those lips.

"Katie?"

Katie turned at the familiar voice, then broke into a smile. "Drew!" She jumped to her feet and gave her former classmate a hug. She and Drew had spent a lot of time in the library, working out math problems and agonizing over physics, which neither of them had excelled at. They'd dated for a while, called it quits and ended up being friends until graduation sent them to opposite ends of the country.

"Lot of hugging going on tonight," Nick quipped from across the table.

Katie shot her brother a look, noted that

Brady had done the same, then turned her attention back to Drew. "You know my brother and Brady, right?"

"You bet." There were handshakes all around, no hugs, and then Drew said, "My uncle mentioned your herb business to me." Katie frowned, mystified as to how his uncle had heard of her herb business, and he explained, "He's a silent partner in Hardwick's." And she'd met with the manager last week.

"I had no idea he was involved with the store."

"That's kind of the point of being a silent partner," Drew said with a smile. "Would you like to meet him?" He gestured with his head toward the opposite side of the room where Mellie and friends had been sitting. "He's over there with my dad and a few friends."

"If it wouldn't be an imposition, yes." She glanced at Brady, who seemed more stone-faced than usual, and at her brother.

"Not one bit of an imposition." Drew put a hand on the small of her back as she started across the room.

"DON'T LET IT get to you." Nick finished pouring his beer as Brady's gaze jerked away from Katie as she crossed the room to what's-his-name's uncle and friends.

"What?"

"She doesn't like him that much." Nick lifted his beer. "And she was definitely jealous of Leni."

"Why are you telling me this?" It wasn't alcohol speaking, because Nick had yet to take a drink.

Nick rolled his eyes in a duh expression. "Why do you think?"

"Who are you meeting here tonight?" Brady asked, suddenly suspicious.

"Nobody. Katie jumped to that conclusion. I thought the two of you could use a night out. I didn't reckon on Prince Charming showing up." He nodded toward where Drew Owens was introducing Katie to his uncle.

"So you're setting us up?" Nick gave a maybe shrug and Brady frowned suspiciously at his friend. "I kind of expected you to warn me off."

Nick shook his head. "Ten years ago, yes, but you never made a move back then, so I didn't have to."

Brady stared at his friend, wondering if he was hearing things right, and Nick laughed.

"What? You thought we didn't know? You practically had a cartoon heart floating over your head."

"Did Katie know?"

"Are you kidding? She was blinded by her own cartoon heart," Nick said as he stretched out his legs. "Katie was a tough read back then, so I get why you might have missed the signals."

More like he'd been so busy avoiding her that he hadn't been receptive to signals.

"You're making me feel a little self-conscious here."

Nick dragged his feet back in and leaned his elbows on the table. "I'm not trying to push you. I'm just telling you that in case you might still have an…interest…I won't punch you in the face."

"Would you have back in the day?"

Nick shook his head. "But you ran a little too fast for Katie. I wouldn't have been happy if you hooked up."

"I was afraid that I'd make her suffer like my mom had suffered because of my dad." Because of the stupid things he kept doing. Racing his truck too fast, spending his money too easily. Riding broncs instead of going to school.

"And now?"

Brady studied the table for a second. "Still a concern, but for a different reason."

"Katie's tough. And she's older. For the record, if you guys try and fail, it won't affect our friendship."

Brady didn't fully buy that. How could it not affect their friendship? And the thought of trying and failing...no. He couldn't handle it.

"One last thing," Nick said, suddenly serious. "Life is short. If you want to present a perfect life and a perfect—I don't know...you?—to Katie, you may never get the chance."

What could he say to that? His friend knew firsthand how quickly life could change. He'd lost his wife. Brady reached for his beer. "I've got things to deal with before I start pursuing interests. I'm in a pretty rotten state economically."

Nick merely raised his eyebrows in a speaking way.

Life is short. Yeah. I got that.

He glanced over at Katie, who was laughing at something her friend had just said, and felt a sharp stab of jealousy. The big question was, what was he going to do about it?

And a bigger question was, what was he going to do about Mellie Taylor, who'd come back into the bar without her beau and was now heading directly toward him?

He looked at Nick, who gave his head a slight shake, then focused back on Mellie, who was approaching like a cat on the prowl. And he, it seemed, was her prey.

KATIE HADN'T SEEN Mellie Taylor return to the pub, but when she glanced toward her table, she was shocked to see Mellie sitting in her chair.

Katie tamped down her territorial instincts and forced her attention back to Drew and his uncle, who seemed interested in her business, and who also had contacts with lending institutions. Katie talked for a few more minutes and promised to contact him if she hit a wall in her search for a business loan, then wished everyone a happy holiday. Drew offered her a drink, but she smiled and asked for a rain check. She had business to attend to back at her table.

As she approached her table, she heard Brady say, "Nick is too much of a gentleman to mention this, but I think your family needs to practice being better neighbors to Gloria and Rosalie."

Mellie's back snapped straight. Nick rolled his eyes—he always had been the most tactful of the three of them when in the heat of battle, never saying anything he might have to unsay later—but Brady showed no sign of backing down. He leaned on the table, looking Mellie in the face. "You guys are gaining a reputation for acting like jerks. Do you really *want* that kind of reputation when you're in the hospitality industry?"

Mellie opened her mouth. Closed it again. Glared first at Brady, then Nick.

"He has a point," Nick said matter-of-factly. "Social media can be a bitch."

"My family has not done one thing that they didn't have a legal right to do," Mellie said with a sputter.

"True. But really? Depriving an old lady of her very cute pet goat? Stealing her antique fence? That doesn't play well at all."

"Don't you threaten me."

Brady lifted his hands. "I'm not threatening. I'm pointing out the pitfalls of acting in a less than neighborly way when you're building a business." Nick gave another nod and Mellie pushed her chair back, practically running over Katie's foot.

"Hi, Mellie," Katie said in pleasant tone.

Mellie let out a low breath and edged her way past Katie without a word.

"I don't know if you just did a good thing or a bad thing," Nick said conversationally as he watched Mellie's pale pink cashmere sweater and the back side of her distressed jeans disappear around the room divider.

"A good thing." Katie jerked her head toward the exit. "I'd like a word, Brady."

Brady scraped his chair back, a mystified look on his face that Katie ignored as she led the way out the rear entrance. The door had barely closed behind them when she slid her hands up around Brady's neck and pulled his lips down to hers.

"What's that for?" he asked against her mouth.

"That's a thank-you for defending my family," she murmured before giving him another kiss. "And that is an acknowledgment of the truth."

"What truth?"

She gave him a look. "I think you know what truth." His hands were on her waist and his forehead was resting on hers. They were so close that their breath mingled and neither made the slightest effort to move back.

"Yeah," he said in a low voice, his fingers tightening on her waist. "I know what truth."

"I was jealous tonight, and I'm never jealous."

"Guess that makes two of us."

"Glad I'm not alone in that." Her expression grew more serious as she met his gaze. "I know you're concerned about the mistakes you've made, and where you are in life, but, Brady, I don't care. I'm not negating the challenges you face, but they aren't deal breakers. The important thing is that you are facing those challenges dead-on and you have a plan for the future."

He let out a breath and Katie's stomach tightened as she waited for his response.

"You're telling me to stop fixating on the past."

"You think?" Katie asked softly.

"Yeah," he said. "I think."

"Going to do better in the future?" she asked in a mock-stern voice.

He fought the smile, but it broke through as he brought his hands up to frame her face. "I'll work on it." He dropped a kiss onto her lips, sealing the deal. "Funny thing. After I kissed you that first time and you told me not to think too hard, all I've been doing is thinking too hard. It hasn't solved a thing."

"What's that tell you?"

"That maybe I've been looking at this all wrong."

Her arms tightened around his neck as she kissed him. "Bingo."

"WE ARE NOT using a hot dog as a nose." Katie set her hands on her hips as she gave Brady an are-you-for-real look.

"If you don't have carrots, and I don't have carrots, I don't know what else to use for a snowman nose."

And it was a fine snowman. The first one he'd built in over a decade and he discovered that snowman making was a lot of fun when bourbon-laced hot chocolate was involved.

Nick was due back in two days with his little girls and Katie wanted to greet them with a snowman since her nieces had never seen snow, so she'd bribed him with alcohol and here he was adding finishing touches to beakless Frosty. Not that he needed a bribe. He'd taken his promise to let go of the past seriously, doing his best to enjoy every second he had with Katie.

He looked around the snow-covered yard, seeking inspiration. They'd used smooth cobbles they'd found below the rain gutter spouts for buttons, eyes and mouth. Katie had found an old stocking hat for the head and Brady had donated a battered wild rag for the neck. All the snowman was missing was the nose—without it, due to the shape of his head, he closely resembled the character that couldn't be named in the Harry Potter stories, and that, they both agreed, might traumatize little girls.

"A screwdriver?" Brady suggested.

"You aren't helping."

Lizzie Belle and Wendell scampered around the yard kicking up snow. The little goats were the reason there were no carrots on the ranch.

"Celery?"

Katie glanced up. "You have celery?"

"It might be a little bit limp."

"No."

He reached out and pulled her closer, leaning down to kiss her nose. The past week had been borderline perfect—so perfect that he was waiting for something to happen that wasn't so perfect. The judge had approved the will and the land sale was moving for-

ward. He would have six months of payments in the bank after the down payment
was made, which would give him time to
nail down another job.

For the first time in a long time, Brady
was feeling confident about the future he
was impatient to start building. Katie was
a good motivator in that regard. They had
pored over the want ads online and in the
local paper and he was in the process of applying for jobs that wouldn't pay enough,
but would see him through if he watched his
pennies. Eventually he'd sell his property,
reinvest…grow something. There would be
tight times, but the payoff would be worth it.

"Want me to go to town and get carrots?"
he asked Katie.

"Actually, I might go. I have to get more
wrapping paper and Grandma said UPS
dropped some packages for me off at her
house."

"You want me to go with you?"

"Nope." She touched his face with her mittened hand. "I'm also going gift shopping."

"Ah."

"And I think I tore you away from your
chores, which I'm sure you're anxious to get
back to."

"Well, it's no fun building a snowman alone."

"Which is why I tore you away from your chores." Katie turned toward the snowman and ran a hand over its head. "I just hope the snow doesn't freeze before I get back."

It was supposed to get colder before it got warmer, so that was a danger.

"I'll get out the drill if that happens."

Katie laughed and he reached for her, wrapping her in his arms before kissing her soundly. Katie kissed him back, then set her hands on his shoulders. "I should get going if I'm going to have time to do everything I planned to do tomorrow."

Twenty minutes later, he waved to Katie as she drove away, then crossed the driveway to the shop where he was tearing into the baler. Nick was a talented carpenter, but Brady was a better mechanic. If he was going to stay until he was able to move on to his own place, he was going to have every piece of machinery on the place running smoothly before he left.

He'd just removed the shroud from the machine when his phone buzzed in his pocket. He pulled it out, glad to see that it was the Larson Stock Company and not Katie dealing with another flat tire. Brady had phoned Chet Jacobs and asked him to transfer the down payment three days ago and Stan was in the process of setting up the title company appointment to sign all the documents. Hopefully he had a date and time.

"Hey." Brady set down the wrench.

"I thought you were wiring the money," Stan said.

"I did."

"It hasn't arrived."

Brady's gut tightened. "I'll contact my guy. See what the deal is."

"Probably just some electronic glitch."

"It has to be." Which meant that he shouldn't have this terrible ominous feeling. *Just a glitch.* "I'll get back to you, Stan."

"If we get the down payment today, Abe Jr. will certify his loan and it's smooth sailing from there."

Brady hung up and took a moment to center himself, just as he'd done before every one of his bronc rides, then pushed his agent's speed dial number. His stomach got tighter with each unanswered ring.

Just a glitch.

He ended the call when it went to voice mail and punched the number again. It was a Wednesday. Chet should be in the office. The guy was a workaholic.

After the third call, Brady tried the cell number and was told that the number was no longer in service.

He tried again and a chill went through him as the robotic voice repeated itself. He ended the call and sat on a hay bale, pressing his fingers against the bridge of his nose.

Don't panic.

He sucked in a breath and dialed a rodeo buddy who'd used the same agent. In less than thirty seconds, he discovered that he wasn't the only guy looking for Chet Jacobs, agent/accountant. Brady set his phone aside and leaned his head back against the haystack, clenching his teeth against the panic swelling inside of him.

What now?

And how could he have been so stupid as to think things could go smoothly?

CHAPTER FOURTEEN

WHITE DIESEL EXHAUST rose from the tail-pipe of Brady's truck as it idled next to Ed's house. Katie smiled, thinking, *Yes*, as she drove over the cattle guard. He'd gotten the call he'd been waiting for. The loan had gone through and he was on his way to Gavin to sign the papers, which meant that a celebration was in order. Tonight she'd cook for him. A steak, and maybe a bottle of prosecco.

The happy thought evaporated as Brady slammed out of the house and stalked down the driveway toward his truck. He stopped dead when he caught sight of her truck and her stomach tightened.

Something was wrong.

Katie pulled up next to his idling rig instead of into her usual parking spot, and got out of her truck without bothering to turn off the ignition. She was barely conscious of closing the door behind her as she headed toward him.

"What happened?"

She couldn't imagine what put that shell-shocked expression on his face.

"Brady?" she prompted when, instead of answering, he looked past her at his truck.

He pulled in a breath then and met her gaze, his expression a mix of determination and defeat. "I'm going to take off for a while. The cattle should be okay, what with the warm front coming in, and Nick will be home—"

It was all she could do not to take him by the front of his coat and shake him.

"Why are you taking off for a while? Where are you going?"

"I have to go to Missoula. I think my agent has taken off with my money."

Katie's heart almost stopped. "The down payment?"

He gave a grim nod. "He was supposed to wire the money to the Larson Stock Company. It never showed up. He's not answering his phone. His cell number is out of service."

"I'll go with you." She'd call her grandmother, call Nick, then pack a quick bag.

"I need to do this alone."

Katie blinked at him, stunned. "No," she

said adamantly. "If the guy did take your money, we'll tackle this together."

He gave her a disbelieving look. "If he stole my funds, then I'm sunk. No savings. No way to fund a land purchase. I'm worse than square one. I'm in square zero."

"And we'll find a way to deal with that."

"*I* need to deal with it."

Katie's heart sank. Brady the solo act. Back again.

She pressed her lips together to keep from saying things that were only going to strengthen his stubborn resolve. But…she had to say something. "Don't shut me out, Brady."

"I need to get to the bottom of this," he said as if she hadn't spoken. "And I need to figure out my next move if it's as bad as I think it is."

"Alone."

His gaze snapped toward her. "Yes. Alone. I'm losing time, Katie." He seemed to realize how harshly he'd spoken, because his expression softened an iota, but he made no move to pull her close. Kiss her. "I'll be in touch."

"In touch." For a moment, she simply stared at him, then she took a step back. "You do that." A tiny spark of anger kept her from saying more. She'd thought they'd made such headway and she'd been flat-out wrong.

"Katie…" Now he did reach out for her, but all she did was shake her head. Two could play this stubborn game, and damned if she was going to try to make him feel that she was accepting of this when she wasn't.

"Like you said, we'll talk when you get back."

It seemed impossible, but his expression shuttered even more than before. The classic Brady response to pain. He hurt. But she couldn't help him if he wouldn't let her in.

"Go. Do whatever you have to do." And then, because she had no idea what to do that didn't involve shaking him or begging or exploding, she turned and stalked toward her truck, yanked the door open and turned off the ignition.

By that time Brady was in his truck. She heard the door slam as she headed for the house, but she waited until she heard his truck bump over the snowy cattle guard before turning to watch him go.

Once he was out of sight, she tipped her head up and closed her eyes. And for the first time since she'd pulled Brady out from under the four-wheeler, she felt as if she wasn't going to be able to break through his defenses.

Oh, she'd chipped away at the exterior, but the core seemed to be made of titanium.

ROSALIE SHIVERED AT the bit of slush that splashed into her boot as she tossed a shovelful of snow blocking the driveway to one side.

"Do you think this was an accident?" Gloria panted a little as she scraped away at her half of the driveway. "Or did Vincent Taylor have something to do with it?"

It did seem suspicious that Vince's driveways were not blocked, but theirs was.

"Maybe it was too much trouble for the driver to continue to pick up his blade," Rosalie said.

Gloria stopped scraping, setting a bright purple mitten on top of her shovel. "Do you believe that?"

"No. I'm trying to keep steam from coming out of my ears."

Gloria laughed. "Maybe it would help melt the snow."

Both women stopped digging as a car slowed, then Rosalie straightened as Vince

Taylor's big pickup rolled to a stop. Carl had always said that you could tell how secure a man was by what he did to his pickup truck. Carl had driven a bare-bones model. Vince's had a four-inch lift and a chromed differential.

He rolled down the window and Rosalie forced a smile. "Good morning, Vince. Quite a snowfall."

"It's not going to work," Vince said darkly.

"Excuse me?" Rosalie and Gloria said in unison.

"Siccing Will McGuire on me. Nice try."

"I did not sic anyone on you," Rosalie said coldly. "I don't know what you're talking about."

Vince gave a disbelieving laugh. "He just decided to attend a city council meeting and to make a public comment about how shameful my behavior was regarding 'overly strict' enforcement of zoning regulations?"

"I wouldn't know."

"And I suppose you don't know that he had the temerity to accost me in the parking lot and tell me to keep my distance from you or else?"

Something in Rosalie's chest went still. He'd done that?

She barely kept from saying the words aloud. Instead, she drew herself up and said, "I have no control over Will McGuire and I certainly did not ask him to speak on my behalf. I am fully capable of speaking for myself."

Vince smirked at her. "Then next time perhaps you should do that." He nodded at the house behind her. "There's a very nice property for sale on the other side of Main Street. Close to the business district."

"We like this house," Gloria said, picking up her shovel and approaching Vince's truck as if she meant to do it, or him, bodily harm. "So I suggest that you tell your friend the snowplow man to lift his blade for our property, too, or I will be at the next city council meeting asking for an explanation." She smiled sweetly. "I've taken photos."

Vince gave another sneering smirk and began rolling up the window. "Good day, ladies," he said before the window shut.

Gloria let out a sigh as he drove down the street.

"I truly dislike that man."

"Yes," Rosalie said in a distracted way, her eyes narrowed as she watched the truck travel down the street.

"Are you all right?"

"I will be—once I settle a few things with one Will McGuire."

"Surely you don't have a problem with him voicing support."

Rosalie gave Gloria a quick look. "No. I have a problem with him putting his nose in our business without giving us a heads-up."

Rosalie knew where to find Will if he was in town—the same place he and Carl had gathered on Wednesday mornings to discuss cattle prices and ranch issues: the feed co-op. And it just so happened that it was Wednesday.

After shoveling the driveway to the point that she could get her car out, Rosalie headed down to the co-op, and sure enough, Will's truck was parked in its usual spot—right next to the spot where Carl had parked. She got out of her car and marched into the store, which was essentially empty, with the exception of the men gathered in the back around a long table.

"Will McGuire. A word, please."

He scooted his chair back and got to his feet, while his friends made no effort to hide their interest in what was happening. Why had Carl Callahan's widow stomped into the co-op?

Well, Will could come up with whatever explanation he wanted, after she'd had her say.

She waited until they were close to the front of the store, out of earshot and hidden from view by a display of various seed types.

"I've been informed that you went to the city council meeting and discussed enforcement of zoning ordinances."

"I did."

"And that you not so subtly threatened Vince Taylor in the parking lot afterward."

Will opened his mouth to speak, and even though Rosalie had fully intended to hear him out, instead she pointed her finger at him and said in a low voice, "Do not ever threaten anyone on my account. Ever. Do you understand me?"

"Rosalie—"

"Ever," she repeated.

"The only thing Vince Taylor understands is threats."

"Then I will do the threatening. You are not to intercede on my behalf again. Do. You. Understand?"

He nodded, his striking blue eyes narrowing. "I was acting as a friend."

"Friends keep the channels of communication open. They do not act without informing the parties involved of their intentions."

"If I'd done that, what would you have said?"

"Exactly what I'm saying now." Rosalie pulled in a breath, wishing her cheeks didn't feel so embarrassingly warm. "I'll fight my own battles. If I need help, I'll call."

WHEN BRADY ARRIVED at Chet Jacobs's office in a strip mall near the Missoula city limits, he found the door locked, and a quick glance through the tinted window showed that the place was abandoned and not simply closed for the holidays. He felt like puking. Instead, he leaned his hands against his truck in the almost-empty parking lot and hung his head.

What now?

With no money, there'd be no land. No selling at a profit and reinvesting. No security.

A car pulled into the lot and parked a few spaces away, bringing his head up. The driver got out, giving him an odd look before locking her car and heading into a nail salon.

On impulse, Brady followed her into the salon on the off chance that someone there might be familiar with Jacobs and his habits. The bored girl at the counter knew nothing about the guy in the offices four doors down. No—she'd never even seen him, but she had seen the lights on recently. It was dark when she started home, so she recalled that small fact, but she couldn't remember the last time she'd seen the lights on.

Brady left the salon and headed for his truck.

He had little choice but to file a police report, even though it was probably a hopeless endeavor. He'd brought what little documentation he had with him, in case he needed it while dealing with Jacobs, but instead he'd be leaving copies with the police report. Not that there was a lot the police could do until Jacobs was located, and chances were that he was far, far away.

Brady called his fellow bronc rider, gave him the bad news about their agent, then started driving back to Gavin before he realized his tank was almost empty. Wouldn't that add insult to injury?

He pulled off at the next exit, filled his

tank and called Nick, who was still on the road between California and Montana.

"What's going on with your agent?" Nick asked. "Did you find him?"

"I take it you spoke to Katie." *And just how angry was she?*

"Yeah. She filled me in when I texted my location. So, what's the deal?"

The deal was that he was in deep trouble.

"His office is locked. I filed a police report." Nick muttered a curse, but before he could say anything, Brady asked, "Do you need me on the ranch over the next few days?"

"I'll be home tomorrow, so feel free to do whatever you have to do." Nick hesitated, then asked, "What do you have to do?" He sounded as if he fully expected Brady to go on a rampage. If Brady had any idea where to find Jacobs, he might just do that.

"I don't know." But the honest truth was that he wanted to avoid a showdown with Katie. "I have to meet with Stan and Abe Jr., tell them what happened and see what they say." The chances of him being able to work out a deal without a down payment were next to nil, but he had to give it a shot.

"You know you always have a place on our ranch."

"I know."

A place his pride would have a hard time letting himself accept unless he had something to give back, and until Nick started farming the ranch and bought more stock, he wouldn't need Brady. Besides that, losing this chunk of money changed everything. Being a day hand wasn't going to build his future. Wasn't going to get him his own place. He wouldn't be able to save enough for retirement and health care… Yeah. Being a day hand would have been enough to make his payments. It wasn't enough to start over with no savings.

He was screwed.

"I need more than a place, Nick." He didn't know how to explain that, after being on top for so long, he couldn't take being on the bottom for much longer. "I need a job and a purpose." Something he could take pride in.

"Yeah," Nick said softly. "I get that. Just… don't do anything reckless. Or at least don't do anything reckless until I come back."

Reckless was his middle name. How was he supposed to change his ways now?

"Yeah. I'll talk to you later."

The Larson Stock offices were closed for the Christmas holidays, but Brady managed to arrange a meeting with Stan and Abe Jr. as he drove back from Missoula.

He explained what happened in a few sentences, then offered up an alternative plan. A balloon payment if Abe Jr. would allow him some time. No go.

While they were sympathetic to his predicament, Abe Jr., in particular, was a businessman and after the meeting Stan told Brady that the rich guy who'd made an offer on the remaining Hayden Valley acreages would snap up the homestead in a second. Abe Jr. was not motivated to make a new deal with Brady, and he wasn't a particularly sentimental man. Brady got no points for being a hometown guy who'd been slapped around by life.

"Sorry it worked out this way." Stan slipped his hands in his back pockets.

Even if he was able to chase down Jacobs and his missing funds, it was clear that his real estate deal was sunk. He could tick Land Baron off his list of possible career opportunities.

"Guess it's time for plan B."

"Do you have a plan B?"

"Yeah. I do." It was called online job search. He was no longer tied to the Gavin area, because he no longer had a land deal to anchor him there. He was free to go anyplace in the state—in the country, really—where he could find a job that didn't involve too much physical labor. And not a lot of training.

Why, the possibilities had to be endless.

Crazy that for more than half a decade he won time and time again. And now he kept losing. But damned if he was going to feel sorry for himself. He was going to pull himself up out of this hole into which he'd fallen—before more dirt got shoved down on top of him.

Stan held out his hand and Brady shook it. "I appreciate the help."

"I'll let you know if I hear anything else from the Bar HM Ranch."

Brady shook his head. "I'll find my own job." He was done reeling in favors. "But thanks."

He left the office and crossed the snowy sidewalk where he stopped at his truck, hesitated for a moment before opening the door. His body felt heavy. His leg hurt.

And he had to talk to Katie when he got

back to the ranch. Explain to her that once Nick got back, he was moving on, because he had to. He was so glad he hadn't let things get as serious between them as he'd wanted to. That some small voice had kept nudging him to hold back until he was certain of his future.

Well, he was certain now—about what he didn't have.

KATIE DROVE TO town after Brady had left on his mission to Missoula. She couldn't relax so she decided to shop. She returned home with the makings for Christmas dinner and all kinds of kid-friendly foods. Nick and his girls would be arriving later that evening and they'd be hungry.

And because food shopping hadn't kept her from worrying about Brady, she'd walked down Main Street, soaking up the Christmas ambience and buying several small gifts for her nieces. Yes, she was going to spoil them. But it was Christmas. What better time to spoil a couple of adorable little girls? A pleasant afternoon visit with her grandmother, during which she took care not to mention Brady or his problems, had helped her relax. She'd even hummed a few Christmas carols on the way home, but the sight of Brady's truck parked in front of Ed's house wiped all thoughts of Christmas straight out of her head as she bumped over the snowy cattle guard.

Okay. There would be answers. To a lot of questions. Had he found his agent? Had it all been a big mistake? And, if not, what was he going to do?

Her stomach worked itself into a big fat knot as she pulled to a stop in her usual spot. She'd got out of the truck and had just opened the rear door when she heard him crossing the driveway toward her. She pulled out an armload of grocery bags, telling herself that she needed to keep cool and not let her anxiety show. Brady did the same, closing the door and then following Katie into the house.

"How were the roads?" she asked as she pulled open the door and then snapped on a light.

"Not bad."

Once inside they stomped the snow off their boots on the rug, then set the bags on the blue quartzite countertop.

"Nick should be home shortly," Katie said.

"That's good. I need to talk with him."

She didn't like the note of finality in his voice, as if he'd come to a decision and nothing was going to deter him from it.

She pulled the milk out of the closest bag on the countertop. "What happened in Missoula?"

"The offices were locked up tight. I filed a police report, but long story short, I won't be getting the homestead property from the Larsons."

Her stomach plummeted. "That's a certainty?"

"Even if I get my money back from Jacobs, which I think is a real long shot, there's another guy hot for the property, and he's offered more money. Abe Jr. is accepting his offer."

She set the milk back on the counter. "What now?"

He shifted his weight. "Nick offered to let me stay on, but we both know that until spring hits, he doesn't need the extra help."

"What are you going to do, Brady?"

He rubbed his hand over the back of his neck. "I had time to think as I drove. I won't stay here and get a check for doing next to nothing. That's not right." She opened her mouth to speak, to tell him that depending on friends during hard times was natural, that it wasn't a reason to be ashamed, but before she could get a word out, he said, "I made calls as I drove. I contacted a bucking school in Vegas that needs staff."

Of course. A bucking school. Did it get any more perfect than that? A job Brady was totally suited for.

"Why didn't you call them before? When you got out of the hospital?"

"I was done with rodeo," he said simply.

"And now you're not."

"Now my other plan has exploded in my face and I'm in a much different position," he said tightly.

"Do you want to go back to rodeo?"

No. She could read it in his face. It must still hurt not to be able to do what he'd once loved. What he'd sacrificed so much to do.

"I don't have any choice. The job's not permanent, but it's a job. Something I'd be good at."

For a long moment they faced off and she wondered if Brady knew what a clear read he was. He wasn't perfect. His life wasn't perfect. Therefore, he was leaving...even though she was certain he had strong feelings for her. That was the kicker. Didn't he realize that by protecting her, he was ripping out her heart?

Lesser of two evils, in his mind.

"Are you going to disappear from my life?" she asked softly.

"No."

"I don't know if I believe you." It was so easy to see Brady meaning to come back, but talking himself out of it in order to protect her from, what? An economically uncertain future?

A flash of pain crossed his face at her flatly spoken words, and then his expression blanked out. Classic Brady protection mode.

She wanted to step forward, to wrap her arms around him and tell him that they could work through this together, but it didn't appear that the word *together* was part of Brady's working vocabulary.

"Are you staying for Christmas?" Two days away.

"Actually, I'm going to start traveling tomorrow."

"You're going to travel on Christmas Eve and spend Christmas alone in Vegas?" If she sounded outraged, it was because she was.

"No one is alone in Vegas."

His joke fell flat.

Katie pointed a finger at his chest. "I know you think you're protecting me—"

"I have nothing to offer." His voice was edged with anger.

Good. Katie was feeling a bit of that anger herself. She just started to speak when lights reflected off the windows. Nick was there.

"Looks like you get to have that talk," she said grimly. "The sooner you quit, the sooner you can escape."

"I'm not escaping. I'm trying to do the right thing."

For a moment, Katie thought her head was going to explode. She pulled in a slow breath and then managed to grit out the truth as she saw it.

"You're a fair-weather relationship guy." He opened his mouth, as if to protest, but she held up a hand. "You don't trust other people to take the bumps in the road with you."

Just outside the window, Nick's truck pulled to a stop next to Katie's, but Brady didn't seem to hear the opening and closing of doors or the excited voices of little girls. Instead, his gaze remained locked on Katie's.

"I don't *want* to make them take the bumps."

Katie gave a scoffing breath as footsteps

sounded on the porch. It was time to act normal, but before that she had one last thing to say. "Yeah. And until you get over that, I think you're going to be one lonely guy."

She may have been hearing things, but as the door opened and her nieces tumbled into the kitchen, she swore she heard him mutter, "Nothing new there."

CHAPTER FIFTEEN

ROSALIE GLANCED OVER at Katie, who was creaming eggs and butter for Christmas cookies with a vengeance, the wooden spoon thumping rhythmically against the side of the stainless-steel bowl as she stirred.

"You're very quiet over there." *With the exception of the wooden spoon percussion, that is.*

Rosalie's best guess was that Brady's abrupt departure had a lot to do with the beating the eggs were taking, as well as Katie's prolonged silence. It wasn't like her not to chitchat while they worked together in the kitchen.

"Sorry." Katie worked up a smile as she added the dry ingredients to the eggs and sugar, but the smile evaporated as soon as she glanced back at the bowl.

Rosalie let out a silent sigh. After raising all these competent adults, it still pained her to see her kids and grandkids hurt. She glanced toward the living room where Kendra and Bailey were sound asleep on the sofa with Nick dozing in between them. Once they awoke, she and Katie wouldn't be able to talk—at least not without making a big deal about it—so she decided to dive in while she had the chance. And she chose to dive straight into the deep end.

"I'm sorry that Brady wasn't able to stay for Christmas." Rosalie figured that when Nick had explained why Brady wouldn't be there for the holiday, he'd probably given her about two-thirds of the facts, holding back the rest in a misguided effort to protect his grandmother from…whatever it was grandchildren protected their grandparents from. Despite his efforts, she had a pretty good idea what was going on.

Katie's gaze flashed up at the mention of Brady, telling Rosalie that she'd hit the nail on the head. If she hadn't, she would have been surprised.

"He has other commitments," Katie said to the bowl she was stirring.

"So I understand."

Come on, Katie, love…give a little.

"This job is perfect for him. I'm surprised he didn't think of doing it before."

"Sometimes it hurts to be involved with something you love but can't do anymore. Brady was quite the competitor."

"Yes." Katie bit her lip as she struggled to stir the last of the sugar and flour into the eggs and butter. She finally lifted the wooden spoon and scraped the remainder of the dough off with a smaller spoon. Then she smiled at Rosalie. "If you don't mind, I'd rather speak of something else."

"Fair enough." Rosalie focused on chopping nuts for fudge. It was hard to accept that her grandkids were adults who had to sort out their lives and deal with consequences of decisions made, just as she and Carl had, but accept she must.

And it was equally hard to accept that when she wasn't thinking about Katie being unhappy, she was thinking about Will McGuire. What was the man thinking, involving himself in her affairs like that? And what was she thinking, noticing, despite everything, that he was a very good-looking man? She'd been widowed for two years, and yes, she had needs, emotional and otherwise, but a rancher...no. She would not look twice at another rancher. She'd lived that life and now she was ready for another.

"He drives me crazy," Katie muttered as she yanked a length of plastic wrap off the roll and covered the cookie dough bowl. Clearly, she might want to speak of something else, but she was having a hard time *thinking* about something else. Rosalie was kind of having the same issue.

"There's peanut butter ribbon in the downstairs freezer. I left the ice cream when I moved." Rosalie loved ice cream and always stocked her freezer with a variety of pint containers—perfect for solo consumption. Carl had not been an ice-cream man.

"This situation is beyond being fixed by peanut butter ribbon."

"It couldn't hurt," Rosalie muttered more to herself than to Katie.

"You're right."

Katie popped the bowl into the fridge and then opened the door leading to the basement where two chest freezers took up almost an entire room. When she came back upstairs, she was carrying two pints of ice cream, both peanut butter ribbon.

"A two-carton problem?"

"I'm saving myself a trip later." Katie started toward the kitchen freezer, then came to a stop when Rosalie held out her hand.

Slowly Katie relinquished the container before opening the flatware drawer and handing Rosalie a spoon. Her eyes never left Rosalie's face during the process.

"What is *your* peanut butter ice cream problem?"

Rosalie shook her head. She wasn't one to unload—especially when she was in new territory and edging toward a situation she wasn't certain how to handle. How did one handle a man like Will McGuire? Why couldn't she stop thinking about the man?

"Something to do with the Taylors?"

"No." She grabbed on to that line of questioning. "But I'm sure it's coming."

Katie leaned her elbows on the counter as she put another spoonful of ice cream in her mouth. "Then what is it?"

"Katie... I'm not telling."

Katie's eyes went wide and then she gestured with the spoon. "No fair."

"Totally fair. I get to have my private concerns, just like you have yours."

A gust of wind blasted rain and sleet into the dark windows, bringing both of their heads around.

"Fine," Katie said as she walked to the window and stared out at the sleet. "It's really coming down. Has the ranch ever flooded?"

"No, I think we're safe in that regard." But the river could get high. It'd taken out the old bridge the year she and Carl were first married, which had led to all kinds of complications since the only other route to the ranch was literally ten miles of bad road.

There was a noise in the hallway and Katie strained her neck to see who it was. "Ah. The first survivor of the nap," she murmured as Nick walked into the room, one side of his face red from sleep.

"The first rule of single fatherhood. Sleep whenever you can." He looked at the ice-cream containers and rubbed his forehead. "Okay, let me guess… Brady." He nodded at Katie, then shifted his attention to Rosalie. "And…the Taylors?"

"Grandma is dealing with a mystery problem."

Nick's eyes narrowed. "No kidding. What's his name?"

To her horror, Rosalie felt guilty color rising from her neckline. Even if Nick *had* been kidding, she'd just given herself away, but judging from the look on his face, he hadn't been kidding.

"I'm not prying into *your* lives," she said firmly.

Nick grinned at her. "Point taken. Any more ice cream?"

"Tons," Katie answered.

"Excellent."

Rosalie smiled as Nick headed downstairs, then shook her head. "It's going to be hard to mind our own business now that the family is back together."

"Maybe we should make a pact."

"Do you think it would do any good?"

"Not one bit," Katie said solemnly. "We have that bad habit of protecting our own."

"Brady's the same way," Nick said as he topped the stairs carrying a carton of Moose Tracks.

"You think that's what he's doing?" Katie asked.

"Don't you?" Nick gave his sister a pointed look.

"I don't want to talk about it." She raised her chin and drilled him with a look.

That made two of them, which meant a change of subject was in order. Rosalie stabbed her spoon into the carton. She needed a distraction, so she went with the obvious.

"About those Taylors…"

Brady could honestly say that the time between his talk with Nick, who seemed to understand his need to head to Vegas, and actually leaving the Callahan Ranch after he and Nick had dug out his trailer were some of the tensest hours of his life.

More than once while he'd been packing his stuff, he'd started for the door with the intention of finding Katie and telling her that she was off base—that she didn't understand why he needed to leave.

Every time he stopped himself. She was wrong about one thing—he would be back. He wasn't walking away from the Callahan family, although falling for Katie, again, had complicated matters.

He was so damned glad to be heading somewhere where they needed him—or would need him. The Christmas break clinic had a full staff, but the powers that be had been happy to squeeze in a rider with his experience, with the promise of a full-time job shortly before the new year. He'd stay in his trailer on the grounds of the school, along with some of the other instructors, and basically his only expenses were propane and food.

It wasn't ideal, but it was a decent place

to land while the search continued for his cheating agent. He could save some money, might even be able to work in some continuing education classes. But for the moment, being a trainer at bronc riding school was good enough. At least it was a step forward.

And Katie…

Every time he thought about her, his chest went tight. But it wasn't like he could ask her to live with him in a trailer in a Vegas parking lot, right?

It took more than love to put together a life. It took opportunity and resources.

Katie was right about him not being good at sharing the bumpy road, so the solution was for him to smooth it out. Get a job that wasn't given to him as a favor from a family he loved. Save money for school. Make something of himself.

He had to try. He'd hate himself if he didn't.

The one thing he couldn't do was ask Katie to share his life while he was at rock-freaking-bottom. And once she had some time to reflect, she'd understand that.

Snow was coming down hard when he pulled out of the RV campground just outside Gavin, having chosen to spend the night there in his trailer rather than on the Callahan Ranch. He lost almost half of his travel day stocking up on groceries, then dealing with a broken bearing on his trailer wheel. Finally, hours after he'd intended to leave, he was almost on his way.

His last stop before leaving town was at the bank where he cashed the check Nick had cut him for wages he'd actually earned, unlike the wages he would have received if he'd stayed through January and February. Once calving started in March, he would have been earning his keep again, but until then, Nick would have essentially been paying him to be on call in case of emergencies. Not much happened on a ranch during the dead of winter.

The wind hit him hard as he left the bank and he put his head down, hunching his shoulders against the arctic blast.

"Some weather."

Brady glanced up to see Will McGuire standing on the snowy sidewalk near the front of his truck. Really? Was he here to rub things in? "Yeah."

"Is that little goat doing okay?"

Brady frowned at the man, wondering why they were discussing goats instead of him making yet another bad decision by trusting his thieving agent. "Wendell? He seemed happy enough the last time I saw him."

Will jammed his hands deeper in his coat pockets. "I owe you an apology for the other day. Out in the pasture with the four-wheeler." He jerked his head toward the café two doors down. "I'll buy you a cup of coffee."

Brady needed to be on his way if he was going to make it to Pocatello that night. With the snow it would be slow-going, but Will was already walking to the Mad Hen Café, leaving Brady with two choices—get in his truck and start driving or follow Will into the café and take his lumps. Again.

He'd barely joined Will in the padded red leather booth when a server wearing jingle bell earrings arrived, glass carafe in hand, asking if they wanted coffee.

"Just coffee," Will said. "We won't need menus." The server turned over the cups and filled them, then moved to the next booth, leaving Brady facing Will McGuire across the table.

Will scowled at him. "Relax, okay? You're making me jumpy."

Neither of them made a move to touch their cups.

Brady propped his forearms on the table. He wasn't certain what had caused Will to think he owed Brady an apology, but it went both ways. "I appreciate the fact that you tried to send me in the right direction with that scholarship. Everything you said that night was true."

"I can't remember exactly what I said. I was a tad frustrated at the time."

"I noticed," Brady said dryly.

"You were salutorian, Brady. With my money and the other scholarships you could have won, you'd have had a full ride. Instead, you had to listen to Stan and take to the rodeo circuit."

Brady studied the table. "I figured I could go to school anytime." He looked up with a matter-of-fact expression. "But it doesn't work as well the other way around. Rodeo wouldn't wait, and I was at the top of my game. It seemed stupid not to continue."

"And you won a lot of money."

Brady swallowed at the mention of money. "Yeah. I did." He held the older man's gaze. "I made the decision that felt right at the time, even though it meant breaking my promise to you."

"And I was afraid you were going to turn out like Colton."

Brady gave a nod.

"You didn't."

Brady gave a small snort. Not according to his mother.

"You were wild, but not like your dad. He had no concept of consequences. It was like there was something in his brain that wasn't fully connected to the fear center." Will smiled grimly. "But he was likable. A guy that made you want to save him from himself." He shook his head. "I heard you're buying property in the Hayden Valley."

Brady pressed his lips together at the change of topic. "Things have changed."

"How?"

He didn't want to talk about it. He wasn't going to talk about it—wasn't going to admit that he was in an even worse place than he'd been after the bronc fell on him.

Will gave Brady a hard look before settling his forearms on the table and leaning across the table. "I know you have a habit of holding things close, but I'm going to hear a version of the story at the co-op within a matter of days. I may as well hear the truth."

"The truth leaves me feeling raw," Brady said darkly. "My agent robbed me and now I'm heading to Vegas to guest star at a bucking clinic."

Will straightened in his seat, a stunned expression on his face. "You were robbed?"

Brady told him the story and Will listened with an ever-deepening frown. Finally he reached for his coffee, which had to be just this side of lukewarm. "How's Katie handling it?"

"Katie's not really involved."

Will's silver eyebrows lifted. "That's hard to believe, given what I've observed."

Did everyone know that he was in love with Katie?

The answer came a split second later when Will added, "From the way she defended you, I just assumed that you two finally figured things out."

"First *I* have to figure it out."

Will gave him a sharp look. "Always back to you."

The older man's words startled him. Brady opened his mouth to fight back, then thought better of it. "Yeah. Maybe so."

"Bad habit, Brady. Take it from one who knows."

"Adversity can tear relationships apart. I'm not ready to risk that." When he came back to Katie, he'd have something to offer her.

"Yeah. It can also glue them together. It depends on the people, Brady. You have to ask yourself, what kind of person are you? And what kind of person is Katie?"

Brady fought for an answer, but before he could say anything, Will stabbed his finger on the table. "Things aren't perfect. They never will be. Neither will you be." His voice lowered a notch as he added, "Don't wait for perfect, Brady. Perfect never comes."

"HIDING?" NICK ASKED as he leaned his head in through Katie's open bedroom door.

"Resting," she said from where she stood at her closet, trying to find something festive to wear on a day when she wasn't feeling all that festive. But Christmas Eve with the family demanded full participation, regardless of her feelings, and that meant dressing the part. She gave Nick a smile that felt pretty genuine given the circumstances. "Someone brought small tornadoes into the house."

As if on cue, Bailey and Kendra came racing down the hallway, their stocking-clad feet thudding on the hardwood floor. They slipped past their father and climbed up onto the bed, cuddling together on Katie's pillows. "We're invisible," Kendra whispered, putting her finger to her lips when Bailey giggled.

Katie cocked her head at Nick. "Did you hear mice?"

The girls dissolved into peals of laughter, then Bailey held her hands at her chest and wrinkled her nose. "Squeak, squeak. Squeak, squeak."

Brady had been right about the ranch being a livelier place after Nick and his family arrived. Katie only hoped that she was successful in hiding her mood, which was not suited for a proper celebration of Christmas Eve, from the rest of the family.

"Very nice, Miss Mousy," Nick said. "Now if you ladies will excuse us, Aunt Katie and I need a moment of privacy."

Katie's stomach dropped, but she managed a careless smile. "Tell Grandma that I'll be there in a few minutes and we'll see about cookies."

"Making or eating?" Kendra asked.

"Could be both..."

The girls exchanged looks, then slipped

past their dad again, racing into the kitchen where Katie heard Rosalie say, "I was wondering where my help had gotten to."

"They're excited for Christmas," Nick said as he glanced down the hall. "Usually Kendra is a lot more reserved."

"It's good to see her play."

Nick grinned. "She'll start enforcing rules soon."

"I figure this will help them sleep tonight."

"Only until about four in the morning. Then all bets are off."

"Bailey Jean Callahan." Rosalie's voice floated in from the direction of the kitchen. "Close that refrigerator. You're letting all the cold air out."

"Ever hear that before?" Nick asked.

"Only a couple hundred times." Katie laughed as she pulled a red sweater with pearls sewn around the neck out of the closet. It would do.

"Uh…what's up with Grandma?"

Katie let out a soft breath, thankful that he didn't want to talk about Brady. She didn't want to talk about him. Didn't want to think about him. She just wanted to enjoy the holiday with her family.

Of course, none of those things were possible. Oh, she'd enjoy the holiday, but missing Brady put a damper on her celebratory feelings.

"What do you mean?"

"Peanut butter ribbon ice cream, straight out of the container?"

"Yeah. I wondered about that, too. Do you think it's the Taylors?"

"She said no."

"Then…" Katie gave a shrug. "I have no idea."

Nick nodded slowly. "If you do discover what's bugging her, will you clue me in?"

"Or, like you said, we trust her to live her own life and settle her own problems."

"I guess," he said heavily. "And how are you?"

Katie shook out the sweater. "Oh, I'm living my own life and solving my own problems."

Nick smirked at her gotcha, but she could read concern in his expression.

"I'm dealing, Nick. Thank you."

"All right. But if you ever need help solving a problem, I'm here."

"Yeah. Well, I don't know if I have a problem that can be solved. But if I need help, I know where to find you."

A bowl clattered in the kitchen and Nick glanced down the hall. "I better go see what's up."

"I'll be right there," Katie said, laying the sweater on the bed. *Just as soon as I once again get a grip.* Talking about Brady...well, it hurt.

BRADY WAS STILL working on the fact that he'd gotten relationship advice from Will McGuire when he started out of town toward the highway, driving slowly due to the rapidly accumulating snow. Pulling a trailer was tricky in conditions such as these and the last thing he needed was to end up in a ditch somewhere.

What was he doing out on roads like this, anyway?

Running. Just like Katie had said. But despite what Will believed, he had reason.

It wasn't like he could turn around and go back to the Callahan Ranch. For all he knew, Katie might be in the process of moving into Ed's house to make room for Nick and his family.

Once he made it over Monida Pass and got into Idaho, the weather was supposed to clear. Getting over Monida Pass was going to be the trick.

Actually, as the wind started blowing directly at him he began to think that getting to the freeway leading south was also going to be a trick. Gavin was thirty miles from the main artery leading through Montana south to Idaho, and despite it being close to the holiday with people no doubt traveling to be home with family, he was one of the only vehicles on the road.

His wipers were barely able to keep up with the snow as the wind blew it directly into his windshield, and he'd slowed to the point that it felt as if he was barely moving. Every now and again, the wind would catch the trailer and buffet it sideways, causing him to slow even more.

Once he hit sunny Vegas, this would all be worth it. The clinic started two days after Christmas, giving the riders time to travel from wherever they'd spent the holidays, and giving them plenty of time to travel back to their respective colleges and universities, since this particular clinic was geared toward college athletes.

Sunny Vegas.

He'd never really liked Vegas. So many people. So darned hot, even in the winter.

Brady closed his eyes for a split second and let out a breath. When he opened them again, the wind suddenly died and the snow that had been swirling around him settled to the roadbed, leaving him in an eerie silvery white world.

And then a movement up ahead of him caught his eye. Something small and white, moving like a bouncing snowball.

Or a rabbit.

He slowed, the trailer skidding behind him, pushing the truck forward for a few feet before coming to a complete stop. The rabbit stood on its hind legs, little front legs dangling at its sides, and tipped its chin up at Brady as if to say, *Hey. What are you doing out here? Why aren't you home?*

Brady glanced in his rearview mirror, concerned about another vehicle barreling up on him. Nothing behind him. Then he shifted his gaze forward again, beyond the bunny, who stubbornly held his position in front of him, studying him through the windshield. Nothing ahead of him, either.

His shoulders slumped as he let out a long breath.

Nothing ahead of him that he really wanted.

What he wanted was in the opposite direction of the one in which he was traveling.

You can't go back. Not now. Not until you've—

Brady told his small voice to shut up.

He'd tried to be noble, do the right thing, tried to keep from dragging Katie down with him. But...maybe she could help him rise.

The thought came out of nowhere, making Brady sit up straighter as he gripped the wheel, and for one brief moment it appeared as if the rabbit nodded at him.

Rabbit approval aside, Katie had made it clear that she wanted to be with him as he figured things out, and he hadn't respected that. Had been utterly convinced he knew what was best.

He started to inch forward, and the rabbit turned and hopped off the road into the snow-covered underbrush, duty done.

Brady smiled grimly as he pulled off the road into the last rest area before the freeway. The snow was deep, and he was hauling a trailer, so he figured that if he didn't get stuck, he was meant to go back.

He didn't get stuck.

Twenty-two miles to Gavin, another nine to the ranch. And then he'd confront his future and see if she was still talking to him.

At the very least she'd have the satisfaction of kicking him off the ranch.

CHAPTER SIXTEEN

ROSALIE FOLLOWED HER great-granddaughters down the hall from the bathroom where they'd taken a rather energetic bubble bath before changing into the warm flannel nightgowns Gloria had made them for Christmas.

It was amazing how two small girls could change the dynamics of the once-quiet ranch house. They were excited for Christmas, which boosted their energy levels, and seemed to have the opposite effect on Nick's. He looked dog-tired, as well he might after traveling from California through all kinds of weather—but Rosalie remembered feeling that same way without driving through a storm. Kids were wonderfully exhausting.

On the mantel, a photo of Kayla, Nick's wife, was placed front and center. This would be the second Christmas the family had celebrated without her, and while Rosalie was thrilled to have Bailey and Kendra there for Christmas, she couldn't help but worry about Kayla's parents, who were spending their first Christmas without Nick and girls since their daughter's death. But they were talking about moving to Gavin to be closer to the kids, which Rosalie thought would be a good solution for everyone. Next year the entire family would be together—even Cassie. If she came up with another work-related excuse to miss the holidays, Rosalie was going to fly to Wisconsin and bring her back by the ear.

"This one's for you, Aunt Katie." Bailey set a small wrapped gift she'd pulled out from under the tree in Katie's hands. Nick rolled his eyes at the ceiling.

The girls wanted to open their presents and three-year-old Bailey kept delivering gifts from under the tree to Katie in hopes that she would get the ball rolling.

"Sorry, sweetie," Katie said. "We have to put this back until tomorrow."

Nick reached down to swing Bailey up in his arms and to touch her forehead with his. "Just twelve short hours, Bill." Nick's pet name for his youngest, taken from the old song *Won't You Come Home, Bill Bailey*.

Her lips started to quiver, and Nick put his own lip out in an exaggerated pout.

"Bailey. We have to wait," Kendra said, taking charge of the present and putting it back under the tree. "I have to wait, and you have to wait."

Rosalie had forgotten how strict five-year-olds could be. Rules were there for a purpose—to make people feel secure, and Kendra never felt more secure than when she was enforcing a rule. It had been good to see her being silly with her sister that afternoon.

"Don't want to wait," Bailey said adamantly.

"Let's go look at the books," Nick said. "We'll read some stories before bed."

Katie, who'd been curled up in the big recliner near the fireplace, rose to her feet and headed into the kitchen.

Rosalie followed. Katie had done her best to put on a brave face after Brady left, but she was clearly miserable—the one hiccup in an otherwise happy evening.

"Hey," Katie said from where she was running tap water into a glass.

"Hey," Rosalie echoed. She stood in the doorway, studying her granddaughter, wishing there was a way to make things better, but knowing that only Katie could do that.

"It's so much fun having the girls here."

Rosalie nodded after her granddaughter stated the obvious.

Katie turned off the faucet and brought the glass to her lips, not quite meeting Rosalie's eyes. Yes, she was hurting, and as the hours passed, she was having a more difficult time hiding it.

"You miss Brady."

Katie's mouth worked for a second or two before she said, "I love him."

"You're certain?"

Katie rolled her eyes. "Yes. I've been certain for about a decade."

"Brady has never been easy," Rosalie said slowly. "He's hard on himself."

"And he always has to be the outsider looking in." There was a note of frustration in Katie's voice.

"True." Rosalie remembered how closed off Brady had been when he'd first started coming to the ranch with Nick and how, with time, he'd loosened up, and eventually accepted the fact that the Callahans considered him part of the family. "His parents treated him like an outsider, so I guess that's to be expected."

Katie perched on one of the high kitchen stools, like she had when she was a teen and had a major issue to work through. "What do I do, Grandma?"

She may as well have asked how to pin down the wind.

"I don't know, honey. Be patient?" A totally inadequate answer, but the truth was that Rosalie didn't have an answer. Katie loved Brady, but until Brady loved and accepted himself, there wasn't much anyone could do.

Katie tipped her chin up and Rosalie saw her delicate throat move as she swallowed. "I'll be patient. For a while."

Rosalie was half afraid to ask, "What then?" so she didn't. Instead, she said, "Why don't you join us for the story? Nick's going to read The Night for Christmas." Bailey's title for the classic story. "Let's enjoy the evening, and then we can talk things out. Make a plan."

"Sure. Just...give me a minute."

Katie glanced down a little too quickly and Rosalie suspected she was fighting tears. But if she needed a hug, she would ask, so Rosalie did the hard thing and let her granddaughter be.

"I'll see you in there."

"Thank you. I'll be in shortly."

What Rosalie wouldn't give to get her hands on Brady and shake some sense into the boy. But one thing life had taught her was that you couldn't force people to see the truth. They had to come to it themselves. And unfortunately, Katie's truth might be that Brady was never going to get over his need to protect her from himself.

Rosalie settled on the sofa with Kendra between her and Nick and Bailey on his other side. "Leave room for Aunt Katie," she murmured to Bailey.

"Hey, Katie," Nick called, unaware that his sister was doing her best to get a grip before joining the family.

"Coming. I just—" Her voice cut off abruptly. "Uh…give me a second, okay?"

"For what?" Nick asked.

The only answer was the sound of shuffling boots by the door. By leaning sideways, Rosalie could see Katie jamming her feet into her brother's oversize winter boots. She grabbed a coat off the hook and opened the door, disappearing outside.

"You're squishing me, Grandma," Kendra complained.

"I'm sorry, honey. You need to excuse me," Rosalie said, doing her best to tamp down her sense of alarm. Was Katie heading out into the storm to compose herself? That seemed...wrong.

"Daddy, the story," Bailey said.

"In a minute, pumpkin."

Rosalie went to the kitchen window and pulled back the curtain, her breath catching in a small gasp as she saw Brady's truck roll over the cattle guard, breaking a good eight inches of snow as he dragged the trailer into the ranch yard. Katie was already past the front gate, slogging through the snow in Nick's boots, a coat thrown over her shoulders.

Nick came up behind Rosalie and leaned down to look out the window with her. "Those two are going to drive me crazy," he muttered.

"This could be good, or it could be bad," Rosalie said in a low voice.

"I'm banking on good. Brady dragged a trailer back through a storm to get here. He wouldn't do that to break her heart." He straightened and looped an arm around Rosalie. "He'd better not, anyway."

"Amen to that," Rosalie said through her teeth.

"We're here if Katie needs us, and in the

meantime, let's go see what my little minions are up to."

"Come on, Gran'ma," Bailey called as they walked into the living room, patting the sofa where Rosalie had sat until she'd excused herself to see what had driven Katie out into the storm. Kendra held the book on her lap, looking very important.

"I'm coming." She and Nick crossed to the sofa and Nick took the book Kendra solemnly handed to him.

"Are we going to wait for Aunt Katie?"

"Aunt Katie has a visitor, so no." Nick drew in a breath and started reading, and Rosalie did her best to sit still and pretend all was well.

Katie will be okay. She has family.

KATIE THOUGHT OF at least a dozen things to say to Brady as she waded through the snow, which was deep and dry enough to fall into the tops of Nick's boots, chilling her bare feet. But when he got out of the truck and shut the door, then stood without moving, tall and silent and everything she ever wanted, words escaped her. She slowed to a stop a few feet away from him, searching his face.

"I couldn't do it," he finally said, his voice raspy, as if he hadn't spoken in a while.

"Couldn't do what?"

"I couldn't leave you."

For a long moment she simply stared at him, hoping this wasn't another instance of the now familiar push-pull.

"I don't want to ever leave you, Katie. I want to stay with you for as long as you'll have me."

Katie launched herself forward. One of Nick's boots nearly came off as she stumbled in the snow, but Brady caught her, pulling her into his arms, holding her against him. She breathed deeply, pulling in the scent of damp canvas coat, soap and guy. The guy she loved.

"I want to come home, Katie."

"I'm going to cry," she murmured against his neck.

"Don't cry." His voice cracked and he held her even tighter.

The air was cold, but Brady was warm and the big wet snowflakes that landed on his coat, on Katie's cheeks and eyelashes, melted on contact. She blinked against the dampness, not all of which came from the snow. She told herself to let go, to stop clinging so that the two of them could get in out of the weather.

She couldn't.

Brady's hand traveled over her back, then he tipped up her chin and leaned down to gently kiss her lips. "I don't ever want to leave you."

"Good thing," she murmured before kissing him back.

A shiver went through her and Brady started toward the house, his arm still around her, but Katie planted her feet, stopping them.

"We won't be able to talk in there."

"We can talk later." His tone promised an important talk. More than that, a positive talk.

Katie's heart skipped, but she had to know one thing before they joined her family— their family. "Why did you decide to come back?"

An odd look crossed Brady's face. "Well, you see…there was this rabbit."

"Another one?"

"And Will McGuire."

She blinked at him as a couple of fat snowflakes hit her cheeks. "This sounds like some story." She shivered again and he propelled her forward. This time she let him, slipping an arm around his back to keep her balance in Nick's oversize boots.

"I'll explain later."

"There's no way you're getting out of that promise." Because she really needed to know how a rabbit and Will McGuire brought the guy she loved back to her on Christmas Eve.

"Wouldn't be brave enough to try."

"It's a little crazy in there." Katie gestured at the house with her chin as they approached. "What with little girls and Christmas."

Brady stopped at the porch steps and raised a hand to stroke her cheek. "Believe it or not, I'm ready for some family crazy."

She smiled up at him and rose up on her toes to lightly kiss his lips. "Wish granted."

FAMILY CRAZY FELT GOOD. Brady sat on the sofa with Katie beside him while Nick's little girls peppered him with questions. Did he see Santa while he was out in the snow? Does he have a tree at his house? Did he unwrap his presents alone?

Katie had answered the last one for him. "I think Brady might come over here to watch you guys unwrap *your* presents tomorrow morning."

He nodded at the girls, who exchanged laughing glances at the mention of their presents. Katie squeezed his fingers and he squeezed back.

Did he feel self-conscious about leaving and returning in such short order? Oh, yeah. But he would address that with the family in short order. In the meantime, he sat with his hand on Katie's knee, soaking up the warm ambience surrounding him.

For the first time in forever, he felt like he was where he was supposed to be. He didn't try to analyze or debate or argue with himself. For once he was content to just let himself be.

When Rosalie told the girls it was time for bed, Nick and Katie and Brady retired to the kitchen, where Nick set out four glasses on the table and then poured from a high-priced bottle of brandy.

"I'm going to tuck my girls in," he said before giving Katie and Brady a stern look. "Don't start without me."

"Wouldn't dream of it," Katie said. She picked up a glass, sniffed the rich liquid and smiled, then set the glass back on the table. "I love brandy."

And I love you.

"I'm going to talk to Nick about renting Ed's house while I look for work in Gavin."

Katie moved closer and set her hands loosely at his waist, tipping up her chin, tempting him to kiss her again. "I think that's a great idea."

"Probably one I should have had before, except that I was too busy feeling like a failure."

Katie gave a slow nod. "Tell me about the rabbit."

"I talked to Will in town. He invited me to coffee after I went to the bank. We didn't talk long, but he had an impact. Kind of hammered the point home that maybe I shouldn't be making decisions for the both of us."

"Smart man," she murmured. "Now about the rabbit?"

"The rabbit essentially stopped me dead in the road on my way to the freeway. And while I was stopped, I suddenly knew what I had to do. I had to get back to you. I had to stop running. I needed to go home. I needed to make decisions with you, not for you."

"Maybe he's cousin to the rabbit who tipped you over in the river pasture."

"That one tried to kill me."

"No...he brought us together." Katie leaned into him, wrapping her arms around him and resting her head against his chest.

He cradled the back of her head, wanting nothing more than to hold her forever. "I love you, Katie."

"I know," she murmured against his chest. He laughed and leaned back so that he could see her face. She frowned up at him. "You are well aware that I love you." Her expression softened. "Thank you for coming back so that I can do something about it."

Footsteps sounded in the hallway, and Brady dropped a quick kiss on Katie's head before stepping back. Katie kept hold of his hand as Nick and Rosalie came into the room. "Prepare yourselves for an early morning," Nick said on a wry note.

"Are you ready for our Christmas Eve toast?" Rosalie asked. When everyone had a glass in hand, she raised hers, looking directly at Brady, and said, "To family and Christmas."

"And to wise neighbors and rabbits," Katie added.

"Do I want to know?" Rosalie asked with a soft laugh.

"Long story." Brady glanced at the woman he loved, their eyes meeting over the brandy glasses.

Maybe they'd tell it at their wedding.

* * * * *

*Be sure to look for the next story
about the tight-knit Callahan family
in Jeannie Watt's next
Sweet Home, Montana book,
available in 2020!*

Get 4 FREE REWARDS!

We'll send you 2 FREE Books plus 2 FREE Mystery Gifts.

Love Inspired® books feature contemporary inspirational romances with Christian characters facing the challenges of life and love.

FREE Value Over $20

Get 4 FREE REWARDS!

We'll send you 2 FREE Books plus 2 FREE Mystery Gifts.

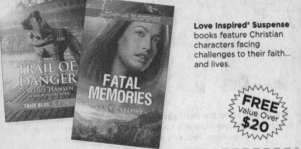

Love Inspired® Suspense books feature Christian characters facing challenges to their faith... and lives.

FREE Value Over **$20**

THE FORTUNES OF TEXAS COLLECTION!

18 FREE BOOKS in all!

Treat yourself to the rich legacy of the Fortune and Mendoza clans in this remarkable 50-book collection. This collection is packed with cowboys, tycoons and Texas-sized romances!

YES! Please send me **The Fortunes of Texas Collection** in Larger Print. This collection begins with 3 FREE books and 2 FREE gifts in the first shipment. Along with my 3 free books, I'll also get the next 4 books from The Fortunes of Texas Collection, in LARGER PRINT, which I may either return and owe nothing, or keep for the low price of $5.24 U.S./$5.89 CDN each plus $2.99 for shipping and handling per shipment*. If I decide to continue, about once a month for 8 months I will get 6 or 7 more books but will only need to pay for 4. That means 2 or 3 books in every shipment will be FREE! If I decide to keep the entire collection, I'll have paid for only 32 books because 18 books are FREE! I understand that accepting the 3 free books and gifts places me under no obligation to buy anything. I can always return a shipment and cancel at any time. My free books and gifts are mine to keep no matter what I decide.

☐ 269 HCN 4622   ☐ 469 HCN 4622

Name (please print)

Address   Apt. #

City   State/Province   Zip/Postal Code

Mail to the **Reader Service:**
IN U.S.A.: P.O. Box 1341, Buffalo, N.Y. 14240-8531
IN CANADA: P.O. Box 603, Fort Erie, Ontario L2A 5X3

THE CHRISTMAS ROMANCE COLLECTION!

10 FREE BOOKS IN ALL!

'Tis the season for romance!
You're sure to fall in love with these tenderhearted love stories from some of your favorite bestselling authors!

Get 4 FREE REWARDS!

We'll send you 2 FREE Books plus 2 FREE Mystery Gifts.

FREE
Value Over
$20

Both the **Romance** and **Suspense** collections feature compelling novels written by many of today's bestselling authors.

YES! Please send me 2 FREE novels from the Essential Romance or Essential Suspense Collection and my 2 FREE gifts (gifts are worth about $10 retail). After receiving them, if I don't wish to receive any more books, I can return the shipping statement marked "cancel." If I don't cancel, I will receive 4 brand-new novels every month and be billed just $6.99 each in the U.S. or $7.24 each in Canada. That's a savings of at least 13% off the cover price. It's quite a bargain! Shipping and handling is just 50¢ per book in the U.S. and $1.25 per book in Canada.* I understand that accepting the 2 free books and gifts places me under no obligation to buy anything. I can always return a shipment and cancel at any time. The free books and gifts are mine to keep no matter what I decide.

Choose one: ☐ **Essential Romance**
(194/394 MDN GNNP)
☐ **Essential Suspense**
(191/391 MDN GNNP)

Name (please print)

Address   Apt. #

City   State/Province   Zip/Postal Code

Mail to the **Reader Service:**
IN U.S.A.: P.O. Box 1341, Buffalo, NY 14240-8531
IN CANADA: P.O. Box 603, Fort Erie, Ontario L2A 5X3

Want to try 2 free books from another series! Call 1-800-873-8635 or visit www.ReaderService.com.

*Terms and prices subject to change without notice. Prices do not include sales taxes, which will be charged (if applicable) based on your state or country of residence. Canadian residents will be charged applicable taxes. Offer not valid in Quebec. This offer is limited to one order per household. Books received may not be as shown. Not valid for current subscribers to the Essential Romance or Essential Suspense Collection. All orders subject to approval. Credit or debit balances in a customer's account(s) may be offset by any other outstanding balance owed by or to the customer. Please allow 4 to 6 weeks for delivery. Offer available while quantities last.

Your Privacy—The Reader Service is committed to protecting your privacy. Our Privacy Policy is available online at www.ReaderService.com or upon request from the Reader Service. We make a portion of our mailing list available to reputable third parties that offer products we believe may interest you. If you prefer that we not exchange your name with third parties, or if you wish to clarify or modify your communication preferences, please visit us at www.ReaderService.com/consumerschoice or write to us at Reader Service Preference Service, P.O. Box 9062, Buffalo, NY 14240-9062. Include your complete name and address.

STR520